D1151737

Aspire to Die (Large Print)

An Oxford Murder Mystery

Bridget Hart Book 1

M S Morris

This book is a work of fiction and, except in the case of historical fact, any resemblance to actual persons, living or dead, is purely coincidental.

Margarita Morris and Steve Morris have asserted their right under the Copyright, Designs and Patents Act 1988 to be identified as the authors of this work.

Published by Landmark Media, a division of Landmark Internet Ltd.

M S Morris® and Bridget Hart® are registered trademarks of Landmark Internet Ltd.

Copyright © 2019 Margarita Morris & Steve Morris

msmorrisbooks.com

All rights reserved.
ISBN-13: 978-1-914537-01-1

CHAPTER 1

"Lust and ambition are the driving forces of tragedy. Discuss."

Sophie Hinton tossed and turned in her narrow college bed. It was hard to sleep when your dreams were filled with bloody daggers and lustful desires.

She'd been up until gone midnight finishing her essay for today's tutorial. Lust, ambition, tragedy. A heady mix. Turned out, Shakespeare thought so too. She had filled twenty closely-typed pages with references to the bard's plays where lust or ambition drove the action. She hoped she'd finally managed to nail down all the pertinent points, but as she turned out her bedside light in the early hours she was suddenly overwhelmed by doubts. No wonder she'd had such troubled dreams.

Now it was too late for sleep. Bright sunlight streamed through the thin curtains of the room, reaching warm fingers across the wooden floor. She slid out of bed, rubbing her tired eyes, and stumbled into the shower.

Lust and ambition. Sophie didn't consider

word.

Lust, ambition and tragedy. Val must be privy to them all.

She showed no inclination to keep her hard-won secrets to herself. 'Whatever it was, the drinks certainly flowed freely, judging by the number of empty bottles and used glasses.' She lowered her voice confidentially. 'I don't care much for this new dean, you know, not that he's all that new, but when you've been around for as long as I have, I feel entitled to call him new. I've seen a few deans in my time and this one reminds me of a politician. Too ambitious by half. Not like the old dean. He was a proper gentleman.'

Val would talk all day long if you let her. Sophie nodded politely and made her exit. She knew secrets too, but unlike Val she kept them close.

She slowed her pace as she made her way across the great quadrangle – Tom Quad, to give it its popular name. The sixteenth-century sandstone walls gleamed golden in the morning sun; in the central pond, surrounded by water lilies, the statue of Mercury – god of financial gain and messages – balanced on one foot atop his pedestal; and on the west side, the great clock tower known affectionately as Tom Tower soared skywards.

Eight muscular rowers and their skinny cox were gathering in the lodge beneath the clock tower, all clad in matching one-piece Lycra rowing suits. It was the men's first team. The tallest of the rowers was Zara's boyfriend, Adam Brady. Adam was a man filled with both lust and ambition. Sophie studied him closely. If she allowed her imagination to roam freely, she could easily feel a stirring of lust herself. Adam seemed to be staring back at her, his eyes shadowed beneath unruly black hair, his powerful arms flexing in preparation for the run to the boathouse.

His gaze held hers for a moment, but she pulled away and pressed on, continuing her path across the quad to Zara's staircase. She pushed open the heavy oak door and stepped inside. The thick stone walls offered shelter from the sun which was already getting hot, and it took a second or two for her eyes to adjust to the dark after the brightness outside.

Two doors opened onto the ground floor – her tutor's room and a seminar room that was being redecorated. She crept quietly past them and up the stairs. Dr Claiborne probably wasn't around yet, but she had no desire to bump into him before the tutorial began.

She went up to the first floor landing. There were two more rooms on this floor. The first was Megan's, a girl who was studying Classics. Megan wouldn't be in her room this early in the morning. She'd be in bed no doubt, but not her own. Megan was no stranger to lust. Sophie turned instead to the other entrance, the door to Zara's room.

She knocked quietly and when there was no

response, knocked again louder. The room beyond stayed silent. She took hold of the brass doorknob and twisted it cautiously clockwise. It turned, and with a gentle push the door opened. Sophie peered inside.

The room beyond was dim, the curtains drawn tightly shut, but even in the semi-darkness Sophie knew that something terrible had happened. Sprawled on the floor was Zara Hamilton, her arms and legs splayed out, unmoving. Beautiful, kind, intelligent Zara. Her head was twisted to one side and her blue eyes stared lifelessly, her mouth hanging open. Her long, angelic hair was sticky with blood which had pooled across the carpet in a crimson stain.

Sophie put a hand on the door frame to steady herself, but all she could feel was the thudding of her heart. She approached the body cautiously, careful not to step in any blood, nor to touch any surface. She knelt down and laid two fingers on Zara's neck. She counted to thirty. There was no pulse. She'd known there wouldn't be.

Lust and ambition. Which was to blame for Zara's tragedy? Sophie shook her head, letting tears fall.

CHAPTER 2

The romantic strains of Verdi's La Traviata thundered from the kitchen's sound system, threatening to overwhelm the little house with pathos and drama. Detective Inspector Bridget Hart was enjoying a rare day off work, and she intended to make the most of it.

First she was going to bake a cake for her daughter Chloe's fifteenth birthday, then she was going to go swimming. She'd worked so hard for her recent promotion to DI that her exercise routine had fallen by the wayside and her work trousers were becoming ever more snug. This was, in fact, the first day of annual leave allowance that Bridget had succeeded in taking since the start of the year. This evening, when Chloe got home from school, she planned to take her out to a nice little Italian restaurant in North Oxford. Just the two of them, mother and daughter. It would be a real treat. And if she managed forty lengths at the pool and didn't eat too much during the day, she'd allow herself a bowl of her favourite tagliatelle with truffle cream sauce. A glass of red wine would be the for joining the force had long since been removed, old attitudes took time to die. Much like Superintendent Grayson himself, who had been in the job as long as Bridget could remember. She didn't participate in the beer-swilling and adolescent joke-telling that constituted police social rituals. She didn't do drinks after work except on rare occasions, and she'd always resisted working overtime as much as possible. And the reason for all that had been simple – Chloe. Being a single parent with a young daughter to get home to had held her back professionally. But now Chloe was older, and this was her chance to finally progress her career.

'All right, no problem,' she heard herself saying. 'I'll be over there right away.'

'Keep me informed.'

'Yes, sir.' But Grayson had already ended the call.

With a sigh, Bridget returned the calorie-laden baking ingredients to the cupboard. Perhaps they were safer kept in there, especially since it didn't look like she'd be getting that much-needed exercise after all.

She went upstairs and changed out of her jeans into smart black trousers, pulling in her stomach as she hauled up the zip. She picked a cream blouse and a grey jacket which she hoped had a slimming effect, although obviously not as effective as actually doing some exercise. She'd planned to wash her hair at the pool, after her swim. The just-got-out-of-bed look didn't suit her at all but there was no time to wash it properly now. She wet her comb under the tap and ran it through her short, dark bob in a futile effort to get both sides to lie flat. A dab of foundation and a smear of nude lipstick – she had the quickest make-up routine in Oxfordshire – and she was ready to go.

Her red BMW Mini convertible was parked outside the house, in front of Wolvercote village green. Tucked just inside the northwestern corner of the Oxford ring road, Wolvercote was a small community with a couple of pubs, a church and a family-run corner shop. Bridget owned one of the small terraced cottages in the heart of the village, just big enough for herself and Chloe. Tiny, in other words.

Two young mothers were pushing their children on the swings by the green, the little boy and girl screaming with delight and chattering animatedly. For Bridget, those early days with her own daughter were a distant memory. When Chloe was younger they used to take a picnic to Port Meadow alongside the River Thames, or explore the ruins of nearby Godstow Abbey. But now Chloe was older she preferred to spend all her time with her friends. She hardly told Bridget anything. Bridget didn't even know if Chloe had a boyfriend. And her carefully-laid plans to make today special for her daughter's birthday had just been shot down in flames by the Chief Super. The working mother could never win.

She climbed into the car and tossed her bag

onto the passenger seat. The little car with its iconic design and twin-power turbo engines was one of her few indulgences – a treat for herself on her thirty-fifth birthday three years ago. Even Chloe thought it was cool, which was saying something. Bridget loved the car. She liked to think it reflected herself – sensible and compact, but spirited, with a keen sense of fun. She turned on the ignition and the engine thrummed into life.

Chloe had already hinted that the Mini would be the perfect car to learn to drive in, but Bridget didn't want to think about that. She'd seen more than enough fatal crashes in her time with the police, too many of them involving young people on the brink of adulthood. But she'd seen worse too, far worse, and not only since becoming a police officer. Darker fears than traffic accidents haunted Bridget's dreams, no matter how well she was able to suppress them during daylight hours.

She pushed her concerns away. She needed to focus on the task ahead. From what the Chief Super had told her, a young woman had lost her life today, and that woman's family would be depending on Bridget to find answers. The full weight of the responsibility removed any lingering thoughts of birthdays, cakes and dress sizes from her mind. She pulled away from the village green, crossing the bridge over Wolvercote Mill Stream before picking up the Woodstock Road that would take her into the heart of Oxford.

Driving from North Oxford to Christ Church, just south of the centre, was not as easy as it should have been. Despite Oxford's main roads having a simple medieval layout – four roads leading north, south, east and west, intersecting at Carfax – the city council had imposed a one-way system that made the journey twice as long as it needed to be.

Bridget tried to stay calm as she navigated the route, silently cursing modern traffic congestion, all the time keeping an eye out for the dozens of cyclists who thronged the narrow streets, not to mention the foreign tourists, many of whom seemed surprised to discover that cars drove on the left in Britain. The rich operatic melodies of Mozart's Così fan tutte soared through the car's speakers, helping to soothe her journey, and on arrival she was pleased to note that she'd only had to honk her horn once.

An ambulance and two marked police cars were parked outside the main entrance to the college on St Aldate's, causing havoc with the double-decker buses that clogged the road in both directions. Bridget pulled up behind one of the police cars on double-yellow lines. A traffic warden appeared in her side-view mirror and began to issue her with a ticket, but she rummaged in her bag and pulled out a permit that stopped the warden in his tracks. She slung the bag over her shoulder and hurried through the arched entrance-way beneath the clock scene, that was the most important task, the one thing he mustn't fail to do. 'Move along, please. Nothing to see here,' he told the students billowing around the perimeter of the taped-off area. He didn't know where the words had come from. They didn't sound like his own. They weren't even true; they were a bare-faced lie. There was plenty to see and that was precisely why he was here. Yet the words had the desired effect, slowly starting to disperse the curious crowds. He was impressed by his own effectiveness. The voice of authority. He was a real policeman now it seemed, or at least he'd fooled these students into believing it. If he carried on like this he might even fool himself.

★

Bridget was met at the porters' lodge by a man whose lined face was sad and drawn. He offered her his hand. 'Jim Turner, ma'am. Head porter of the college. I was told to expect you.'

His silvery grey hair was combed neatly in a side parting, but his bushy eyebrows seemed to have a will of their own, and arched upwards, reaching for the sky. Bridget was reminded uncomfortably of her own hastily-tamed hair that so often seemed to mimic her daughter's rebellious nature.

'Detective Inspector Bridget Hart,' she said, shaking his hand.

She was struck by the man's quiet dignity. He

spoke with a soft country accent, marking him out as one of the Oxford locals. He'd probably devoted his working life to the college. Calm and capable, he was just what she needed.

He clasped his hands behind his back. 'If you'd like to follow me.'

Bridget was no stranger to the many colleges that made up the university, and she had visited Christ Church on several occasions. Not only was it Oxford's largest and grandest college, it also housed the city's cathedral. It was hard not to be impressed by its architectural magnificence. Bridget herself had been an undergraduate at the more modestly proportioned Merton College. She preferred the smaller colleges with their more intimate quadrangles, perfect for enjoying a glass of Pimm's after a summer concert or an al fresco performance of Shakespeare. The vast number of tourists who visited Christ Church each year, voting with their feet – and their money – clearly didn't share her opinion, however.

They entered Tom Quad and turned left towards the staircases on the north side of the quadrangle. Today, the architectural symmetry was rather spoilt by the crime scene tape surrounding the doorway to one of the staircases. A group of students had gathered on the opposite side of the quad, watching as the drama unfolded.

'It was one of the students who found her,' the porter was saying. 'Poor girl. She was shaken up something dreadful.'

'I can imagine.'

'I've worked here all my life. You see a few things working in a place like this, but you don't expect to come across something like that.' They stopped a short distance from the cordoned-off area. 'If you need anything, I'll be in the lodge.'

She watched him walk, head bowed, back to the lodge, then turned to meet the young sergeant who was striding towards her. He was tall. Well, most people were compared with Bridget. She was used to that. He looked to be about late twenties, no more. His keen face was splashed with freckles and framed by ginger hair and a thick beard that reached up to his ears. He stepped easily over the crime scene tape with his long, gangling legs and held out his hand.

'Detective Sergeant Jake Derwent, ma'am.'

She noted his northern accent and wondered where he was from. She'd seen him around the office a few times, but hadn't worked with him before.

'DI Bridget Hart.' They shook hands. 'You're new to Oxford, DS Derwent?'

'Been here six months, ma'am.'

'Where were you before?'

'Leeds. West Yorkshire.' He had a firm grip, and answered straightforward questions with straightforward answers. Bridget had a feeling they'd get on well together.

'So what have we got?'

Jake took a notebook out of his breast pocket.

His handwriting was a spidery scrawl, but he seemed to have no problem deciphering it. 'A suspicious death – almost certainly a violent one. I spoke to the officer who was first on the scene when the alarm was raised. He spoke to the girl who found the body – her name is Sophie. The dead girl is Zara Hamilton, second year English student. She has a twin brother in the college called Zac and, according to Sophie, her boyfriend is a guy called Adam Brady.'

'Anyone spoken to Adam yet?'

Jake shook his head. 'Sophie says she saw him about to run down to the boathouse this morning with the other rowers. They're not back yet.'

'Okay, well we know where to find him if we need him. What about the parents? Have they been informed?'

'Some officers from the Met have gone to their London home.'

'Their London home? Does that mean they have more than one?'

'The porter said something about a country house near Oxford in the Cotswolds.'

Bridget raised her eyebrows. A home in London and a country house in the Cotswolds? She was starting to form an impression of the sort of people she was dealing with here.

'And where are we with the scene of crime officers?'

'They're upstairs now, going through everything. The photographer's taken pictures.'

'Good, then maybe we can...'

19

course, they mostly just want to see the dining hall since it was used in the Harry Potter films, although personally I think the cathedral and art gallery are of more interest.'

Bridget was rapidly losing patience with this man who seemed to find the police presence nothing more than an inconvenience. She drew herself up so that she was level with his chin. 'Dr Reid, a student has died in one of your college rooms. Therefore, the splendours of Hogwarts notwithstanding, I must ask that you keep the college closed to visitors for the rest of the day and for the foreseeable future, at least until we have completed our initial investigations.'

The look of surprise on the dean's face suggested that she'd make a good match for Professor Severus Snape when it came to delivering a snarky riposte. Dr Reid blinked, then quickly recovered himself. 'Well, yes, of course I do understand that.'

'So, if you'll excuse me, the sooner I can get on with my job, the sooner all this tape can be cleared away. But until then I must ask that you allow my team unhindered access to the college, the students, and anyone else we need to speak to.'

The dean was momentarily lost for words.

'And,' continued Bridget, 'I understand that the dead girl has a twin brother in the college. Has he been informed yet?'

A shadow passed across the dean's face. 'A twin brother, yes. I doubt Zachary is up yet. He's

His handwriting was a spidery scrawl, but he seemed to have no problem deciphering it. 'A suspicious death – almost certainly a violent one. I spoke to the officer who was first on the scene when the alarm was raised. He spoke to the girl who found the body – her name is Sophie. The dead girl is Zara Hamilton, second year English student. She has a twin brother in the college called Zac and, according to Sophie, her boyfriend is a guy called Adam Brady.'

'Anyone spoken to Adam yet?'

Jake shook his head. 'Sophie says she saw him about to run down to the boathouse this morning with the other rowers. They're not back yet.'

'Okay, well we know where to find him if we need him. What about the parents? Have they been informed?'

'Some officers from the Met have gone to their London home.'

'Their London home? Does that mean they have more than one?'

'The porter said something about a country house near Oxford in the Cotswolds.'

Bridget raised her eyebrows. A home in London and a country house in the Cotswolds? She was starting to form an impression of the sort of people she was dealing with here.

'And where are we with the scene of crime officers?'

'They're upstairs now, going through everything. The photographer's taken pictures.'

'Good, then maybe we can…'

Their conversation was interrupted by the arrival of a man in a sharply cut suit striding across the quadrangle towards them. He had a proprietorial air, as if the college belonged to him. The new arrival looked to be in his late fifties or early sixties. His thick hair was surely too dark to be natural. 'Who's in charge of all this' – he indicated the cordoned off area with a wave of his hand as if he found the matter rather distasteful – 'business?'

He was looking at Jake, clearly making the assumption that it must be the man running the show, even though Jake was ten years Bridget's junior. It was no more than she had come to expect.

She stepped forwards, making herself as tall as her five foot two inch frame would allow, and held out her hand. 'Detective Inspector Bridget Hart.' She waited for the man to introduce himself.

He glanced down at her, momentarily nonplussed, then accepted her hand. 'Dr Francis Reid. I'm the dean of Christ Church.'

That would explain the sense of ownership he exuded.

Some colleges had a principal, some had a warden, some had a master, but Christ Church had a dean. It was something to do with Christ Church's special status as both a college and the cathedral. Basically, this was the man in charge and the person she would have to deal with if this turned – as she anticipated it would – into a murder investigation. 'My sergeant has just been filling me in on the details.'

The dean drew her to one side and spoke very precisely as if communicating with a child. 'You must understand, this case needs to be handled with the utmost discretion. We can't possibly have the police here for longer than is absolutely necessary, and I must insist that you keep the story out of the press.' He glanced in Jake's direction as if he suspected him of already selling the story to the highest bidder. 'The bad publicity would be disastrous for the college's reputation. I take it you know who you're dealing with here?'

'I believe the dead girl is called Zara Hamilton.'

'Quite. She's the eldest daughter of Sir Richard Hamilton.'

Bridget wondered for a moment who he meant, then she remembered the media tycoon who owned television and film companies. No wonder they had a town house and a country pile. He probably owned properties abroad as well. Keeping this out of the press was going to be tricky, even if she decided that she wanted to.

'How quickly do you think you can clear away all this tape?' asked the dean. 'We would normally have opened the college to tourists hours ago. Visits are a major source of income for the college and summer is our peak time for visitors. More people come to Christ Church than any other Oxford college, you know. Of course, they mostly just want to see the dining hall since it was used in the Harry Potter films, although personally I think the cathedral and art gallery are of more interest.'

Bridget was rapidly losing patience with this man who seemed to find the police presence nothing more than an inconvenience. She drew herself up so that she was level with his chin. 'Dr Reid, a student has died in one of your college rooms. Therefore, the splendours of Hogwarts notwithstanding, I must ask that you keep the college closed to visitors for the rest of the day and for the foreseeable future, at least until we have completed our initial investigations.'

The look of surprise on the dean's face suggested that she'd make a good match for Professor Severus Snape when it came to delivering a snarky riposte. Dr Reid blinked, then quickly recovered himself. 'Well, yes, of course I do understand that.'

'So, if you'll excuse me, the sooner I can get on with my job, the sooner all this tape can be cleared away. But until then I must ask that you allow my team unhindered access to the college, the students, and anyone else we need to speak to.'

The dean was momentarily lost for words.

'And,' continued Bridget, 'I understand that the dead girl has a twin brother in the college. Has he been informed yet?'

A shadow passed across the dean's face. 'A twin brother, yes. I doubt Zachary is up yet. He's not known to rise before lunchtime.'

Bridget glanced at her watch. It was ten minutes before noon. 'In that case, I'll go to the victim's room now with my colleague, and then I would like to talk to Zachary straight afterwards.'

'I'll speak to the porter and make sure there's someone to take you to him.'

'Thank you.' Things were starting to go a little more smoothly with the dean. She watched as he took his leave and headed off towards the porters' lodge.

'Well done, ma'am,' said Jake, coming up behind her. 'He needed a bit of firm handling.'

'Most men do,' said Bridget. 'Come on. Let's go upstairs.'

CHAPTER 3

Bridget donned protective clothing and stepped somewhat inelegantly over the crime scene tape, followed by Jake. The group of students gathered on the opposite side of the quad was steadily growing in number. She would have liked to restrict access to the whole quadrangle, but it was such a large area, cordoning it off would be almost impossible. As well as functioning as the main entrance to the college, Tom Quad also provided access to the dining hall – the one of Harry Potter fame – and to the cathedral.

She smiled at the young uniformed police constable standing guard outside the door to the staircase as he moved aside to let her pass. Having been a student at Oxford, Bridget was familiar with the layout of these types of college buildings – a series of doors around the quadrangle, each leading to a staircase from which rooms were accessed. The staircases were usually numbered, often with a Roman numeral etched into the stone above the doorway. On each floor there were normally two rooms facing each other. This staircase looked to be no exception. By Bridget's reckoning the cordoned-off doorway should give access to four rooms in total – two on the ground floor and two upstairs.

On entering, she immediately felt the slight chill that always came from old, stone buildings even in the height of summer. On the ground floor was a seminar room on the left side and a tutor's room on the right. The door to the seminar room stood ajar and from the strong smell of paint and the various ladders, dust sheets and paint tins, it was clear that this room was currently being redecorated. She sniffed again. The paint was masking another smell. Vomit? She peered around the door and saw that someone had been sick over the newly-painted wall. The decorators were not going to be happy.

The door opposite bore a brass plaque with the name Dr Anthony Claiborne engraved on it.

'Any sign of Dr Claiborne this morning?' she asked.

'None, ma'am. We did knock.'

Most probably the room was only used during the day for tutorials.

Their footsteps echoed on the hard bare steps as they climbed the stairs. The plain walls were painted a dull shade of magnolia. For all their external grandeur, there was a certain asceticism to these colleges, originally built for the education of the clergy in days when people were concerned more about their souls in the afterlife than about their physical comforts in this life.

Upstairs, two doors faced each other. Zara's

door stood wide open and the room beyond was a hive of activity as the Scene of Crime Officers went about their jobs. Bridget recognised the head of the SOCO team, Vikram, from previous cases she'd worked on when she was still a detective sergeant like Jake was now. She had always found his calm, professional manner reassuring and was glad to see him. He nodded at her to acknowledge her arrival.

The door opposite, like Dr Claiborne's on the ground floor, was closed. 'Do we know whose room this is?' asked Bridget.

'I got a name from Sophie,' said Jake, pulling out his notebook. He flipped efficiently through the pages. 'Another second year student. Her name is Megan Jones. But she hasn't been seen this morning.'

'Has someone been into her room to check?' asked Bridget, suddenly fearful that there might be a second dead body behind that door.

'Yes,' said Jake. 'I got a spare key from the porter. The room was empty.'

'Okay,' said Bridget, 'let's take a look at the victim.' She took a deep breath. This might well turn out to be her first murder case as a detective inspector, but years of being a single parent had taught her that she could cope with any new challenge as long as she acted the role that people expected of her. I've got this, she thought, and stepped into Zara's room, doing her best to exude an air of confidence.

Jake followed in her wake. 'Pretty big for a

student room,' he said, gazing around. Bridget thought he was trying to mask his nerves by focusing on the room rather than the figure under the white sheet in the middle of the floor.

'Yes, it's one of the more spacious ones,' she said. The fact was, college accommodation at Oxford ranged from the palatial to the poky, from the charmingly historic to the utilitarian and modern. She'd seen rooms that were little better than garrets and others that looked as if they'd been furnished for a remake of Brideshead Revisited. Her own room in her first year at Merton had been practical, but nothing special. In her second year she'd lived out of college in a shared house with five other girls just off the Cowley Road in East Oxford. The less said about that dump, the better. For her final year she'd been able to choose a beautiful room in college with views over the Fellows' Garden.

Zara had been lucky to have two rooms, in fact – a study/sitting room and an adjoining bedroom. At present both rooms were filled by the white-suited SOCO team and their gear. They were busy photographing, videoing, dusting for prints and bagging potential evidence.

In the centre of the sitting room, next to a small coffee table, lay the body, discreetly covered by a white sheet.

Bridget and Jake waited by the door until the head of the SOCO team waved them over.

'Hello, Bridget,' said Vikram from behind his

protective face mask, 'or perhaps I should call you DI Hart now?' His eyes crinkled to show that he was grinning. She couldn't see his mouth.

Bridget smiled back gratefully. If all of her colleagues were as friendly and helpful as him, her job would be so much easier. 'Bridget will do just nicely. And this is DS Derwent.' She indicated Jake. 'Is it okay if I call you Jake?'

'Yes, ma'am,' he said with a quick grin. She noticed his reluctance to use her first name in return. She was getting to like the young sergeant more, the longer she spent with him.

'Vikram Vijayaraghavan,' said the SOCO head to Jake. 'People call me Vik. Excuse me if I don't shake your hand.' He indicated the plastic gloves he was wearing. 'We've nearly finished here. We'll be taking the laptop away for analysis but we haven't found a mobile phone anywhere.'

'Any initial thoughts, Vik?'

'Could have been an accident, I suppose. But it doesn't look likely. I'd guess someone did this to her.'

'What about a murder weapon?'

Vikram shook his head. 'Looks like she was hit on the back of the head with a blunt object, but there's nothing matching that description here. We'll know more after the pathologist has done the post-mortem.'

'Any other obvious signs of violence?'

'Nothing I could see.'

'May we take a look, please?'

'Of course.' Vikram stepped nimbly to the side

and, with delicate fingers, pulled back the white sheet that covered the body.

Zara lay on her front, her head turned to one side. She was dressed for the weather in a simple summer dress in pale yellow. A sticky trail of half-congealed blood tangled her hair and ran across her shoulders onto the carpet. That long, blonde hair must have been stunning once, the sort of hair that had a starring role in shampoo adverts, the sort of hair Bridget had dreamed of having when she was little but which she'd never been able to grow.

She crouched down next to the body for a closer look. Beneath the mass of hair and blood, Zara's eyes were closed and her face looked almost peaceful. It reminded Bridget of Chloe when she was asleep. With corpses, it was never the physical damage that got under her skin, but the thought that this was someone's child or partner or parent. The question that always went through her head was, How would I feel if it was my own daughter lying there? That was why she had to find the killer – for Zara's sake and for the sake of the dead girl's friends and family.

She nodded at Vikram and he replaced the sheet. Jake had already looked away, a slightly queasy look on his face.

'Is this the first dead body you've seen, sergeant?' she asked.

'No, ma'am.'

'It won't be the last one either.' She wanted to tell him that it would get easier with time, but

29

that would have been a lie. 'This body is evidence of a crime, and if you want to find the person who committed that crime – who killed Zara – you need to study the evidence. All of it.'

'Yes, ma'am.' He met her gaze. 'You're sure it's murder, then?'

She softened her voice. 'It looks that way, but we won't know for certain until we get the post-mortem report.' She turned to Vikram. 'When do you think that will be?'

'The pathologist said he'd try and do the PM on Monday morning.'

Today was Friday. Bridget couldn't afford to wait three whole days for the autopsy. She fully expected to be working this weekend, and she didn't see why the pathologist should be any different. 'I'll have a word with him and see if I can hurry it along,' she said. 'How long before you have your provisional results?'

'First thing tomorrow. I'll make it my top priority.'

'Excellent,' said Bridget, treating him to a smile. 'I'll be in touch.'

While the corpse was zipped into a body bag in preparation for removal to the morgue, Bridget and Jake took a look around the room.

In many ways it was a typical student room, filled with books, pens, pencils, sheafs of paper and other stationery. Arty posters covered the walls – black and white photos of obscure musicians jostled for space with fine art prints, and political slogans in bold typefaces.

'Studying English by the look of it,' said Bridget, examining the bookshelves.

The shelves were laden with classics of English literature: Shakespeare's plays and sonnets, Chaucer's Canterbury Tales, Beowulf in the original and Seamus Heaney's translation, numerous anthologies of poetry and short stories, plus a slew of nineteenth-century novelists including Dickens, Hardy, Eliot and the Brontë sisters.

'That's a lot of reading to get through,' said Jake.

Bridget turned to the desk by the window, with its view of Tom Quad and the Mercury fountain. Its surface was littered with handwritten papers – essays, revision notes, and carefully annotated copies of texts. Bridget read the words on the top sheet. Lust and ambition are the driving forces of tragedy. Underneath Zara had brainstormed a list of ideas about Hamlet, Macbeth and Julius Caesar. She certainly appeared to have been a hardworking student.

Above the fireplace hung a cork noticeboard. Alongside a lecture timetable and a notice about opening hours at the Bodleian Library, Bridget found a ticket to the upcoming end-of-term Christ Church ball in just over a week's time, a leaflet from Shelter, the homeless charity, and a flier from the Oxford University Labour Club. That, together with the political posters strongly suggested that Zara's politics were left of centre. Bridget was pretty certain that Sir Richard

Hamilton was no supporter of the Labour Party. Hadn't he recently made a big donation to the Conservatives? She wondered how Zara's political leanings had gone down with the rest of the family. She'd presumably find out soon enough, when she spoke to the twin brother, Zachary.

She took a quick look in the bedroom. It was smaller than the sitting room, just big enough for a single bed, a chest of drawers and a minuscule en-suite bathroom that had been shoehorned into one corner. The original Tudor occupant of the room had probably had to walk across the quadrangle to reach the nearest primitive wash facilities, which certainly wouldn't have included a shower with hot running water. Even in Bridget's time, she'd shared a communal bathroom with half a dozen other students. She'd never questioned it, but young people evidently expected better these days.

Clearly a lot had changed in the twenty years since Bridget had first joined the university as a student. Twenty years. Was it really that long ago? In some ways it felt like yesterday. But seeing Zara's beautiful, youthful face had suddenly made it seem like an eternity. What hopes and dreams had the young woman held? Very little of what the eighteen-year-old Bridget had imagined about her own future had come true. But at least she was still alive.

What would she do differently if she could rewind the clock and live those twenty years again? Everything. Then Chloe's face flashed before her, and she thought: nothing. She would live it all again, just as before. All the joy. All the pain. No regrets.

'I think we've seen enough here,' she said. 'We'll see what forensics have for us later.'

As she and Jake made their way back down the stairs, they heard the sound of raised voices coming from the quad.

'She's my sister, for Christ's sake!' The male voice sounded haughty and angry. It was the voice of someone used to getting their own way.

'I'm sorry sir, but I must ask you to move back. Please return to the other side of the cordon.'

'Get your hands off me or I'll have you done for police assault!'

'What's going on here?' asked Bridget as she stepped around the constable guarding the doorway. She was met by a red-faced young man who, from his wavy blond hair and finely chiselled features, was unmistakably Zara's twin. This had to be Zachary, the brother who never surfaced before mid-day, but from the look of him it was impossible to tell if he'd been to sleep in his clothes of the night before, or hadn't yet gone to bed. The stink of alcohol on his breath was still strong. He was wearing a crumpled dress shirt that appeared to have blood on the collar and his cheekbone was cut and freshly bruised. He ran a hand through his hair and Bridget noticed a smear of magnolia-coloured paint on his palm.

'What's going on is that this bonehead' – Zachary indicated the uniformed PC with a flick of his hand – 'is refusing to let me see my sister.'

'I'm sorry,' said Bridget, 'but you won't be able to see her.'

The young man staggered backwards a couple of steps, the fight gone from him momentarily. 'Oh shit, so it's true then?'

'I'm sorry.'

He spun away from her and looked as if he was about to keel over.

'Zac, come here.' A girl standing on the other side of the cordoned-off area was holding her arms out to him. He fell into her embrace and hugged her across the crime scene tape. He sobbed wildly as she stroked the back of his head. It was either genuine grief or the most over-the-top acting Bridget had seen for a long time.

'Go to the boathouse and find the boyfriend, Adam,' said Bridget to Jake. 'I'll see what I can get out of the brother. See you back at headquarters in about an hour.'

'No worries,' said Jake, striding effortlessly over the tape.

Bridget made her way over to Zac and his girlfriend. The boy was still weeping savagely. His face shone with real tears. 'Could we go and talk somewhere more private?' she suggested.

CHAPTER 4

Jake walked briskly along the edge of Christ Church Meadow on his way to find the dead girl's boyfriend, Adam. He took off his jacket, undid his top button and loosened his tie. It was going to be another hot day. If he hadn't been on a murder investigation he'd have been tempted to sit down under one of the many trees lining the footpath and enjoy five minutes of peace and quiet. He hadn't been living in Oxford long and would never have guessed that the city contained what appeared to be a country meadow complete with grazing land for animals right in its centre. But perhaps he shouldn't have been too surprised. Oxford was a strange place, stuffed full of ancient, medieval colleges, with churches everywhere you cared to look, and so many dusty libraries that there was probably one for every person who lived here. And all of it bunched right up against overcrowded shopping streets that were literally impossible to drive around.

The college porter had given him directions, informing him that, 'The meadow is private land belonging to Christ Church, but access is granted to the public during daylight hours.'

Jake had got the distinct impression he was expected to show gratitude for having been granted access. 'Cheers, mate,' he'd said to the porter. As he strode along the dusty path leading down to the river boathouses, a small herd of cud-chewing cows regarded him nonchalantly. He had no idea what a college might want with a meadow. Maybe they had plans to teach the cows Latin.

Oxford was certainly a very different world to Leeds, where he had grown up, and Bradford, where he'd studied Criminology. He'd never imagined himself moving to the south of England, but his long-term girlfriend had got a job in Oxford and he'd transferred down here to be with her. But the relationship hadn't lasted. Towards the end she'd done a lot of crying and, it turned out, a lot of lying. He still missed her, but he was better off without her. So now here he was, alone in Oxford, unwilling to admit defeat and return home with his tail between his legs, and instead trying to make the best of things. His mates up north teased him about becoming a soft southerner, but in truth he was finding Oxford quite a challenging place to live. The traffic was mad. The people were strange. The house prices were insane. Even on his detective sergeant's salary, buying a place to live was out of the question. Instead, he was renting a cramped, one-bedroom flat above a launderette on the Cowley Road, sandwiched between an Indian restaurant and a Chinese. Well, at least it was convenient for doing his washing and getting takeaways.

He reached the river and turned left along the bank towards the boathouses. The River Thames, for some unfathomable reason, was known in Oxford as the Isis, apparently after the Egyptian goddess. Jake shrugged. Whatever. He could handle that.

A women's boat powered along the water, the cox shouting orders to her crew. On the opposite bank a coach cycled along, also yelling commands through a loudhailer. All eight rowers in the boat were red-faced and panting. Rowing looked like hard work. Jake didn't fancy getting up extra-early to do that every morning. It would be even worse in the middle of winter. The boat shot past, surprising him with its speed.

The boathouses were square, flat-roofed structures topped with viewing balconies. He walked along the bank until he spotted the Christ Church college crest above the open doorway of one of the buildings. It was the very last one at the end of the row of boathouses and looked older than its neighbours, constructed from red brick. It wasn't as old as the college itself though, not by a few hundred years. A boat was just coming in to dock beside the floating raft in front of the boathouse.

The cox, a short, skinny guy, sprang out of the boat and started giving orders to the rest of the crew to disembark. The eight rowers executed a well-practised manoeuvre, getting themselves, the eight oars, and the boat out of the river. They hoisted the boat upside down and carried it at shoulder height as if it weighed practically nothing. The sleek carbon-fibre hull gleamed in the sun. It must have been getting on for twenty metres in length.

Jake ducked out of the way as the rowers swung the boat around, missing him by no more than a foot. They lowered the boat onto a set of sliding rails in the boathouse and then jogged back to the landing raft to collect their oars.

Jake approached the cox. 'Impressive team you've got there, mate.'

'They're not too bad,' said the cox grudgingly. 'They need to work harder, pull together as a team. Can I help you with anything?'

'I understand that one of your rowers is called Adam Brady.'

'That's Adam over there. He's the stroke.' The cox pointed to the biggest guy in the team. None of them were midgets – the men's average height must have been over six foot – but Adam was taller and more muscular than all his teammates.

'He's the what?' asked Jake.

'The stroke.' The cox sounded impatient. 'He's the one who sits right in front of me in the stern. The others sit behind him. They follow Adam's lead, or at least that's what they're supposed to do. With a bit more discipline, they might yet learn to.'

'I see. Well, thanks for your help.' Jake walked

over to Adam, who was chatting to one of the other rowers. From their gestures Jake guessed they were discussing rowing technique. 'Sorry to interrupt, but could I have a word?'

The other rower slapped Adam on the back and walked off.

'It'll have to be quick. We're just about to run back to college.' Adam interlocked his fingers and stretched his arms behind his back, tilting forward from the waist. 'Who are you, anyway?'

Jake drew his ID from his pocket. 'DS Jake Derwent, Thames Valley Police.'

Adam seemed taken aback. He unlocked his fingers and straightened up. 'Police? Really? What's this about?' He ran a hand through his hair. Both hands were bandaged around the knuckles and palms.

'We can talk while we walk back to the college if you like,' said Jake. He had no intention of letting Adam run off anywhere, and he certainly wasn't going to run alongside him. The cox was taking the rest of the team through a series of stretching exercises that looked painful. They appeared to be limbering up to start jogging.

'All right,' said Adam grudgingly. He started walking along the river bank, back the way Jake had just come. His long legs carried him at a fast pace, but Jake was almost as tall and had no problem matching him.

'I need to ask you where you were last night and first thing this morning,' said Jake.

'What the hell for?'

'It's about Zara, your girlfriend.'

Adam stared straight ahead and didn't break his stride. 'She's not my girlfriend anymore. We split up yesterday afternoon.'

Interesting, thought Jake, mentally storing this new information. 'Well, I'm sorry but I have some bad news to tell you.'

Adam came to an abrupt halt and turned to face him. 'What?'

'I'm afraid that she was found dead.'

Adam clenched his fists so that his biceps bulged. 'If this is some sort of sick joke –'

'I'm sorry, this is no joke. She was found this morning by her tutorial partner.'

Despite his overt machismo, Adam seemed to crumple. His shoulders slumped and he buried his face in his bandaged hands. 'Oh, God. How did it happen?'

'We don't yet know the cause of death.'

The rest of the team ran past, staring at them.

'Come on,' said Jake. 'Let's keep walking.'

After a moment, Adam seemed to recover. They continued at a slower pace, more comfortable for talking. Jake tried to keep his tone conversational. 'So what were you doing last night?'

'Drowning my sorrows in the college bar.'

'Because you'd split up with Zara?'

'Yes.' Adam sniffed.

'What time did you go to the bar?'

'Just after seven.'

'And what time did you leave?'

'I don't know. Perhaps about ten.'

'Where did you go afterwards?'

Adam shrugged. 'I dunno. I wandered around for a bit. Tim – that's the cox – saw me at some point and reminded me I had to get up early for training today. He could see I was in a bit of a state. So I went to bed. I didn't want to let the team down.'

'And did you see Zara at all last night?'

'No.' Adam shook his head. They had almost reached the top of Christ Church Meadow by now. One of the bandages had come loose and Adam tore it off angrily.

'Rowing injury?' asked Jake, nodding at the damaged hand.

'What? Oh yes, you get blisters rowing.'

But not cuts and bruises on your knuckles you don't, thought Jake, staring at the backs of Adam's hands. 'You might want to put some antiseptic on that, mate. It looks nasty.'

★

Zac's room was in a different quadrangle – Peckwater Quad – this one dating from the eighteenth century. That made it two hundred years newer than Tom Quad. By Oxford standards, it was a modern addition. Bridget followed Zac and his girlfriend into the neo-classical building and up to a well-proportioned room on the second floor. Wood panelling lined the walls and an elaborate chandelier hung from

41

the central ceiling rose.

And yet the room was squalid. Empty champagne bottles littered the floor; dirty glasses and stained coffee mugs were strewn around; items of female clothing hung over the backs of two armchairs and a small sofa that occupied the centre of the room. There was little evidence of much work being done. The desk was less a place of study, more a repository for glassware – half a dozen shot glasses, a half-empty bottle of vodka, a large bottle of scotch, and a glass paperweight in want of any papers to hold down. The place looked and smelled like the aftermath of a Bacchanalian feast. Zac collapsed onto the sofa, his head in his hands.

'Sorry about the clutter,' said the girl as she moved languidly around the room picking up lacy underwear, a silk camisole and a little black cocktail dress. She was startlingly pretty, with long, auburn hair drawn into perfect lines that framed her face. She tossed the clothes into the adjoining bedroom and closed the door. 'Do you want to speak to Zac alone?'

'Please don't go, Verity,' said Zac. 'I can't do this without you.' He reached out a hand and she went to him, wrapping her slender arms around his shoulders.

'It's all right,' said Bridget. 'I'm happy for you to stay.' She took a seat on one of the armchairs opposite.

'Tell me what happened,' said Zac. His voice was barely more than a croak. 'Was it an accident? It wasn't suicide was it? Please tell me it wasn't suicide.'

'We have to wait for the post-mortem,' said Bridget, 'but at the moment it doesn't look like an accident or suicide.'

'What does that mean? She was murdered?'

'We're treating the death as suspicious.'

Zac shook his head in disbelief. 'It isn't possible. It must have been an accident.'

'No one would want to murder Zara,' insisted Verity. 'Everyone loved her.'

'When did either of you last see Zara?'

Zac bit his lower lip. 'I saw her briefly at lunch. Yesterday, I mean. She was just leaving hall as I was arriving. But she wasn't at formal hall in the evening was she?' He looked to Verity for confirmation.

'No.' Verity shook her head. 'Zara didn't often eat with us. She preferred to eat at informal hall at six twenty. Formal hall is an hour later. You could try asking Sophie. That's her tutorial partner. Or Megan. She has the room opposite Zara's.'

'I'll do that,' said Bridget. She had dined once at formal hall in Christ Church as the guest of a guy she'd met at a student party. It had been a very grand affair with all the students and tutors dressed in academic gowns. Latin grace was said before the three course meal, which was served by college staff wearing white shirts and black waistcoats. Informal hall, as its name suggested, was a more relaxed self-service meal, more in keeping with the twenty-first century. 'And what did you do last night, Zac?' she asked.

'Me? I went to the Oxford Union.'

'Zac's the president of the Union, this term,' said Verity with a pride that she found impossible to conceal.

Well, that would explain the dress shirt, thought Bridget, but not why he was still wearing it the morning after. Oxford's debating society had never really appealed to her when she was a student. Maybe because it had seemed to be so full of people like Zac and Verity. Not much had changed there, by the look of it.

'And what time did you get back from the Union?'

'Just after eleven, I think. I wasn't really paying much attention to the time.'

Verity had though, it seemed. 'Yes, it was twenty past eleven when you came back to your room. I was chairing a meeting of the ball committee until eleven. You were back twenty minutes later.'

Uh-huh, thought Bridget. Even during a police investigation into the violent death of her boyfriend's sister, the young woman hadn't been able to stop herself mentioning that Zac was president of the Oxford Union and that she was chair of Christ Church ball committee. She obviously felt it was a big deal. But even Bridget had to concede that they made quite the high-powered couple.

'So you were here when Zac returned?' she

asked Verity.

'Me?' said Verity. 'Sure. I was waiting for him.'

'You have a key to his room?'

'He left it open for me.'

'And what did you do after that?'

'We both stayed here,' she said, stroking the side of Zac's face with the back of her fingers.

'What was the debate about at the Union, Zac?' Bridget wanted to move the conversation on.

'Oh, just some boring debate about veganism.'

'Get a bit violent, did it?'

'What?'

'The cut on your cheek. The blood on your shirt. Looks like tensions were running high.'

'Oh, no,' said Zac, touching his cheek. 'That was something else entirely.'

'Care to elaborate?'

Zac squirmed in his seat. 'Not really.'

'You look like you've been in a fight.'

Zac's eyes narrowed. He sat up straight and looked Bridget in the eye. For just a moment she saw a glimpse of the powerful, overbearing media tycoon who'd fathered this privileged young man. 'I don't know what you're implying, detective. If you think I had anything to do with the death of my sister, you couldn't be more wrong. I loved Zara with all my heart. Now she's been murdered, and you're sitting here asking me questions about some stupid argument that has nothing to do with anything. I suggest you get off my back and catch whoever did it.'

'So you think it might be murder after all, then?'

'What?'

'Previously you insisted that your sister's death must have been an accident.'

'I don't know!' shouted Zac. 'Just leave me alone. Get your people out there and find out what happened.'

The angry outburst was not entirely unexpected in the circumstances. Bridget let it pass. 'I fully intend to find out what happened, and to catch whoever did it,' she said, standing up. 'But before I leave, I must ask you to hand over your shirt for forensic analysis. I'm sure you understand.'

CHAPTER 5

Bridget left Zac to be consoled by Verity. The girl didn't seem to need much encouragement, and set about her task with zeal. Zac was lucky to have such a devoted girlfriend who was willing to overlook his arrogant manner. She also didn't seem to mind the mess in his room which, to be fair, was at least half hers, nor the fact that he went to sleep in his outfit of the night before and woke up smelling like an empty wine bottle. Young love.

Bridget had married young – too young – and look how that had turned out. Pregnant at twenty-three and a single parent at twenty-five. None of which had helped her career, although it hadn't harmed her ex-, Ben, who was now a senior detective with the Metropolitan Police in London.

As she walked back across Peckwater Quad, her thoughts turned again to Chloe, and Bridget felt a fresh round of guilt. Guilty feelings seemed to be an inescapable part of motherhood, or at least Bridget's experience of motherhood. She had to face facts – that homemade birthday cake she'd planned so carefully was never going to happen. Was there somewhere she could stop off and buy a cake on her way back to Police HQ?

She arrived back in Tom Quad to find the PC outside Zara's staircase engaged in a heated discussion with a man dressed in slim-fitting chinos and an open-necked blue shirt in a good quality twill fabric. The studied smart-casual look was offset by the slightly battered leather briefcase he carried under one arm.

'Can I help?' asked Bridget.

The man regarded her through large designer glasses. 'I was just trying to explain to this policeman that I have a tutorial in five minutes and really must be allowed into my room. I've been in the library all morning.'

Bridget remembered the name she had seen on the door of the ground floor room. 'Would you be Dr Claiborne?'

The young tutor ran a hand through his foppish hair. 'Yes, I'm Dr Claiborne.'

'I was hoping to speak to you.'

The tutor raised one eyebrow.

'What is it that you teach?' asked Bridget.

'English. I'm the college's English tutor.'

Bridget remembered the books in Zara's room – all works of English literature. 'So Zara Hamilton was one of your students?'

'One of my best students.' His gaze shifted nervously from Bridget to the PC and back to Bridget. 'Why? And why are you referring to her using the past tense?' Trust an English tutor to pick up on her use of tenses, thought Bridget.

'I'm afraid that Zara was found dead this morning in her room.'

'Oh, God.' Dr Claiborne's briefcase fell to the ground. He took off his glasses and rubbed his eyes with one hand. 'Was she… I mean, how did she…'

'We're currently investigating the circumstances of her death,' said Bridget. 'But since you have a room on the same staircase, and you were her tutor, can I ask when you last saw her?'

Dr Claiborne pushed his glasses back on and his forehead creased into a frown. 'I think it must have been yesterday afternoon. Yes, that's it, I saw her coming into the staircase in the afternoon. It must have been about four o'clock because I'd just finished a tutorial with some first years.'

'What about later on? Did you see her in the evening?'

'No, I…er…There was a drinks reception in the dean's lodgings. I went to that.'

'And what time did the drinks reception finish?'

'About eleven I think.'

'Thank you. We'll need to take a statement from you. And I'm afraid that you won't be able to have access to your room until we've finished taking physical evidence from the scene.'

'Not even to…'

'If there are any items you need to get from

your room, please tell the constable and he will retrieve them for you.'

'Yes. I...' Dr Claiborne's cheeks reddened. 'Of course.' He turned away and headed in the direction of the porters' lodge, taking his briefcase with him.

'Any sign of the student who has the room on the top floor?' Bridget asked the PC.

'Not yet, ma'am.'

'When she comes back, get someone to go up with her. She'll need to collect her stuff and be allocated a new room.'

As she turned to leave, her phone rang. She checked the caller display. Oh God, not now. It was her sister. She supposed she'd better answer it or she'd get no peace. She descended to the lower level of the quad and wandered over to the Mercury fountain in the centre for some privacy.

'Vanessa, hi. What is it?'

'Is that how you answer the phone these days? How about How are you?'

'Listen, I'm really busy right now. I can't talk.'

'I won't keep you long. I just wanted to check that you're coming for lunch on Sunday.' Vanessa sounded anxious. But then she always sounded anxious.

Bridget sighed. She'd forgotten about that. 'Sure, if I can, but I'm in the middle of an investigation and...'

'Don't say that. I've invited a plus one. Mid-forties, but looks very good for his age. Widowed, three years ago. Cancer,' she added in a stage whisper.

Bridget grimaced. Her sister was on a mission to fill the man-sized void she saw at the heart of Bridget's existence.

'His name is Jonathan,' she continued, oblivious to Bridget's lack of interest. 'He runs an art gallery in Oxford.' She spoke the words in hushed, reverential tones. 'Very successful apparently.'

'Great. I have to go now. See you Sunday.'

Bridget finished the call and pocketed her phone. If Vanessa called again she'd let it go to voicemail.

She set off briskly towards Tom Gate, the arched gatehouse that led from the college back onto the bustle of St Aldate's. One of the bowler-hatted custodians who manned the entrance was trying to disperse a group of curious tourists who were crowding around, taking pictures on their phones. 'Perhaps you should consider keeping the gates closed until all the crime scene activity is finished,' she suggested.

She looked around the vaulted entrance space until she found what she was looking for. Just as she'd hoped, a CCTV camera was mounted on the stone wall beside the gate. She entered the lodge and found Jim Turner, the head porter, sorting through a pile of mail.

He looked up when he saw her. 'Inspector Hart. Is there anything else I can do for you?'

'Yes, there is, actually. I see you have a security camera on the main gate. Is it operational? Are

51

there any others?'

'We've got state-of-the-art CCTV at all the entrances to the college.' Now this was what Bridget liked to hear. The porter continued to elaborate. 'One here at Tom Gate, another at Canterbury Gate off Peckwater Quad, and we also have one at Meadow Gate, which is the tourist entrance. The Meadow Gate closes to visitors at quarter past four, Canterbury Gate is locked at dusk, and Tom Gate closes at nine in the evening.'

'There are no other ways into the college?'

'Just the three gates. So whoever did it, they're bound to have been caught on one of these cameras when they entered the college.'

Unless they were already inside, thought Bridget.

'In fact,' continued the porter, 'I thought you might ask about CCTV, so I've already made copies of last night's tapes for you.' He handed her a small padded envelope. 'I call them tapes, but of course they're memory sticks these days. Everything's gone digital. This is everything from the three gates from noon yesterday through to nine o'clock this morning, which was when the alarm was first raised.'

'Wow,' said Bridget. 'You're a star, Jim. You wouldn't believe how difficult it is sometimes to get hold of this material. You've just made my job a whole lot easier.'

'Ah, well,' said the porter gravely. 'I want to do everything I can to help you catch whoever did this.' He leaned over the counter and lowered his voice. 'She was a lovely girl, Zara. Heart of gold. Everyone here's really cut up about it.'

'Thank you for your help,' said Bridget. 'You take care, and I'll let you know if there's anything more I need.'

★

Bridget returned to her car, checking to see if any over-zealous traffic warden had issued her with a ticket, but mercifully her car was unmolested. She retraced her route through the one-way system and headed up the Banbury Road, passing through Oxford's most expensive residential area. The parade of shops here catered to the middle-class inhabitants of leafy North Oxford, including Bridget's sister, Vanessa. As usual there was nowhere to park. With barely a trace of guilt, Bridget pulled up on double yellow lines outside her favourite pâtisserie, leaving her police permit defiantly on the dashboard. She popped into the artisan bakery and bought an iced chocolate cake in a fancy presentation box. She laid the box carefully on the back seat of the car then pulled away, singing gutsily along to Despina's soprano aria, as other drivers in search of a parking spot threw furious glares in her direction. Bridget often felt that life would be so much easier if she'd simply been born Italian.

Although Oxford's main police station was

situated on St Aldate's, just a stone's throw from Christ Church, Bridget was based at the headquarters of Thames Valley Police in Kidlington, just north of Oxford. The small town was something of a town planner's afterthought, the sort of place you passed through on your way to somewhere else, without even noticing it. There was little worth noticing. The town's old, historic centre was stuck out on a limb, hidden from casual passers-by and dwarfed by the sprawl of bland houses, low rise offices and retail space that constituted modern Kidlington.

Bridget found a small space in the car park at Thames Valley HQ and squeezed her Mini between two much larger vehicles. The smell of chocolate wafting from the back seat was making her hungry. Should she leave the cake in the car and risk the icing melting in the heat, or bring it inside? She decided it would be safer in the car. If she left the cake on her desk there was little chance any would be left by the end of the day.

'Thought you were taking the day off,' said the duty sergeant as she walked in.

'That was the plan, then something came up.'

'That Oxford student?'

Bridget nodded. Word had got around fast. Sex, death and chocolate cake – it was impossible to keep any of them a secret for long at Kidlington.

Upstairs, the CID suite was humming with the clatter of fingers on keyboards, the ringing of telephones, and not entirely work-related conversations. Bridget acknowledged her colleagues with a smile here and a nod there. She hadn't even made it as far as her desk by the window – one of the perks of being promoted to detective inspector – before she heard the hectoring tones of Chief Superintendent Grayson summoning her into his office. She would have liked five minutes to grab a coffee and straighten her thoughts before seeing him, but Grayson, who had come from the military, always wanted answers straight away. If not sooner.

Taking a deep breath, she entered the inner sanctum of the Chief Super's office – more of a glass fishbowl really – and closed the door behind her, shutting out the comforting background noise of the open plan work space.

Grayson sat in his comfortable leather chair behind his voluminous desk, which was always remarkably free of the teetering piles of paperwork that littered Bridget's much smaller desk. Well into his fifties, with short salt and pepper hair, a strong jaw and an upright posture from years of standing to attention, Grayson was more respected than liked. He was known not to suffer fools gladly and could come across as abrupt and even abrasive. On the plus side, he was considered to be fair, even-handed and loyal.

Pride of place on his desk was a photograph of himself and his wife, a good-looking woman who dressed well and looked as if she kept regular appointments at the hairdresser's, standing next to the Mayor in Oxford's elaborate Town Hall. Further photographs showed each of his three children – a girl and two boys – graduating from top universities. Grayson liked to keep himself fit by playing golf, and photographs of him playing at various courses hung on the wall behind his desk. At least that solved one problem – what to buy him as a leaving present when he retired in a few years, an event Bridget was greatly looking forward to.

'Sit down.' He indicated the chair in front of his desk.

'Sir.' Bridget could never enter Grayson's office without feeling as if she was being called in to see the headmaster about her grades.

'You've been to Christ Church,' said Grayson. The Superintendent had a strange way of turning simple statements into both questions and rebukes.

'I've just come from there now,' said Bridget, omitting to mention the quick stopover in North Oxford, which didn't actually take her out of her way, so didn't count.

'Your assessment of the situation? What are we dealing with?'

'Definitely a suspicious death,' said Bridget. 'The girl sustained a serious injury to the back of the head, which couldn't have been deliberately self-inflicted. I can't completely rule out accidental death at this stage, but murder looks much more plausible. The post-mortem should confirm, one way or the other.'

'Right,' said Grayson. 'I'm taking you off the case.'

'What? Sir?'

The Chief Superintendent leaned forwards with his forearms on his desk, his big hands clasped together. 'You do know who we're dealing with here?'

The dean had asked her exactly the same question. 'I understand that the dead girl is Zara Hamilton, daughter of Sir Richard Hamilton, the media magnate.'

'Quite.' Grayson sat back in his chair, gripping the armrests. 'The media spotlight will be shining brightly on this case. There's no room for error. I need a more experienced detective as senior investigating officer.'

Bridget's cheeks burned with indignation. 'But sir, you said –'

'I'll reassign someone else to the case. Baxter. Davis. Leave it with me.' He dismissed her with a sharp nod and opened a report to read.

Bridget stayed where she was. 'Sir?'

'Yes?' The Chief Super looked surprised to see her still sitting there.

'I can handle this case. I've already identified the victim's boyfriend and sent a sergeant to take his statement. I've interviewed several key witnesses and spoken to the SOCO team. The head porter has given me CCTV footage...'

'But can you handle the press coverage?' interrupted Grayson. 'They're like wolves. If they smell blood...'

'They won't, sir. I won't let them.'

Grayson leaned back, studying her face, his dark eyes boring into hers. She held his gaze steadily. Despite the interruption to her plans for today, now that she had made a start – now that she had actually seen the dead girl – she didn't want to let this case go. She felt a sense of duty to the victim. She wouldn't let Zara down.

'I've encountered Sir Richard once or twice on the golf course. Take it from me, the man's a bully. He has friends in high places, too. Any slip ups and he'll be on our backs. More to the point, he'll be on my back.'

'I won't slip up, sir.'

The Chief Super tapped his finger on the desk and seemed to come to a decision. 'Very well, you can stay for now. But I want regular daily updates on progress. We'll have to move quickly on this one. Sir Richard will want to see results, fast. But it's not just Sir Richard we have to worry about. The college won't put up with more intrusion than is absolutely necessary. They'll be worried about the damage this will do to their reputation.'

'I already got that impression from the dean,' said Bridget.

'Any dirt you unearth stays under wraps until we have cast-iron evidence. Oh, and by the way, the Met phoned just before you arrived. Sir Richard and Lady Hamilton are being driven from London and should be at the morgue in about an hour and a half.'

'I'll make sure I'm there to meet them.'

Grayson nodded. 'You'd better get on with it, then.'

'Thank you, sir.' The meeting was over.

Bridget returned to the open plan office, desperate to get herself a coffee. A slice of that chocolate cake wouldn't go amiss either. She'd surely burned off at least a hundred calories under the Chief's intense grilling.

A young woman with a pixie haircut and clad in green motorcycle leathers was perched on the edge of Bridget's desk. She was typing on her phone, using both thumbs at breakneck speed, a skill that Bridget had never mastered, and was oblivious both to Bridget and to the appraising glances from the male officers seated nearby.

'Can I help you?' asked Bridget. She wondered if the new arrival was being deliberately rude, or simply had no awareness of personal space.

'DC Ffion Hughes.' The young detective constable stood up straight, speaking with a lilting Welsh accent. She held out her hand.

Bridget took the hand in hers. It was slim, the fingers long and delicate, the nails painted the same green hue as the motorcycle leathers. Ffion's almond-shaped eyes were the same emerald green.

'I was told to report to you. About the Christ Church death.' Ffion picked up the crash helmet that she'd left on top of Bridget's bulging in-tray. 'I just need to get changed,' she said. 'Then I'll be ready to start work.'

'Of course,' said Bridget. She felt short and dumpy next to this elfin beauty in her skin-tight leathers. 'DS Jake Derwent should be here shortly. Team meeting in ten minutes. Oh, and could you drop this off in forensics for me?' She handed Ffion the evidence bag containing Zac's shirt.

'Already on my way,' said Ffion, striding off across the office floor.

★

Noticeboards covered one wall of the incident room, displaying names, roles and tasks to be assigned. Pinned to the central board were photographs of the crime scene – the victim viewed from every angle, gory close-ups of the wound to the back of her head, images of blood spatter that resembled abstract works of art. The atmosphere in the room was tense with expectation. A new case, everyone keen to make a start and gather as much information as quickly as possible. They all knew the first twenty-four hours were critical.

Bridget walked to the front of the room and surveyed her hastily assembled team. Half a dozen detective constables and a similar number of sergeants had been pulled from other, less high-profile cases. She'd worked with some of them before, and knew the rest by sight. Jake had returned from the boathouse and was munching a chocolate bar, his other hand gripping a mug of coffee with Leeds United emblazoned on it. Next to him, Ffion was holding the string attached to a herbal teabag, dunking the bag up and down in a mug sporting a bright red Welsh dragon. All Bridget had managed since she'd got back to Kidlington was a quick coffee from the vending machine down the corridor. The machine dispensed hot water willingly enough, but grudgingly held back any hint of flavour.

She waited a moment to make sure she had everyone's attention. It wasn't easy to stamp your authority on a case when everyone else in the room literally looked down on you. She stood up straighter and pulled her shoulders back. The hubbub of voices gradually died away.

'Okay, let's make a start. I think you all know me. DI Bridget Hart.' She pointed to the first photograph on the noticeboard. 'The dead woman is Zara Hamilton, daughter of Sir Richard Hamilton.'

A murmur went around the room. They'd all heard of the influential media magnate who owned a string of newspapers and television channels in the UK and across Europe.

'Zara was twenty years old, and a second year student studying English at Christ Church. She has a twin brother in the college. Zachary, known as Zac.' Bridget took a sip of water before continuing. 'The victim was found this morning in her room by Sophie Hinton, her tutorial partner. Judging from the obvious damage to her skull and the blood spatter, I'd say she died after being struck with some considerable force by a blunt object.' Eyes swivelled to the more gory photographs on the noticeboard.

'The body was fully clothed and there's no obvious indication of any sexual assault. No trace of a murder weapon was found in the room or in the vicinity, and we'll have to wait for the post-mortem to be sure of the cause of death.' Bridget picked up the summary report that Vikram had given her. 'Initial findings from SOCO indicate that her mobile phone is missing. They also couldn't find her wallet, which could mean that this was a random burglary. It's possible that someone wandered into the college off the street, found their way to Zara's staircase, and attacked her. But it's unlikely, given that Christ Church has some of the tightest security in Oxford.'

'You're not kidding,' said Ryan Hooper, one of the local coppers, from the back of the room. 'Those custodians guard the place like it contains the crown jewels. They used to call them bulldogs in the old days.' Smiles and light laughter greeted his comment and Bridget acknowledged him with a nod. A bit of banter always helped to break the ice and bond the team. He was referring to the bowler-hatted custodians who were on constant duty at the entrances to the college. The tourists thought them a quaint curiosity, until they tried to get past one.

'Plenty of visitors going in and out, though,'

said Harry, one of the young constables. 'Could someone have entered with a tourist ticket and lingered behind?' It was a fair point.

'The head porter's already given me the CCTV recordings from the three entrances,' continued Bridget, 'so we'll be able to check who came and went throughout the day and night. While we can't rule out a stranger, most likely it was someone Zara knew. Jake, how did you get on at the boathouse?'

Jake nervously swallowed the last mouthful of his chocolate bar and scrunched the wrapper in his hand as he stood to address the team. 'I spoke to the boyfriend, Adam. He's now the ex-boyfriend. They split up yesterday afternoon.'

There were audible inhales of breath around the room. A boyfriend or husband was always a prime suspect, and a jealous or angry ex- doubly so.

'How did he seem?' asked Bridget.

'Pretty shocked, to be fair,' said Jake. 'He certainly gave the impression he didn't know anything about it. But he's a dodgy character. There's definitely something he's not telling us.'

'Such as?'

'Well, his hands were bandaged. He said it was because of blisters from the rowing, but one of the bandages came loose and there were clearly cuts and bruises on the back of his hand. You don't get them from rowing.'

Bridget nodded. She already had a pretty good hunch where those cuts and bruises might have come from. 'Did he say what he was doing last night?'

'Drowning his sorrows in the college bar. Should be easy enough to check.'

'Good,' said Bridget. 'Thanks.'

Jake sat down, a look of relief on his face.

'I spoke to Zac, Zara's twin,' continued Bridget. 'He claims to have been in the Oxford Union until around eleven, and his girlfriend, Verity, confirms that he got back to his room in college at twenty past eleven. Zac had blood on his shirt – it's been sent to forensics – and a cut on his cheek. He'd obviously been involved in a fight, but when I questioned him about it, he got angry with me and refused to discuss it. He says that the last time he saw Zara was at lunchtime, and that she wasn't at formal hall at seven twenty. Her tutor says that he saw her at four o'clock. We need to find out if anyone saw her later than that.'

'Ryan' – Bridget looked at the DS who'd made the quip about the bulldogs – 'could you take a couple of constables over to the college and start establishing Zara's whereabouts last night. Where did she go? Who was she with? Who were her friends? Any enemies in college, that sort of thing. Get as much background as you can.'

'I'm on it,' said Ryan. He nodded at a couple of DCs standing nearby and they left.

'Jake, Ffion, I'd like you to start by going to the Oxford Union and checking that Zac was actually there, what time he left, who he had the fight with.'

Jake glanced across at Ffion and his face lit up. The DC had changed out of her motorcycle leathers and was wearing tight black trousers, ankle boots and a designer shirt that hugged her toned figure. Bridget became conscious that she was holding her own stomach in, whether through nerves or a subconscious desire to appear slimmer, she wasn't sure. 'Then check Verity's alibi. She's vouching for Zac, so we have to be sure she's not lying. Then check Adam's alibi with the college bar staff. Might be worth having another word with him.'

'Andy' – she nodded to one of the other sergeants she knew – 'take the rest of the team. Find Megan, the student who has the room opposite Zara's. No one's seen her since yesterday. Take a full statement from the tutorial partner, Sophie, who discovered the body. Talk to anyone who can vouch for Adam's whereabouts. Start questioning all the students who were in college yesterday and see if anyone saw anything. Start with everyone who has a room in Tom Quad, including tutors and academics. Oh yeah – and there was a drinks reception in the dean's lodgings yesterday evening. Find out who was there.'

Had she covered everything? Something else was nagging at her, but she couldn't think what.

'What about you, ma'am?' asked Jake.

Bridget checked her watch. 'I've got to run. I'm expected at the hospital in half an hour to meet the parents.' Thirty minutes to get to the morgue and grab some lunch en route. One of these days, she'd find a way to live a healthier life. Until then, it would have to be a packet of crisps and a can of Diet Coke, like so many times before. That bloody vending machine would be the death of her.

CHAPTER 6

'So, who's driving?' asked Jake as they made their way to the car park.

Ffion looked directly at him with her startlingly green eyes. She really was quite stunning. 'I don't have a spare crash helmet,' she told him, 'so we'd better take your car.'

'Oh, right,' said Jake, feeling slightly foolish, although how was he to know she was a biker?

They passed a line of motorbikes and she patted a futuristic-looking lime green model at the end.

'That yours?' he asked.

'Kawasaki Ninja H2. Four cylinder 998cc engine with a centrifugal supercharger. Top speed of 183mph.'

'Wow,' said Jake, stumped for words. Not only was she a looker, but she rode a bloody cool bike. He imagined what his mates in Leeds would say if he turned up with her on his arm. Some crude Anglo-Saxon phrases sprang to mind.

'I'm parked over here.' He clicked his remote and his Subaru eagerly flashed its lights in response. The orange hot-hatch stuck out a mile from all the identikit grey, silver and charcoal cars in the car park. He'd picked it up secondhand two years ago from a dealer in Bradford and had then spent almost as much again pimping it up. He hoped Ffion would be impressed. He hastily brushed some chocolate wrappers off the passenger seat before she got in.

'Subaru Impreza WRX. 2.5 litre turbocharged engine,' she said, sitting next to him. 'Nice car.' It was impossible to tell if she was being sarcastic with that lilting Welsh accent of hers. He sensed her smirking but didn't dare look.

'You know your motorsport, then,' he said cautiously.

'Critics say the Impreza's a good value sports hatchback, but the suspension is soft, and the interior feels cheap and outdated.'

'Uh-huh,' countered Jake weakly. He pushed the start button, and the sound of the Arctic Monkeys blasted out of the souped-up speakers. He turned the music off before she could offer an opinion. 'I've not seen you around before,' he said, as he reversed out of the parking space.

'I transferred from Reading two weeks ago.'

'Reading? I thought you were from Wales.' Stupid comment. Why couldn't he think of something more intelligent to say?

'I can see why they recruited you to CID.'

Ouch. He deserved that. He signalled left and pulled out onto the main road. 'When I was a kid we used to holiday in North Wales,' he said, trying to recover the conversation. 'Prestatyn,

Bangor, Rhyl.' There were other seaside towns his family had visited, but he couldn't be confident of pronouncing them correctly. He wasn't a hundred percent sure he'd said these right. 'They're nice places when it isn't raining. Trouble is, it always was.' It was a weak joke, but it was all he had to offer right now.

Ffion looked distinctly unimpressed. 'If you're going to make a joke about sheep shaggers, don't bother. I've heard them all before.'

Sheep shaggers? Where on earth had that come from? He'd been going to ask if she followed the rugby, but thought better of it.

'So, um, whereabouts in Wales are you from?'

'Cwmclydach.'

The strange word seemed to fill the space between them. An unpronounceable, unspellable word that sounded like it had a surplus of consonants and not enough vowels. He had no idea where it was. Did Welsh people make these names up just to confuse the English?

'It's a former mining village in the South Wales valleys,' explained Ffion, answering his unasked question. 'I couldn't wait to get out and come to Oxford.'

'Oh, did you study here, then?' he asked, surprised.

'They do let Welsh people in, you know.'

Christ, she was prickly. Weren't the Welsh supposed to be into poetry and singing, that sort of thing? 'So which college did you go to?' He'd learnt that this was always the question to ask.

There were over thirty separate colleges making up the university, and Oxford graduates often seemed to feel more fondness for their college than for the university itself.

'Jesus College,' said Ffion, a hint of warmth and affection creeping into her voice for the first time. 'Lots of Welsh people go there. They say, if you stand in the front quad and shout "Jones", half the windows will open.'

He had no idea if she was being serious.

He slowed down as they approached the twenty-mile-an-hour zone in the centre of Oxford and parked on the wide street of St Giles', just outside St John's, another grand college. Ryan had told him once that you couldn't walk from St John's in Oxford to St John's in Cambridge without once stepping foot off land owned by one or other of the two colleges. He didn't know if Ryan was pulling his leg, but he wouldn't have been surprised if the story was true.

'So what's this Oxford Union, exactly?' he asked as they skirted around the tourists at the foot of Martyrs' Memorial, the tall stone monument in the middle of St Giles'. His dad had been a union representative at Tetley's Brewery in Leeds before he'd been made redundant, but somehow Jake didn't imagine this Oxford Union standing up for workers' rights and balloting for strikes.

'It's the university debating society,' said Ffion. 'It attracts aspiring politicians. Zac being president is a pretty big deal.' They darted across Magdalen Street in front of the Woodstock bus. 'Several British prime ministers were president of the Union in their student days – Edward Heath, William Gladstone, Herbert Henry Asquith, not to mention Boris Johnson.'

They crossed the busy road into Cornmarket, one of the four main streets that intersected at Carfax. A young woman was playing something classical on a cello outside the medieval church of St Michael at the Northgate. That was the kind of busker you got in Oxford. They turned down the narrow side road of St Michael's Street, and there, tucked just behind Oxford's main pedestrianised shopping street, was another of the peculiar discoveries that sometimes made Jake think he was living on a film set.

Just a short walk away from the bustling shops and fast-food restaurants of Oxford's main shopping street, a wrought iron gate opened into the grounds of a building that resembled a grand manor house with fancy brickwork, octagonal towers, and full-height leaded bay windows. A gravel path led them past clipped shrubs to an elaborate wooden doorway.

Jake swung the door open. 'After you.'

Inside, the impression of stepping into the country house of an earl or lord was only further enhanced by the wood panelling and oil paintings in gilt frames that adorned the walls.

'Looks like a private members' club,' said Jake.

'That's effectively what it is.'

Ffion seemed to know her way around. She strode confidently across the entrance hall and through a doorway. Jake followed her into a student bar like none that he had ever been in, and he'd tried a fair few in his time at Bradford and when visiting a couple of his mates who'd studied at Newcastle and Sheffield. Those places had either been modern – all chrome and neon lighting – or cave-like holes, not decorated since the seventies. Either way, the walls in those bars had been plastered with posters for gigs, and the atmosphere was generally loud and raucous, especially on a Friday or Saturday night. The Oxford Union bar, on the other hand, was the sort of place he could have brought his grandmother. Floor-to-ceiling burgundy curtains framed the large windows, and comfortable leather chairs and sofas were positioned around wooden tables. The walls were covered in photographs of all the famous people who had debated at the Union, and there seemed to be no shortage of them. He recognised the Dalai Lama, Mother Theresa and Albert Einstein, and they were just the ones that happened to be nearest. Incongruously, a chalk board next to them advertised the soup of the day.

A couple of students were seated by one of the windows, drinking lattes and chatting.

The barman was polishing glasses. 'May I help you?'

Jake showed his warrant card. 'DS Jake Derwent and DC Ffion Hughes, Thames Valley Police. I wonder if we could have a word?'

The barman immediately put down his cloth and looked uneasy. 'Sure. What about?'

'Were you working here last night?'

'Until we closed at 2am. Why?'

'Did you see Zachary Hamilton here?'

A shadow fell across the barman's face. 'Oh, yeah. I saw Zac all right. Couldn't miss him. In fact, I threw him out.'

'Why was that?'

'Is this on the record?'

'Not yet, but we may ask you to provide a written statement later.'

The barman glanced across at the two students who had stopped talking and appeared to be listening. He stared at them until they turned away and resumed their conversation. 'Zac was blind drunk. He often is, by the end of the night. He got into a fight with another student. I know he's the president, but I had no choice. I threw them both out.'

Jake found it hard to believe that a punch up would happen in this place. It seemed far too civilised. 'Who was the other student?'

'I don't know his name, but he was a big guy. Well over six foot tall' – the barman stretched up a hand to demonstrate – 'and muscular with it. Black hair. Tanned skin. I'd have put money on him being a rower or a rugby player. You get to recognise the type.'

Adam. He certainly fitted the description and there was no way those grazes on his knuckles were from rowing.

'Any idea what the argument was about?' asked Ffion.

The barman shook his head. 'Sorry, no.'

'And what time was this?'

'I kicked them out just before eleven o'clock. Zac was here for at least an hour before that.'

'Thanks, mate,' said Jake. 'You've been a big help.' He turned to Ffion. 'Time to go?'

'Just a minute.' Ffion was watching the two students. They looked to be about nineteen or twenty. One was wearing glasses, the other had long, floppy hair. To Jake, their manner screamed privately educated. Ffion approached their table. 'Mind if we have a word with you?'

The two guys clearly didn't mind in the least. Their eyes tracked her closely as she sat down at their table and crossed her long legs. Jake pulled up a chair and joined her.

'Do you attend the debates here?' she asked. 'Or do you just make use of the bar?'

'We go to the debates,' said the one wearing glasses. His accent was very posh. 'We were just discussing last night's speakers. Bloody awful. I'm Reuben by the way and this is Michael.'

Ffion didn't bother to introduce herself or Jake. 'So do either of you know Zachary or Zara Hamilton?'

'God, everyone knows Zac and Zara,' said Michael. 'Zac's the president this term, although

74

a lot of people would have preferred it to be Zara, but she didn't stand. She's not studying PPE like her brother.'

'PPE?' asked Jake. Another Oxford term to add to his lexicon.

Reuben and Michael looked at him as if he'd just landed from Mars.

'Politics, Philosophy and Economics,' explained Ffion. 'It's popular with people who have political ambitions.'

'And would you say Zac had political ambitions?' Jake asked the students.

Reuben nodded his head vigorously. 'I should say so. He aspires to be prime minister one day.'

'Do you think he actually could be?'

Michael spread his hands. 'It's an established career path – read PPE at Oxford, become president of the Union, work for one of the main political parties for a few years before standing for Parliament, then onward and upward. But plenty of people fall by the wayside. There are no certainties in politics.'

Jake wondered what the barman would make of the guy he kicked out for brawling being put in charge of the country. 'So what about Zara? Does she take an active part in debates?' He was careful to use the present tense as if she were still alive.

Michael guffawed. 'You should see those two. Sparks fly when they're debating. They're always on opposite sides. Basically, Zac is a dyed-in-the-wool Tory, and Zara's a banner-waving socialist.

Makes for some lively arguments.'

'Next week's debate is going to be standing room only,' interjected Reuben. 'You see, Zac has invited Catriona Hodgson as one of the speakers.'

'The newspaper columnist?' asked Jake. Catriona Hodgson was always causing controversy by tweeting her antagonistic views on social class, immigration, Muslims and 'benefit scroungers'.

'The very same,' said Reuben. 'But some people are arguing that we shouldn't even be giving a platform to someone like Catriona because allowing her to speak only legitimises her views. Zac says it's all about the right to free speech. There's a Twitter campaign saying we should ban Catriona and boycott the debate.'

Ffion took her mobile phone out. 'What's the hashtag?'

'NoOxfordPlatform.'

'Here we go,' she said, flicking at her screen. 'It's trending. There are hundreds of tweets against the debate going ahead.'

'All right,' said Jake, standing up. 'Thanks for your time. It's been helpful.'

It was time to head back to Christ Church and confront Adam and Zac.

CHAPTER 7

The aroma of partially-melted chocolate cake drifting from the back seat of the car tormented Bridget as she drove to the hospital. All she'd managed since breakfast was a packet of prawn cocktail crisps, hardly a healthy choice, and yet they'd somehow also conspired to be completely tasteless. She was pretty sure that no prawns had been harmed in their making. She wondered when she'd next manage to eat a meal that wasn't grabbed from a machine, or heated in a microwave.

This evening, she promised herself. She'd take Chloe out for a birthday dinner that evening come what may. She'd already sent Chloe a quick text to say that she was bringing home a special birthday treat. Her daughter knew her well enough to know that treat meant cake.

Oxford's John Radcliffe hospital, known locally as the JR, was a vast, sprawling site of mismatched buildings situated on a hill in the north eastern corner of the city. The JR was practically a small town in its own right. You needed a map to find your way around.

Every time Bridget visited the hospital she was reminded that it was here she had given birth to Chloe. Fifteen years ago today, in fact. Ben, her ex-husband, had driven her to the maternity unit at breakneck speed, then mysteriously vanished for much of the following fifteen hours of agony that had preceded the intense joy of holding her newborn daughter in her arms for the first time. The explosion of love she'd experienced then had never quite left her, even during Chloe's most rebellious phases. The love she'd felt for her husband had not endured as long. It certainly hadn't survived his serial cheating.

A queue of cars was waiting to enter the pay-and-display car park. Bridget drove past them, straight to the area reserved for doctors and other visiting professionals, making sure her well-used police permit was prominently displayed.

She switched her phone to silent as she made her way, not to the maternity ward but to its opposite: the mortuary. From cradle to grave. As she walked, she thought of Zara's parents and how they would never get to celebrate another birthday with their child. Just a few years separated Zara from Chloe, and yet Zara's life had already been brought to a brutal end. She quickly tapped out another text to Chloe: Love you lots xxx.

Zara's parents had already arrived at the hospital when Bridget entered. She was met by a uniformed police woman from the Met who'd accompanied them from London.

'They're in the waiting room,' she said, when Bridget showed her warrant card. 'You're late.'

'How are they?'

'As you'd expect. Angry. Shocked.' The woman's manner suggested that this might somehow be Bridget's fault.

Bridget composed herself carefully before entering the room. Meeting bereaved relatives was unquestionably the most difficult part of her job, even worse than coming face to face with the actual corpse. The corpse's suffering was over. Theirs was only just beginning.

She knew better than most of her fellow officers that bereavement after a violent death could take many years to come to terms with. She'd had to deal with it herself once, not for a daughter, but for a murdered sister. But that was a long time ago.

She pushed open the door to the waiting room and stepped inside. Despite the whisper of the air conditioning, the small room seemed stuffy and airless, the atmosphere tense. A vase of flowers on the central table was starting to wilt, the petals dropping onto the glass tabletop.

Sir Richard was on his feet and looked as if he'd been pacing the room, an urgent appointment beckoning. At the sound of the door opening, he swung abruptly to face her. She recognised him instantly from television appearances – the thick silver hair that gave men of that age a certain gravitas, the well-cut suit designed to disguise the middle-aged paunch.

Lady Hamilton, by contrast, was too thin for a woman of her age and height, her cheekbones too prominent, her shoulders too angular. Her forehead was unnaturally smooth. Her platinum hair, which she wore shoulder-length, had that professionally blow-dried look that Bridget never managed to attain. She was wearing a grey silk dress, casually understated, and clasping an expensive designer handbag. She perched on the edge of one of the chairs, rigidly upright, her face a mask. Only the slight puffiness around the eyes gave a clue to the sorrow and pain she must be feeling.

'So sorry to have kept you,' said Bridget, extending a hand to Sir Richard. 'DI Bridget Hart.'

He didn't take her hand. Instead he glared down at her, nostrils flaring, failing to hide the surprise in his voice. 'Where's the person in charge? That other woman said the senior investigating officer would be coming to meet us.'

'I will be leading the investigation into your daughter's death.'

'And how old are you?'

Bridget ignored the rudeness of the question. Nothing would be gained here from confrontation. She didn't need the Chief Superintendent's warning to tell her that. 'I'm thirty-eight, I'm a detective inspector, and I have many years of experience as a police officer.'

'Hmm. And you're sure it's actually her?'

'Richard, please…'

He ignored his wife. 'I mean, we haven't seen her yet.'

'If you'd like to come with me,' said Bridget. 'I need you to formally identify the body. I know this is going to be difficult. Please, when you're ready.' She stepped out, holding the door open wide.

Lady Hamilton appeared first, her heels clipping loudly in the silent corridor. Her husband followed, his hands clasped tightly behind his back, chest puffed out, eyes narrowed, as if this might still turn out to be some elaborate and cruel hoax. They followed a waiting mortuary assistant to the chapel of rest.

Bridget stood discreetly to one side as the assistant pulled back the white sheet covering Zara's face. The injury to the back of her head had been carefully concealed, the bloody hair tucked discreetly away. Her beauty was still striking, even with the cold, waxen skin of a corpse.

Bridget was reminded starkly of her own dead sister Abigail, only sixteen when her life was taken from her. And Chloe, just turned fifteen, her whole life still ahead of her. People told her that she must never make this job personal, but how could she not? Abigail's death was the force that drove her. It was the single reason she was a police detective and not just working in some anonymous office somewhere.

Lady Hamilton let out a sob, and Bridget

stepped outside to give the parents some time alone. She knew that until this moment they would have been in denial, clinging onto the hope, however faint and unlikely, that there had been a terrible mistake, that it wasn't their daughter lying on the table. But when the sheet was pulled aside, all hope vanished. Nothing needed to be said in that instant. Identification was confirmed in the sudden widening of the eyes, the intake of breath, the slump of the shoulders, the visceral cry of grief.

Ten minutes later they reappeared. Lady Hamilton's eyes were raw red. She looked as if she might crumple. Sir Richard had a protective hand around his wife's shoulder and the other guiding her arm. He had clearly been badly shaken too, but not defeated.

'Do you know yet who did this?' Despite everything, it was unmistakably the voice of a man who demanded results and expected them quickly. That was how a man like Sir Richard came to be the head of such a large corporation, Bridget guessed. No matter how bad the news, all that mattered was the next move, and how to get ahead again.

'We're making enquiries and following up a number of leads.' Bridget knew that the bland, formal phrase said nothing.

'In other words, no,' said Sir Richard. They returned to the waiting room and he resumed his pacing. 'I'm going to speak to the Chief Superintendent. I want to make sure the best person is leading this case.'

'Of course,' said Bridget. She didn't think that Grayson would be too surprised to receive Sir Richard's call. But she knew the Chief Super would back her. Unless she screwed up, of course. If that happened, her head would be on the chopping block. She turned to Lady Hamilton. 'Would you like to sit down? Shall I fetch you some water?'

Lady Hamilton sank onto her former chair and nodded. 'Please.' Her voice was barely above a whisper.

Bridget fetched two plastic cups of water from a cooler in the corridor. She handed one to Lady Hamilton and placed the other on the table beside the wilting flowers. She took a seat next to Lady Hamilton. 'Do you mind if I ask a few questions about the family? Zara had a twin brother. What were they like together? Did they get on?'

Lady Hamilton turned to look at her. Up close, Bridget could see a few grey roots in the otherwise immaculate coiffure. Fine wrinkles traced lines around her mouth and eyes. Her hands, crossed neatly in her lap, couldn't disguise her true age. 'Zara and Zac, they were always so...' Lady Hamilton stared into the middle distance and her gaze softened as if she was remembering something. Bridget sensed that she was ready to open up and talk about her daughter.

'Is this really necessary?' interrupted Sir

Richard. He pulled back his cuff ostentatiously to reveal an expensive gold watch. 'Unless you have any relevant questions, I think that you' – he glared at Bridget – 'should be out tracking down the killer.'

Beside her, Bridget felt Lady Hamilton flinch at her husband's tone of voice.

'I can assure you,' said Bridget, 'that my people are already doing everything they can to find the perpetrator. I am just trying to build up a better picture of Zara as a person.' It was always important to remember that the dead person once had a life, had hopes, dreams, desires and fears like the rest of us.

Sir Richard shook his head firmly. 'No. Zac texted me to say he's travelling to our country home. We should be there to meet him when he arrives. Come on, Celia. It's time we left.'

Lady Hamilton rose to her feet.

'You can call me at any time,' said Bridget, handing Lady Hamilton her card.

'Thank you.' She dropped it into her leather handbag with barely a glance.

Outside in the corridor, the family liaison officer from London was waiting to accompany Sir Richard and Lady Hamilton to their country house in the Cotswolds. Bridget handed them over gladly, and they left without another word.

CHAPTER 8

If Ffion had been alone and on her Kawasaki, it would have been much quicker to get around. Parking was always simpler on two wheels. But as it was, it was easier to walk straight from the Oxford Union to Christ Church than to go back and pick up Jake's car and then follow the circuitous traffic system that wound its way around the city centre.

They walked together down Cornmarket, deftly avoiding the attempts of various leaflet-toting activists to change their views on religion or animal rights.

Jake strode along briskly, slightly ahead of her, his hands in his pockets, saying nothing.

She knew she'd been mean to him, mocking his car and snubbing his efforts to make conversation, and he'd really done nothing to deserve it. He was all right actually, even if he did own a stupid car and have terrible taste in music. Her response to him had been purely defensive – defence in advance of any actual attack. Excessive, perhaps. But effective.

She'd learned to deal with men this way over

the years. It wasn't that she wasn't attracted to men. She just liked women too. And experience had taught her that her relationships with women were simpler to navigate. There was no misunderstanding for one thing. If she dated a woman then that woman was either gay or bisexual. But when she dated men, most of whom were straight, they tended to assume that any woman they went out with would be straight too. And things could get awkward when guys discovered her true nature. She'd yet to meet a man sensitive and understanding enough, so she'd largely given up on them. She could do without the hassle.

If he asked, she would simply tell him, 'I'm bisexual,' and everything would be out in the open and simpler going forward. Perhaps she ought to have volunteered the information, so that things were clear from the start.

As it was, they weren't even talking, and it was probably her fault. She remembered when she had first come to Oxford. Big city. Strange faces. She'd been lucky to make friends quickly. Jake was still new to Oxford. Perhaps he was just looking for a friend. But with men, it was always so complicated.

They crossed Carfax and headed down St Aldate's, weaving their way through the crowds of people waiting for buses.

They stopped in the porters' lodge and asked for directions to Zac's room. The porter's name badge read Jim Turner, Head Porter. 'Mr

86

Hamilton has left the college. A car came to pick him up half an hour ago. He's gone to his parents' house in the Cotswolds. Understandable in the circumstances.'

'Uh, right,' said Jake. 'What about Adam Brady, Zara's boyfriend? Do you know where we can find him?'

'Just a moment, sir.' The porter tapped some keys on his computer. 'Ah, here we go. Mr Brady has a room in Blue Boar Quad. I'll make a note of the room number for you.' He wrote the staircase and room number on a piece of crested notepaper and handed it to Jake. 'Do you know the way to Blue Boar Quad?'

'Yeah, I know,' said Ffion. 'No problem.'

'Anything else I can help you with?' asked Jim Turner.

'That's all for now,' said Jake. 'Thanks.'

They walked through a largely deserted Tom Quad, past the crime scene tape at the foot of Zara's staircase. The uniformed constable standing guard nodded to them as they passed.

'It's a funny name,' ventured Jake. 'Blue Boar.'

'Not really,' said Ffion. 'It's named after the adjacent street. Blue Boar Street,' she added helpfully.

'Makes sense. Still funny, though.'

She supposed it was, but strange names started to sound normal after you'd heard them a few times. 'The Blue Boar was the symbol of the De Vere family. They were the Earls of Oxford, back in the fifteenth century.'

'You're interested in history, are you?' asked Jake.

'I just have a good memory.'

She led the way left into Peckwater Quad, then left again through a walled walkway into Blue Boar Quad, pausing to see what Jake would make of it.

'Jesus,' he said, stopping to look around. 'How did this get planning permission?'

Ffion smiled to herself as she watched Jake take in the quad's strikingly modernist design. The L-shaped building was all brutal horizontal and vertical lines. It was pure 1960s, and Ffion rather liked it, but compared to the sixteenth- and eighteenth-century quads they'd just passed through, it did rather resemble an architectural alien whose ship had blown off course.

'Don't you like it?' she asked, keeping a deliberately straight face. 'It's a Grade II listed building, you know.'

'Couldn't they have built something that fitted in a bit better?' asked Jake, staring at the grey concrete accommodation block.

'I'd never have had you down as an architectural snob.'

'I didn't think I was. But still…'

He wasn't a snob exactly, she decided, just someone with fixed and firm expectations. She was glad she'd kept him at a distance.

They found Adam's staircase and climbed the stairs to his room on the third floor. Jake knocked loudly.

'Who is it?' called a grumpy-sounding voice.

'DS Jake Derwent and DC Ffion Hughes,' said Jake.

The door opened, but only halfway. 'What do you want?'

'Could we come in and have a word, please?'

The scowl on Adam's face said they were not welcome, but he withdrew into the room, leaving the door open. Ffion followed Jake inside.

Like the building, the room was modern and functional, with fitted cupboards and an en-suite bathroom. The wide window looked out onto more traditional architecture to remind you that you were still in Oxford. But the room was a complete tip. Energy bar wrappers, Lycra rowing suits, track suits, pairs of trainers and assorted muddy socks littered the floor.

Adam stood in front of the window and Ffion got her first proper look at him. He was even taller than Jake – six foot five, perhaps even six six – and heavily built too. She estimated his weight at fourteen stone. He was certainly made to be a rower. He'd obviously changed out of his kit since Jake had interviewed him down at the boathouse, and was now dressed in a black T-shirt and tight black jeans that matched his hair.

Rugged good looks – that was the phrase most people would use to describe him, but Ffion had an eye for detail. His face was long and his brow broad and prominent. His eyes were a dark chestnut. His coal-black hair was untamed, and rough stubble cast a dark shadow across his neck and face. If he'd shaved this morning, he hadn't spent a lot of time on it.

She studied his hands. They were large and bristling, with dark hairs on the back. His fingers and palms were callused from the rowing, but the bandages that Jake had described had disappeared. Instead they'd been replaced by sticking plasters applied directly over the knuckles of his right hand.

Adam stared at them sullenly for a moment, then sat down on the unmade bed. Jake took the desk chair and Ffion sat on the window seat, her back to the view. She crossed her legs and watched as Adam's gaze drifted in her direction.

'We'd like to ask a few more questions,' said Jake. Adam turned away from her. 'First of all, where were you last night?'

'I already told you. I was in the college bar, drowning my sorrows. You can check with the bar staff and about a hundred students if you don't believe me.'

'Because you split up with Zara?'

'Yeah.'

'So, how did that happen? Did she dump you?' Jake somehow managed to inject the right amount of blokeish sympathy to take the sting out of the blunt question.

Adam nodded, looking miserable.

'Did she say why?'

Adam sank his face into his huge hands, clearly revealing his injured knuckles. 'She didn't say. Just that she didn't want to see me anymore.'

'And what time did you leave the bar?'

Adam shrugged. 'I don't know. It wasn't like I was watching the clock or anything. Does it matter?'

'Earlier, you told me you left at ten,' said Jake.

'Ten, then.'

'Were you with anyone in particular?'

'Mostly by myself. I didn't feel much like talking.'

'I can understand that, mate. And where did you go after you left the college bar?'

A moment's hesitation. 'Popped out for a kebab, if you must know.'

'You didn't go to the Oxford Union?'

A guarded look crossed his face for the first time. 'Why would I want to go there? I'm not even a member.'

'Zara was though,' prompted Ffion.

Adam turned towards her, studying her face, frowning. 'We didn't do everything together. She wasn't a rower, for instance.'

'So what did you have in common?' she asked.

Anger flashed in his dark eyes. 'I don't have to explain my relationship to you. Do you have a boyfriend?'

'No,' said Ffion levelly. She sensed Jake glance in her direction. Adam turned away, a look of misery replacing the momentary aggression.

'Tell us about you and Zara,' said Jake in a more conciliatory tone. 'How long had you been together?'

'Most of the year, I guess.'

'How serious was the relationship?'

Adam shrugged. 'I don't know. How do you tell?'

Jake scratched his nose carefully. Ffion had seen him do that before. He did it when he was thinking. 'Well,' he said. 'Did you love her?'

Adam gave the question some consideration. 'I think I did. I thought she loved me too. Until the break-up.'

'Did you ever visit her parents?' asked Ffion.

'No. Zara didn't talk much about her family, apart from Zac.'

'Was she ashamed of them?'

'No.'

'Was she ashamed of you?' asked Ffion.

Adam glared at her. 'You're very rude. Has anyone ever told you that?'

'Yes,' said Ffion. 'So, was she ashamed of you?'

'No. She just liked to keep different parts of her life separate. To be honest, I was glad. Her father comes across as a bully.'

'Have you met him?'

'Just once. I think it's fair to say he didn't think much of me, and wasn't shy about saying so.'

'And how is your relationship with Zac?'

'I try not to spend much time with him. We tend not to agree on much.'

'So,' said Jake, 'we've just come from the Oxford Union and the barman there says he threw two students out last night for getting into a fight. One of them was Zachary Hamilton and the other matched your description. Now, we could check on CCTV or you could just save us all a shitload of work if you admit that you went to the Oxford Union and had a bust-up with Zac.'

A scowl crossed Adam's heavy brow. 'Yeah, all right then. I did see Zac. I knew he'd be at the Union and I went to see him.' He stopped.

Ffion prompted him. 'So you went to see Zac. What happened?'

Adam looked up again, morose. 'Something snapped. I guess that after losing Zara I felt I had nothing more to lose. I should have hit him a long time ago. Finally, I did. It felt good, if you want to know.' He clenched his right fist, showing the plasters covering his knuckles.

'That's how you got the cuts on your hand?' asked Jake.

'Yeah.'

Ffion studied his face. There wasn't a mark on it. Zac had no doubt come off the worse in this altercation. 'What was the argument about?'

'Doesn't matter. Could have been about anything. The guy's a tosser.'

'Why didn't you tell me about the fight with Zac when I asked you before?' asked Jake.

Adam snorted with derision. 'Seriously?'

'Yeah, seriously.'

Adam looked at Jake as if he was stupid. 'What do you think will happen to me if the college finds out I had a fight with Zachary Hamilton? I'll be sent down. That's what's going to happen,

93

isn't it? After all my hard work, I'm going to be kicked back to where I came from.'

'But wouldn't Zac be sent down too?'

Adam laughed mirthlessly. 'You don't get it, do you? Look, I didn't go to Eton. My parents aren't Sir and Lady whoever. I'm from nowhere. Coming here to study at Oxford was a dream come true for me. And meeting Zara... she didn't care where I came from. She treated people however she found them, no matter what their background. But the dean will kick me out on my arse if he finds out about this fight. He wouldn't dare lay a finger on Zac because his father's too important. People like Zac can get away with murder.' He flinched at his own words. 'Sorry, that came out wrong, but you know what I mean.'

Ffion sensed that Adam's outburst wasn't quite finished. She motioned for Jake to stay quiet.

After a moment, he continued. 'The thing is, Zac's father, Sir Richard Hamilton, is making a big donation to the college so they can build a new block of student accommodation off-site. It's going to be called Hamilton House. So even though Zac's a lazy shit who hardly ever does any work, he gets to swan around, playing at being president of the Union and generally being a dick.' He lapsed into silence again.

'Do you know why anyone might have murdered Zara?' asked Jake.

Adam shook his head. 'No. I have no idea. She

was the golden girl, you know? Everyone loved her.'

'Including Zac?'

'Yeah, they were really close.'

'We heard they often clashed in debates.'

He shrugged. 'They had different views, that's all. It wasn't personal. Like I said, Zara never held grudges.'

'One last thing before we go,' said Ffion. 'I'm going to ask you again what the fight with Zac was about.'

The look Adam shot her was pained and furious. 'Nothing. I already told you.' He stood up, his physical size dominating the room. 'I think it's time you left now.'

Ffion nodded. 'We will, just as soon as we've taken your fingerprints.' She smiled sweetly at him. 'Just for elimination purposes, you understand.'

★

'He's still hiding something, isn't he?' said Ffion, as they left Adam's room in Blue Boar and headed back to Tom Quad.

'He's been acting shifty right from the start,' said Jake. But Adam's words had touched a raw nerve with him. Coming from a working class northern background himself, he couldn't help feeling some camaraderie with Adam. 'Is he right about being kicked out of college, but Zac being let off because of his father?' he asked.

Ffion shrugged. 'Some people like to pin blame for their misfortunes on others. The truth is that Oxford has been bending over backwards in recent years to offer places to students from diverse backgrounds. Look at me. A girl from a Welsh mining village and' – she paused and looked away – 'I'm as diverse as they come,' she concluded.

They rounded the corner and found the PC guarding Zara's staircase having a lively discussion with a female student. When Jake and Ffion arrived he turned to them. 'This young woman says her room is upstairs and she needs to get access to it, but I can't allow her to enter.'

'It's all right, we'll handle this,' said Jake. 'What's your name?' he asked the student.

'Megan Jones. Can I get my stuff, then?'

'You're the student with the room opposite Zara's on the top floor, aren't you?'

'Yeah.'

'Has the college found another room for you?'

'Yeah. Some shitty corner of Blue Boar.'

Jake suppressed an urge to smile. Moving from the stone cloisters of Tom Quad to the concrete bunker of Blue Boar sounded like a fall from grace. Yet he'd actually felt more at home in Blue Boar Quad. It reminded him of the student accommodation he'd lived in when he was at Bradford. Plain, functional and no-nonsense. He didn't really trust the decorative arches and crenellations of Tom Quad. It looked too fairytale, as if it might all disappear in a puff of smoke.

'Still,' he said to Megan, 'it's good they've found you a place so quickly. I'm DS Jake Derwent and this is my colleague DC Ffion Hughes. We'll take you upstairs so you can fetch your stuff. We'd also like to ask you a few questions, if you don't mind.'

Megan seemed to relax at the offer of being escorted to her room. 'Sure.'

On their way up the stairs they passed the seminar room on the ground floor that was being redecorated. 'What's happening in there?' Jake asked. 'Isn't it a bit odd to get the builders in during term time? I'd have thought they'd wait until all the students have gone home.'

'There was some water damage,' said Megan. 'The room was unusable so they had to sort it out.'

On the top landing, she glanced anxiously towards Zara's room, but the door was closed and there was nothing to see. She drew out her own key but paused before unlocking her room. When she turned to face Jake her eyes were shining with tears. 'What happened to Zara? How did she die?'

'I can't give you any further information at this stage, but we are treating her death as suspicious.'

Her mouth twisted down. 'I hope you find the bastard who did it.'

'We'll do everything we can,' Jake assured her. 'First, we'd like to know where you were yesterday and what you saw.'

Megan pushed into her room and sat down on the sofa, wiping her eyes. Her room was a mirror image of Zara's. Only the posters on the wall and the books on the shelves were different.

'I saw her coming out of the dining hall at half past six,' she said, her voice thick. 'I was just going in, but Zara had already eaten and was rushing off somewhere. She must have been there when they started serving food at six twenty.' She stopped and more tears ran down her cheeks. 'Zara was such a bright student. Her death is such a tragic waste.'

Jake gave her a moment, then prompted her gently. 'What then?'

'After dinner I went back to the library. I had a Latin translation to finish. Tacitus. Bloody awful it was, too.'

'Did you see her again?'

'No. That was the last time.'

'Do you know what Zara was planning to do with her evening?'

'I think she might have been going out. But I don't know where.'

'And what about you? Did you get your translation finished?'

'Yes, eventually.' She bit her lip, hesitating.

'What is it?'

'It's probably nothing, but I came back here about eight thirty to do some reading in my room. I like to read with my headphones on. I finished a bit after eleven and then I went out to see my boyfriend. Anyway, as I was leaving, at about half past eleven, I saw Zac banging on Zara's door.'

'How did he seem?'

'He was in a foul mood, actually. I think he was drunk. Nothing unusual there.'

'Did you speak to him?'

'No. I try to avoid him when he's like that.'

'And did Zara open the door to him?'

'No. Like I said, I think she was out. But Zac wouldn't give up. He just kept hammering away. I left him there.'

'How long did you spend with your boyfriend?' asked Ffion.

'All night. He lives over the road in Pembroke College. I was supposed to have a tutorial at three. I got back to college an hour ago and found out what had happened.'

'Thanks for telling us,' said Jake. 'Can we give you a hand carrying your gear?'

'Please.' She gave them a thin smile. 'Now I think about it, I'll be glad to move out. I don't want to stay on in this staircase after what happened.'

CHAPTER 9

'You're too late,' muttered Dr Roy Andrews as Bridget pushed open the door to his office.

This time on a Friday afternoon, hospital consultants and registrars were already beginning to disappear for the weekend, but the senior pathologist was old school and Bridget had been confident he'd still be at work. Sure enough, he was sitting behind his squat desk, scratching notes in his writing pad with a gold fountain pen. A protective clutter of books, papers and typed reports partially screened him from the outer office.

Roy regarded her arrival mournfully over the top of wire-frame reading glasses, his gloomy, hang-dog expression belied by his signature brightly-coloured bow tie which protruded above his white coat. Today's bow tie was purple with a design of tiny buzzing bees. A graduate of Magdalen College, he possessed a sharp mind and an acerbic wit. Other detectives found him difficult to work with, but Bridget liked him.

'My secretary's already gone home,' he told her. 'It's close of play for this week.'

'That's not like you, Roy. Since when have you been a clock watcher?'

'Always have been. Nothing like being a pathologist to make you realise that time's running out for all of us,' he said darkly.

'Good. Then let's not waste any.'

He finished his writing and folded away his glasses. 'You're here about the girl, no doubt.'

'Zara Hamilton. I've just shown her body to her parents.'

'Sad business. And you want me to tell you the time of death?'

'That would be helpful. Time of death. Cause of death. Any initial thoughts?'

'Can't help you. Not until after I've done the post-mortem.' He peered at the computer screen on his desk. 'Monday morning sound good to you?'

'I was hoping for something sooner.'

'No peace for the pathologist, eh? What makes you think I have nothing better to do on my weekend?'

Bridget knew for a fact that Roy Andrews was a confirmed bachelor and a workaholic. But it always amused him to play these games with her.

'You have better company to keep than a corpse?' she enquired.

'Hmm,' he sighed with more than a touch of theatrical melancholy. 'You're right. I'll come in tomorrow afternoon.'

Bridget smiled at him.

'I'll start promptly at two o'clock, if you want

to send someone over.'

'I'll be there.' She turned to leave.

'Aren't you going to insist that I give you a provisional estimate of the time of death?' he asked. 'Even though I have yet to give the corpse more than a cursory inspection?'

She turned back, one eyebrow raised.

'All I can say at the moment is sometime between eight o'clock in the evening and midnight. That's an estimate, you understand. I can't be more precise until tomorrow.'

'But you're confident it's between those hours.'

'Have I ever let you down?'

'What about the cause of death?'

'Blunt force trauma. I'm sure that even you could have worked that out.'

'Thanks. I'll see you tomorrow.'

'Don't be late,' he cautioned. 'Time and tide wait for no man.'

She left the chilly and claustrophobic confines of the morgue behind her and made her way out into the warm summer evening. The bright sunshine seemed wrong after spending so much time in the proximity of death. But evening shadows were already beginning to reach across the hospital grounds. It was five o'clock and Chloe would have arrived home from school half an hour ago.

As she walked back to her car, her phone buzzed. A text from Chloe, presumably in response to the ones Bridget sent earlier.

Just going into Oxford to celebrate. See you later x.

Bridget frowned at the screen. Going into Oxford? But what about her plans to take Chloe out? She hadn't actually told her daughter she intended to take her for a birthday meal, of course. She'd simply assumed she would be waiting when she arrived home.

She dialled Chloe's number. The phone rang half a dozen times before her daughter picked up.

'Hi Mum.' Giggling and chattering in the background.

'Chloe, where are you?'

'Chill, Mum. I'm on the bus into Oxford.'

'But where are you going?'

Big sigh. 'Just out. We might grab a pizza later.'

'But I –'

'It's not like you planned anything for my birthday, did you?'

'I –' She should have told Chloe about the Italian restaurant. 'I'm sorry. I was hoping we could eat out tonight, but actually I'm really busy in any case.'

'Yeah, whatever.' More giggling and chattering. 'Listen, I've gotta go, this is our stop.'

'Chloe?'

'What?'

'Stay safe and don't be back late.'

'Oh, yeah. I forgot to say. Olivia said we could all sleep at her place. I've really got to go now, Mum.'

From the traffic sounds in the background, Bridget guessed they'd got off the bus.

'Call me when you get to Olivia's, so I know you're safe.'

'Yeah. Bye.' The line went dead.

Bridget pocketed the phone and trudged over to her car. She opened the door, only to be tormented by the sweet, cloying smell of melted chocolate cake. Damn. She'd had virtually nothing to eat all day. The smell taunted her all the way back to Kidlington.

Most of the team were already back at HQ when she arrived. Ryan and his sub-team had spent the afternoon collecting witness statements from everyone with a room in or around Tom Quad. They were busy entering the details into the Holmes police database.

'How did you get on?' Bridget asked.

Ryan studied his notes. 'We spoke to loads of students. Lots of people saw her at various times and locations yesterday. We should be able to piece together a detailed map of her movements. Everyone knew Zara, and about half of them claimed to be best friends.' His tone suggested some scepticism.

'Any enemies?'

'We didn't hear a single bad word against her.'

Andy's team was similarly occupied, entering their findings into the database.

'We took a detailed statement from Sophie, Zara's tutorial partner,' he reported. 'We spoke to people who were in the college bar. Several of them saw Adam there, getting pissed. We also managed to get a guest list for the drinks reception at the dean's lodgings.' He held up a sheet of letter paper with the college crest at the top. 'Quite a crowd of bigwigs there last night, including the leader of the city council.'

She left them to it and went to speak to Jake and Ffion who were just returning from Christ Church. Ffion was striding into the incident room with Jake trailing a few feet behind her. Bridget wondered if they had hit it off, working together. Their body language wasn't encouraging.

'The bartender at the Oxford Union confirmed that Zac was there last night,' said Jake. 'Zac got into a fight with Adam. We weren't able to speak to Zac or Verity, because they'd already left for the Cotswolds by the time we got to the college, but we went to see Adam again. He admitted he got into a punch up with Zac, but refused to say what it was about.'

'We also spoke to Megan Jones, the student who has a room opposite Zara's,' said Ffion. 'She was out most of last night, but she saw Zara leaving dinner at six thirty. She thinks she may have been going out somewhere. And interestingly, she also bumped into Zac later that evening.' She paused for dramatic effect.

'Go on.'

'He was banging loudly on Zara's door. Megan says he was drunk and angry.'

'What time was this?'

'About half past eleven.'

'That's ten minutes after Verity claims he got back to his room.'

'We also learnt something interesting at the Oxford Union,' said Ffion. 'Zac and Zara always took opposing sides in debates. And there's an aggressive Twitter campaign against one of the speakers that Zac has organised for next week. Catriona Hodgson, the journalist who's always sounding off and offending people.'

'Interesting,' said Bridget. 'Well done. Jake, tomorrow morning you and I will be taking a little trip to the country home of Sir Richard and Lady Hamilton. I want to speak to Zac myself.'

She turned to Ffion. 'I hear you're good with computers.'

Ffion's face lit up.

'I'd like you to find out all you can about Zara online. What's her social media profile like? Did she have any obvious enemies? And see if you can learn any more about this Twitter campaign. Find out if Zara was involved in any way.'

Ffion looked delighted to have been given a technical job.

'Right,' said Bridget, looking at her watch. 'I suggest you both go home and get some rest. It's going to be a long week.'

With the birthday meal off the table, she fetched herself a coffee and logged on to her computer to read through the case notes and check her emails. Dozens of messages had arrived throughout the day. She scanned through them quickly, looking to see if Vik from the SOCO team had sent her anything. He had. She opened his message and found a short summary of the team's initial findings, together with a list of all the items that had been collected for further analysis.

One interesting detail caught her attention. The team had found a handprint in fresh paint in the ground floor seminar room that was being redecorated. A bloody towel had also been recovered from the same location. Bridget already had a pretty good idea whose handprint it was. She hoped to be able to confirm that tomorrow.

Before leaving, she knocked on Superintendent Grayson's glass door and brought him up to date. 'So far we've gathered a lot of intelligence about Zara's movements throughout the day and evening leading up to her death. The pathologist has given us a provisional time of death, and we're seeing how that fits with the timeline of events. We've also verified the whereabouts of several persons of interest, and we have a couple of leads.'

'Who?'

'Zara's brother Zac had a fight with her ex-boyfriend, Adam Brady, at the Oxford Union yesterday evening. Zac was seen banging on Zara's door later that night, though we can't be sure yet whether that was before or after she was killed.'

Grayson's brows knitted together. 'Remember

what I said. Tread very carefully, especially with regard to Zac. Don't make a move without notifying me first.'

'No, sir. I met Sir Richard and Lady Hamilton today when they came to ID the body. I'm planning to drive over to the Hamiltons' country home tomorrow and talk to Zac again. Also, I've persuaded the pathologist to bring forward the PM to tomorrow afternoon, and forensics should have some preliminary results for us too. We should have a much clearer picture by this time tomorrow.'

She remembered then what she'd forgotten earlier. The CCTV footage. The memory stick was still in her bag. She'd make sure to get someone to study it tomorrow.

She suddenly felt very tired. There were so many jobs to remember, and despite having a great team, the responsibility fell on her. Already the strain of running her first murder enquiry was making her feel exhausted. Just this morning her biggest concern had been the ingredients for a birthday cake. Now she was charged with a matter of life and death. She hoped that Grayson couldn't detect any signs of stress.

He fixed her with his dark eyes. 'Keep me informed.'

★

It was gone nine o'clock when Bridget parked her car by the village green in Wolvercote. On this

June evening it wasn't yet dark, but the children who'd been playing on the swings were long gone, probably tucked up in bed by now. The lights were on in the village pub and sounds of music and laughter drifted across the green as its door opened and closed.

She carried the box containing the chocolate cake into the empty and silent house. On a day like today, after dealing with a murder enquiry and visiting the morgue, she'd have liked to come home to the sound of Chloe's music playing upstairs, or see her watching TV in the front room. She wanted to ask her daughter how her day had been, wanted to see her, hug her, know that she was safe. She checked her phone for messages, but there were none.

She went through to the kitchen and put the cake on the kitchen table next to her swimming kit which was still sitting where she'd left it this morning. She was far too tired to go swimming now. She was too tired even to cook, or to change out of her work clothes.

She was suddenly starving. What had she eaten today? A packet of crisps. She opened the fridge and peered at its brightly-lit contents. An open packet of chicken slices curling at the edges; a tub of low-fat cottage cheese past its sell-by date; half a dozen fat-free yoghurts; some vegetables and salad. Healthy ingredients. Good intentions.

Oh, what the hell. She let the fridge door swing closed and lifted the lid off the cake box. Parts of the cake had collapsed. The icing had completely melted and pooled around the bottom of the box. It no longer looked like the sort of cake you could give to someone as a birthday gift. She dipped a finger into the melted icing and licked it. Delicious.

She cut herself a generous slab of the cake, poured herself a large glass of Pinot Noir, and took both through to the lounge. She dimmed the lights and switched on the CD player. Soon the stirring overture from Mozart's Marriage of Figaro began to soothe her nerves, and she leaned back on the sofa with her feet up.

'Cheers!' She raised her glass. The wine was full-bodied and aromatic, with strong hints of cherry and raspberry. She couldn't think of a better match for the rich chocolate cake. 'Happy birthday, Chloe!' she said. It was surprising how much cake she was able to put away, once she got going.

CHAPTER 10

Bridget drove down the Cowley Road in East Oxford to the uplifting strains of Bizet's Carmen playing on the car stereo. She'd arranged to collect Jake from home to save them both having to drive into Kidlington. The trip to the Hamiltons' house in the Cotswolds should take them about forty-five minutes, depending on traffic.

She quickly located the launderette and Indian restaurant that Jake had described and managed to slot the Mini in between a builder's van and a bus that had stopped to collect and set down passengers. Her parallel parking skills were well-honed from practice, and it helped having such a nifty little car. She texted Jake to tell him she was outside.

She closed her eyes while she waited for him. Finishing off the bottle of wine and half of the chocolate cake last night hadn't been such a smart move. Her sleep had been disturbed by bad dreams and indigestion. And what kind of mother ate her own child's birthday cake, anyway? One whose daughter went off with her mates, not caring about her mother, she thought. But it was her own fault for not sharing her plans to take Chloe out for a meal. And for not being there when she got home from school. And for generally being an inadequate mother in too many ways to count.

Chloe had finally sent a text at eleven thirty to say she was at Olivia's house and was having an epic time. At least Bridget had been able to go to sleep knowing that her daughter was safe. Unlike Zara's mother. She wondered whether Lady Hamilton had managed any sleep last night, and imagined that smooth, pale face raw with fresh, senseless grief.

She jumped at the sound of a knock on the side window.

'Morning ma'am.' Jake opened the door and squeezed his tall frame into the Mini's passenger seat.

'There's a lever under the seat,' said Bridget. 'You can adjust the position.'

He slid the seat back as far as it would go but still looked cramped. Maybe they would have been better off taking his car. He fastened his seatbelt without complaining.

She tapped the address into the SatNav then pulled out neatly from her tiny parking space, switching off the music in case Jake didn't appreciate her taste. Few people did, she'd found.

The Saturday morning shopping traffic hadn't got into gear yet, but the road was already busy with buses, cyclists and delivery vans. Cowley Road was somewhat different to the broad tree-lined roads of North Oxford, and to the tourist-crammed medieval streets of the centre. Few visitors ventured this far from the colleges, unless they were lost or staying in one of the cheap bed & breakfasts or family-run hotels to be found in the eastern quarter of the city. It was a lively, diverse part of Oxford characterised by ethnic restaurants, trendy bars, traditional pubs, shared student digs, small businesses and a live music and clubbing venue, the O2 Academy, which Bridget had so far banned Chloe from visiting. Cowley Road was the best place in Oxford to get a really good curry.

She took a short-cut right into Howard Street and navigated her way deftly along the narrow one-way street past all the parked cars. 'Breathe in!' she told Jake as she squeezed the car through a particularly tight spot.

'Where exactly do the Hamiltons live?' asked Jake.

'Shipton-under-Wychwood,' said Bridget. She loved the way little English villages often had such fanciful names, like something Tolkien might have invented. 'Or two miles outside Shipton-under-Wychwood to be precise. It's in the middle of the Cotswolds.'

'I don't really know what the Cotswolds are.'

'Well, the Cotswold Hills stretch from north of Oxford west to the River Severn and the Welsh border.' Bridget could still remember most of her school geography lessons when they'd studied the local area. Jake seemed interested so she carried on. 'Most of the Oxford colleges and university buildings are built from stone mined in the Cotswold Hills. The hills aren't really very high, it's mostly just an area of farmland with villages scattered about. All very picture-postcard. People pay a lot of money for a big country house with a view.'

'I can imagine. So do you mind if I ask, ma'am, are you from around here originally?'

'I grew up in Woodstock, just north of Oxford,' said Bridget. 'So yes, I'm local. I even studied at the university here, too.'

Sometimes she regretted going away to university given what happened at home in her absence, but her sister's murder could not have been foreseen. The girls' school she'd attended always pushed its brightest pupils into sitting the Oxford entrance exam. She'd passed the exam, been offered a place, and had – of course – accepted it. Looking back, it was as if she hadn't really had a choice in the matter. Everything had just slotted into position, and her life had unfolded, almost without conscious design. Meeting Ben. Getting pregnant. Having Chloe. Divorcing Ben. Where had she been while all that was happening to her? But she knew where – coping with grief, even if she'd refused to acknowledge it at the time. Perhaps she was still just coping, even seventeen years after Abigail's death. Perhaps grief still had the power to bubble up and overwhelm her if she ever dropped her guard.

'What subject did you study?' asked Jake, oblivious to the dark train of her thoughts.

'History.'

'So how did you end up joining the police, if you don't mind me asking?'

'What else could I have done with a history degree?'

Jake laughed. It was Bridget's stock reply to the question – a flippant response that concealed the darker truth. She had been driven to join the police force in a desire to restore order to the world, to right wrongs and bring justice. No doubt she was hoping at some deep subconscious level to bring her dead sister back to life, or at least to obtain retribution for a young life snatched so cruelly away. That was an impossibility. Abigail's killer had never been caught, and there was nothing Bridget could ever do to put that right. But perhaps she could stop someone else's sister or daughter from being murdered.

Zara Hamilton's face flashed before her, lying on the floor of her college room, her golden hair fanning out, clotted with blood, then laid out in the morgue, beautiful and serene, yet cold and lifeless. There was no possibility of bringing Zara back from the dead either, but at least Bridget still had a chance to find whoever had murdered her. She would find that person, whatever it took.

'So where did you study?' she asked Jake.

'University of Bradford. Criminology.'

'Well, at least one of us has some relevant qualifications, then.'

They crossed the River Thames at Donnington Bridge and joined the Abingdon Road. From there they would pick up the southern by-pass and proceed north-west through the village of Eynsham. It was a perfect day for a drive through rural Oxfordshire, the hedgerows luxuriant and green, the grass verges bursting with wild flowers, the landscape dotted with fields of glaringly yellow rapeseed. They passed half-timbered pubs, thatched cottages and ancient barns. Just outside Eynsham they joined a small queue of traffic at a narrow stone bridge over the Thames. The bridge was barely wide enough for vehicles to cross in both directions. Bridget fished a five pence coin out of her pocket, lowered her window, and handed over the money to a young man at a toll booth.

'What on earth?' asked Jake, looking back at the toll booth as they drove on.

'Either a quaint and charming curiosity, or an annoying and ridiculous waste of time, depending on your point of view,' Bridget informed him. 'King George III granted the owner of the bridge the right to collect a toll, and no one can stop it. Think yourself lucky – if we were towing a trailer, we'd have had to pay twelve pence.'

The SatNav directed them through the centre

of the picturesque village of Shipton-under-Wychwood, past the chocolate box houses, church and pub, all built in the same golden Cotswold stone, and down a country lane. Bridget slowed to twenty miles an hour, partly because the road was so narrow and winding, and partly because she didn't want to miss the entrance to the Hamiltons' house.

She needn't have worried. The entrance was impossible to miss.

Huge wrought-iron gates flanked by stone pillars were guarded by carved stone lions. Bridget pulled up beside an electronic intercom and pressed the buzzer. No one answered, but the gates glided open and she drove through, following a single-lane road. Open fields rolled before them, edged with dry stone walls made of the same material that had been used to construct the village. They continued along the curving, narrow road, passing trees, meadows and pasture. There was still no sign of the house.

'Wow,' said Jake, peering out of the window. 'So this is what you can buy if you have a couple of million to spare.'

Sir Richard's house and land was probably worth a lot more than that. Bridget knew that these grand estates changed hands for twenty million pounds or more. Of course, the millionaire businessman hadn't been born into money, nor was his title hereditary. The Hamiltons' money wasn't old money, the sort that was handed down from generation to generation along with land, a title and an entry in Debrett's Peerage. It's what was sometimes still referred to derisively in some quarters as new money. As far as Bridget was concerned, earning money was more laudable than being handed it on a plate. And all money, whether old or new, always conveyed a certain power, and Sir Richard clearly liked to wield it, and wanted everyone to know it too.

They followed the road along a tree-lined avenue, passing a stable block and a swimming pool. Then the driveway swung to the right in a great sweeping arc and suddenly they were face to face with a Georgian mansion that looked as if it had stepped straight out of the pages of a Jane Austen novel.

'Wow,' said Jake for a second time.

The house was certainly impressive with its ageing red brick and decorative sandstone edgings. It was worth two wows. A flight of stone steps led up to the porticoed entrance. Three windows flanked the front door on either side, and seven ranged along the upper floor. A further storey of dormer windows protruded from the slate-tiled roof. The otherwise perfect symmetry of the design was softened by an abundant sprawl of wisteria covering one half of the building. The Mini's tyres scrunched gratifyingly on the circular gravel drive in front of the house, which was bordered by a row of sharply-clipped yew hedges.

Bridget tugged on the brass bell-pull and a

chime sounded somewhere deep inside the house. A minute later the front door was opened by a tight-lipped woman who appeared business-like in a crisp white blouse and tailored black trousers. A housekeeper or secretary, Bridget supposed.

'May I help you?'

'DI Bridget Hart and my colleague DS Jake Derwent,' said Bridget by way of introduction.

The woman studied their warrant cards carefully. Satisfied at last, she nodded and invited them to enter. They stepped into a marbled hallway, the panelled walls hung with oil paintings of hunting scenes. A grand staircase swept upwards, turning both left and right onto a first floor gallery. Bridget caught a glimpse of someone – a girl, maybe sixteen or seventeen years old – leaning over the balustrade, but as soon as she looked up, the girl turned and vanished into one of the bedrooms.

'This way please.' The housekeeper led them to a door on the left of the hall. 'If you'll wait in the drawing room, I'll inform Lady Hamilton that you're here.'

The room was the epitome of elegance. Cream silk curtains made from an excess of fabric framed the windows and trailed on the polished parquet floor. A crystal chandelier dangled from the central ceiling rose. In front of the marble fireplace a Chesterfield sofa and armchairs were arranged around a Persian rug of exquisite design. In the far corner of the room a grand

119

piano stood with its lid open as if in readiness for a soirée of classical music.

Bridget wandered over to a polished table by the fireplace on which were arranged family photographs in silver frames. They included numerous shots of Zara and Zac at different ages, and photographs of a younger child, presumably the girl she had seen on the landing.

The door opened and Lady Hamilton appeared. She looked paler than yesterday and even thinner, if that was possible. Bridget wondered if she'd eaten or slept since their last meeting.

'Inspector.' Lady Hamilton held out a delicate hand. 'Judith said you were here. How may I help?'

'We were actually hoping to speak to Zachary,' said Bridget. 'Is he here?'

'Zac? Why do you want to speak to him? Do you think he knows something?'

'It's routine, nothing to worry about. We'd just like to check a couple of facts with him.' Bridget tried to make it sound as if it were no big deal. She didn't want to alarm Lady Hamilton who looked as fragile as a blade of dried grass.

Tread very carefully, Grayson had warned her. There's no room for error.

Lady Hamilton wrung her hands together. 'Well, yes, Zachary is here. Would you like me to fetch him for you?'

'That would be very helpful, if you wouldn't mind.'

'Please take a seat,' said Lady Hamilton, indicating the sofa and armchairs. 'I won't be a moment.'

Bridget and Jake took the two armchairs that faced each other either side of the fireplace. Zac would have to sit on the sofa between them, which would give them a good opportunity to observe him. They waited in silence, the only sound the ticking of the antique clock on the mantelpiece.

After about five minutes the drawing room door swung open again and Zac stomped into the room. Both Bridget and Jake stood. Zac looked no better than he had done yesterday. The cut on his cheek was now covered by a plaster, but dark purple swelling had blossomed below his right eye.

'Thank you for agreeing to see us,' said Bridget.

He regarded them warily from beneath the shock of uncombed fair hair that flopped down in front of his eyes.

'Shall we sit down?' she said.

She and Jake resumed their seats and Zac took up position in the middle of the Chesterfield sofa, slouching, one arm running along the sofa's low back. Jake took out his notebook and pen.

'We'd like to ask you a few questions about what happened on Thursday,' said Bridget.

'What about it?' His tone was sullen, uncooperative.

'We know that you went to the Oxford Union

that evening, and we have eyewitness reports that you were involved in a fight there with Adam Brady, Zara's ex-boyfriend. We've already interviewed Adam, but we'd like you to tell us exactly what happened.'

'What's that got to do with anything?'

'That's what we're trying to establish.'

Zac shrugged. 'Adam's a jerk. Zara dumped him at long last. She was better off without him. He's an uncouth yob. He has no class.'

Bridget refrained from pointing out that both men had been kicked out of the bar for fighting. 'Did Adam come to meet you at the Union, or was he already there when you arrived?'

Zac sneered. 'He's not even a member. They shouldn't have let him in. I'll be having a sharp word with whoever was on the door that night.'

'So Adam came there to see you?'

'I was enjoying a drink with some friends, when that Neanderthal showed up. He obviously wanted to lash out at someone because Zara had left him.'

'What exactly did he say to you?'

Zac shifted on the sofa. He was no longer slouching casually. 'I don't remember. Some bullshit about how life was so unfair. I told him to get used to it.'

'And then what?'

'He threw a punch at me.' He touched his cheek and winced. 'You've seen how big that gorilla is. I think I handled myself pretty well, considering.'

'The barman says he asked you both to leave.'

'Yes. I'll be speaking to him too. That was well out of order. Adam was the one who needed to leave. He started the fight. I'm the president of the Union, for God's sake.'

'So you told me. What happened after you left?'

'Adam skulked off. I went back to college.'

'Did you return directly to your room?'

'Yeah.'

'Your girlfriend, Verity, says you were with her in your room from eleven twenty. But we have a witness who says they saw you banging on Zara's door at half past eleven.'

He gave her a calculating look. 'Was that Megan?'

'Please just answer the question.'

'What of it? Why shouldn't I visit my sister?'

'It's just that it contradicts what you just told us.'

'It's only a detail. I'd been drinking. I'd been in a fight. How am I supposed to remember every smallest thing?'

'And yet since Verity is providing you with an alibi, we need that alibi to be watertight.'

'Alibi?' His eyes flashed with anger. 'What the fuck are you talking about? Why do I need a fucking alibi? You think I killed Zara? I was her brother for Christ's sake. She was my twin. You have no idea.' He moved to the edge of the sofa, balling his hands into fists.

Jake was on his feet before Zac's fury crossed

over into rage. 'Take it easy, mate. There's no need to get angry. We're simply trying to build a clear picture of everyone's movements.'

His words had the desired effect. Zac visibly calmed down and Jake resumed his seat.

Bridget continued as if nothing had happened. 'Finding your sister's killer may well depend on small details. What we'd really like to do is eliminate you from our enquiries. To help us do that, we'd appreciate it if you could provide us with fingerprints and also a handprint.'

He frowned. 'A handprint? Is that a normal thing to request?'

'In some circumstances,' said Bridget.

While Jake took the prints, Bridget asked, 'So are you staying here until the investigation is over?'

'God no. I only came home to support Mummy. I'll be going back to college this afternoon. There's an important debate coming up at the Union.'

'And Verity, is she still here with you?'

He nodded. 'We'll both be returning today. She has the end of term ball to organise.'

They had just finished with the prints when the door banged open and a red-faced Sir Richard stormed into the room.

'What the bloody hell do you think you people are doing?' he bawled. He didn't wait for a reply. 'Have you no respect? This family is grieving for a daughter and a sister. You should be out there looking for the murderer, not coming here hounding my son. How dare you! The Chief Superintendent will be hearing from me personally about this.'

'We were just leaving,' said Bridget, trying to keep her cool.

Sir Richard followed her back into the hallway. 'This is the last time you come here without a warrant,' he said. 'And it's the last time you speak to my son or any member of my family without a lawyer being present. Do you understand?'

On their way out, Bridget glanced up at the staircase. The girl she'd seen earlier was sitting on the top step, looking down. As they left the house, Verity appeared and sat down beside the girl, putting her arm around her.

★

From her bedroom window Celia Hamilton watched the red Mini execute a nimble U-turn and head back down the drive towards the gate. She would have liked to spend time alone with the detective inspector. Bridget Hart seemed like an understanding sort of person, ready to listen and not quick to judge. But she had come to speak to Zac and, inevitably, Richard had sent her packing. Celia supposed the police must be terribly busy and didn't really have time to let you cry on their shoulders. There was the Family Liaison Officer from the Met, of course, but Richard had sent her away too. It seemed he didn't want the police intruding into their lives.

What lives? Celia thought. Her life had been destroyed by this tragedy. What was the point of pretending otherwise?

People often made the mistake of thinking that life was easy when you were rich. They couldn't have been more wrong. Of course, some things were easier. She'd never been short of domestic help, but then she wouldn't have needed it if they didn't own two enormous houses – one in London and one in the country. Sometimes she fantasised of living in a little cottage by the sea.

And it wasn't easy being married to a man like Sir Richard. In the early days of their marriage Richard had always been so busy, building his media empire, rubbing shoulders with the rich and powerful, doing deals. Celia had found herself having to socialise with other wives with whom she had little in common. It had been a relief when she fell pregnant and had an excuse to say she needed an early night.

But when the twins were born she had been ill for quite a while. Richard had solved the problem the only way he knew how, by throwing money at it. He hired help for her. Nursemaids and nannies, a string of young women with impeccable qualifications. But something had gone wrong somewhere along the line. Celia could never be sure when it had happened. Maybe the twins had missed out on her motherly love during those early weeks and months when she was laid low. But they had always had each other, and as they grew older they had developed a bond that almost excluded other people. They even had their own language which no one else could understand. She had thought that was just how twins were.

It had been a relief when they'd gone away to university together. She'd thought they would look after each other. Now she wondered if she'd been terribly wrong.

Between her fingers she twisted the inspector's contact card. DI Bridget Hart, Oxford CID. The inspector's telephone number was printed below her name. Celia longed to call that number and tell her everything.

But she knew she never would. A mother's duty was to her family.

★

Ffion would have been the first to admit she was more comfortable with computers than with people. Machines were predictable. They followed rules and she knew what they were thinking. So she was perfectly happy to be left in the office in the company of Zara's laptop while Bridget and Jake swanned off to the Cotswolds to speak to the brother.

'Need any help with that?' asked Ryan, bounding over to her desk like an over-enthusiastic puppy dog.

Often men were just as predictable as machines, she mused. And it was all too obvious what the young sergeant was thinking. 'I thought you were supposed to be interviewing students in the college,' she said coolly.

'Yeah, guess so,' said Ryan, grabbing his jacket from the back of his chair.

She made herself a green tea and settled down to work. The forensics team had finished going over the laptop and had released it to her for further investigation. Zara's phone still hadn't surfaced, but Ffion hoped she'd be able to access all the relevant information via the laptop.

She began by checking out social media. Zara had been very active, with thousands of friends and connections online. Her Facebook page had the usual collection of personal posts – photos of Zara alone or with friends, sometimes travelling in exotic parts of the world, a few pictures of her posing with Adam. She looked amazing in every one, even when trekking up a mountainside or when snapped late at night in a dimly-lit bar. Zara didn't seem to want to draw attention to her wealthy background and there were hardly any mentions of her family. In addition to the personal stuff, she had relentlessly posted about progressive and environmental issues, frequently reposting items from charities and protest movements. She'd been a keen supporter of the homeless charity, Shelter.

Zara was even bigger on Twitter. Her focus here had been campaigning for various left-wing causes. Intriguingly, she appeared to have run not one, but several Twitter accounts. As well as one that was publicly identifiable as hers, Ffion uncovered two anonymous accounts that Zara had used in her campaigning efforts. Both accounts were heavily involved in marshalling support for the #NoOxfordPlatform campaign against Zac's invited speaker, Catriona Hodgson. It didn't take Ffion long to establish that the entire campaign had been orchestrated by Zara. She had clearly been vehemently opposed to her brother's choice of speaker and had done everything she could to drum up opposition to it. She had even pushed for a rally to take place outside the Union building to physically deny entry to the controversial guest.

Did Zac know how closely his own sister had been involved in trying to disrupt his planned debate? The fact that Zara had used anonymous usernames suggested that she hadn't been keen for anyone to know she was responsible.

Next Ffion moved on to Zara's emails. Fortunately Zara had been very organised with her email, saving all her messages in clearly marked folders. Ffion clicked on a folder entitled College Building Project.

The folder contained dozens of emails from Zara addressed to the dean of Christ Church. Ffion clicked on the earliest email which had been written just over six months ago. The message was long and read like an essay. She speed-read through it to get an overview of Zara's concerns.

I am writing to protest about the college's plans to demolish the homeless shelter in Oxford in order to build more student accommodation...

This action is morally indefensible...

Christ Church is one of the wealthiest colleges in Oxford...

It is unthinkable that we should be taking from the poorest in society to expand our property portfolio.

Ffion remembered what Adam had said about Zara's father giving a donation to the college to build new student accommodation. Reading between the lines, it sounded as if this might be the proposed accommodation block, Hamilton House. It looked as if Zara had been determined to block her own father's efforts to donate money to the college. Judging by what she'd written, the new building would come at the cost of knocking down a shelter for homeless people.

A reply from the dean's secretary thanked Zara for her input and drew attention to the fact that the new building would provide high quality affordable accommodation and would be of most benefit to students from less well-off backgrounds, the implication being that Zara herself was too privileged to understand the issue.

Talk about a red rag to a bull. Zara had immediately embarked on an email campaign, lobbying the dean mercilessly. She'd been met with ever terser responses. In the end, the dean's secretary had refused to reply to any further correspondence, suggesting that Zara take up her concerns with the city council's planning department.

A further angry exchange of emails between Zara and the council planning officer, a Mr Michael Protheroe, had ensued. Her persistent demands had been thwarted by endless and petty bureaucracy.

The last email in the folder was dated the day Zara died. She had emailed both the council and the dean again, threatening a campaign of mass peaceful protest if work began on the demolition of the shelter. She had not received any replies.

Ffion leaned back in her chair and stretched out her arms. She reached for her mug of tea and found that it had long since gone cold. It was already past noon. The morning was over, but hadn't been wasted. Ffion had established two key facts. Firstly, Zara Hamilton had been a one-woman protest machine, operating both in the open and covertly, behind the scenes. And secondly, whatever causes her father and brother stood for, Zara had vehemently opposed.

CHAPTER 11

'DI Hart, my office.'

It was just after lunchtime when Bridget returned to Kidlington, having stopped to grab a sandwich for herself and Jake from the drive-thru on the ring road. As soon as she walked into the CID suite, Chief Superintendent Grayson summoned her into his lair.

He sat behind his desk, twisting a ballpoint pen between the fingers and thumb of his right hand. It was a clear sign that the Superintendent was angry, and Bridget already had a pretty good idea what he might be angry about.

'I've just had Sir Richard Hamilton on the phone giving me an earful about you harassing his family.'

'Well, sir, I wouldn't put it –'

'Sit down.'

Grayson began stabbing the pen repeatedly against the desktop. 'Did you listen to a single word I said?'

'Yes, sir, I –'

'What did I tell you?'

'That Sir Richard's a bully.'

'And?'

'Not to do anything without telling you first. And I did, sir. I told you I was going to the Hamiltons' house this morning.'

Grayson frowned. The pounding of the pen on the desk became more vigorous. 'You did. But you didn't tell me you intended to accuse Zachary Hamilton of murdering his sister!'

'Is that what Sir Richard told you?'

'Pretty much.'

'Well, it's not true. I simply asked him some questions about his movements the day of the murder. I wanted to make sure of his alibi.'

'You have reasonable grounds to suspect him?'

'No. But I can't rule him out, either. I was just doing my job, sir.'

The ballpoint pen snapped under the strain of its repeated battering. Grayson tossed the pieces into a wastepaper basket. 'All right. Carry on, then. Catch the bugger who did this. The sooner we can close this case, the better. But remember –'

'Keep you informed,' concluded Bridget.

She returned to the CID suite feeling frustrated. She and her team needed to be free to investigate all leads without hindrance from the dead girl's father. And that included shining a spotlight on Zac Hamilton and his activities the day Zara was killed. Right now, Zac was looking very much like a suspect in this case.

She called her team together for a meeting. She began by letting the others know how she and

Jake had got on with Zac, and reiterating Grayson's warning about treading warily around the family. 'I know you've all been busy this morning. Tell me what you've found.'

The interviews that Ryan and his sub-team had carried out hadn't revealed much at all. 'We took statements from a few people who saw Zara at informal hall at six twenty. Apparently she was one of the first in line, and left again soon after, as if she was in a hurry to get somewhere. But no one saw her leave college or return. In fact, no one saw her again. We interviewed everyone who has a room in Tom Quad. If these are the brightest minds of the next generation, then God help us. No one seems to have noticed a damn thing.'

'Okay, thanks. Andy?'

'So, we made enquiries about the movements of Adam and Verity.'

'And?'

'Yeah, it all checks out. Adam was in the bar, knocking back beers, just like he says. Verity was chairing the ball committee – whatever the hell that is – from half past eight until gone eleven. Sounds like they were telling the truth – about that, at least.'

'Anything else?'

'We worked through the guest list for the dean's drinks reception and spoke to everyone who was there, including the leader of the council. Sounds like one big piss up for the great and the good. The canapés were first-rate, the booze flowed freely. No one told us anything worth mentioning.'

'Okay.' Bridget wasn't too bothered about any of that. She still had her trump card to play. 'Jake, any luck with that handprint we got from Zac this morning?' She'd sent him directly to the forensics team as soon as they got back from the Cotswolds.

'Bingo!' said Jake, looking pleased with himself. 'I just got a call from the lab. The handprint that SOCO found in the room being redecorated is definitely a match to Zac's.'

Bridget nodded. It was as she'd expected. Their trip to Shipton-under-Wychwood had been justified after all, despite what Sir Richard might think.

'They've also got a match for the blood on the towel that was found right next to the handprint.'

'Zara's?'

Jake nodded. The room filled with murmurs as everyone started to speculate. A clear trail of evidence was beginning to emerge.

'So what do we have?' asked Bridget, holding up her hand for silence.

Ryan was the first to voice what they were all thinking. 'So, Adam's pissed off after being dumped by Zara. Meanwhile Zac's busy playing at being president of the Union. Adam goes to see him, possibly hoping for some sympathy, or at least an explanation of why Zara dumped him, and instead Zac tells him what an arsehole he is. Adam lands a few punches, and Zac goes back to

Zara's room –'

'– and is seen banging on her door by Megan,' put in Andy.

'Right. He's drunk, he's hurting after the fight, he's angry with Zara, maybe even blames her for Adam hitting him, they exchange words, he hits her, she collapses. He tries to stop the bleeding with the towel, then runs away in panic, dumping the towel in the room below. Verity lies to give him an alibi, and he thinks he's got away with it.'

'Yeah,' agreed Andy. 'And it was probably Zac who threw up in the seminar room, when he was getting rid of the bloody towel. Too much booze and a nasty shock would make anyone puke their guts up.'

Bridget nodded. 'It's certainly a possibility. But we don't have hard evidence.'

'Zac's handprint?' ventured Jake.

'It proves he was in the seminar room. Nothing more. We can't ask for a sample of his DNA, not unless we arrest him. So there's no proof that it was Zac who was sick in that room.' She turned to Ffion. 'How did you get on with Zara's laptop?'

Ffion's green eyes lit up and she smiled. 'Some interesting background. Zara didn't just oppose Zac in debates at the Union. She was very politically active online. In particular, she was running a campaign to stop the college from building new student accommodation with money donated by her father.'

Bridget frowned. 'Why would she do that?'

'Because the site that the college wants to develop is currently used as a shelter for homeless people.'

'So the donation put Zara at odds with her family.'

'And with the college authorities. I found dozens of emails between her and the dean, or the dean's secretary to be precise. Also emails with the city council.'

'Any evidence that Zac was involved in any way?'

'None that I found. She'd gone to some lengths to hide her activity. She used anonymous Twitter accounts to orchestrate the campaign to ban Catriona Hodgson, Zac's invited speaker, from speaking at the Oxford Union. My guess is that she wanted to keep the full extent of her campaigning a secret from her family.'

'What is Catriona Hodgson supposed to be speaking about?'

'This House believes that giving money to the homeless encourages homelessness. No prizes for guessing which side of the debate Catriona Hodgson is on.'

'Wow,' said Bridget. 'Incendiary stuff.'

'All right,' said Ryan. 'All this just strengthens the case against Zac. If Zac discovered that Zara was behind the campaign, he wouldn't have been at all happy with her. That alone might have been enough to trigger an argument.'

'Circumstantial,' said Bridget. 'We need cast

iron proof if we're going to arrest Zac Hamilton. We won't even be able to interview him again unless we can put a strong case in front of the chief. We need evidence, and for that we need solid police work.' She checked her watch. 'Who wants to come with me to the post-mortem?'

She wasn't expecting a big show of hands. Both Jake and Ryan pulled a face, but Ffion said, 'I'll do it.'

'In that case,' said Bridget, 'Jake, Ryan, Harry, you three can start watching the CCTV footage from the college entrances. I want to know precisely who came and went and at what time. Andy, take your team back to the college. Widen the door-to-door enquiries. Speak to anyone and everyone. Someone must have seen Zara after she left the dining hall. And Andy, get on to the phone company and find out why they're taking so long to get hold of Zara's call records.'

★

'You're just in time,' said Dr Roy Andrews, greeting Bridget and Ffion with an effusive handshake. Today's bow tie, Bridget noted, was blue with white dots. She wondered how many the pathologist had in his collection. She'd never seen the same one twice. The bow peeked shyly above the top of the plastic apron he wore over green scrubs, as if it knew it was too cheerful for a mortuary. The lower part of his face was covered by a surgical mask. 'Julie is preparing everything as we speak. Would you like to go in there and get changed?' He pointed them towards the female staff changing rooms. 'The chaps from forensics are just getting ready.'

Five minutes later Bridget and Ffion emerged in their scrubs, rubber boots and masks. Even in this get-up Ffion managed to look like the sexy female-lead in a TV crime drama, while Bridget knew she looked ridiculous. The forensics guys acknowledged their arrival with a nod. They were ready with their cameras and evidence bags. Julie Pearson, Roy's assistant, was laying out the instruments Roy would use for the autopsy – a selection of lethal looking cutters, saws and drills that looked like they'd come from the toolbox of a serial killer. She gave them all a cheery wave. How did people in mortuaries manage to stay so relentlessly upbeat? It was the only way to survive the job, Bridget supposed.

She would have hated to work in this environment all day long. The atmosphere was cool and clinical, even in the middle of the summer, an effect enhanced by the harsh strip lighting and the background hum from the ventilation ducts. The white-tiled, windowless room was edged with stainless steel worktops. In the middle of this impersonal space stood a slab on which Zara Hamilton lay like an effigy, a sheet covering her body from the shoulders down. Her golden hair fanned out around her, yet her skin seemed more like pale stone than flesh. There was something Pre-Raphaelite about her, as if she was waiting to be rowed to the Isle of Avalon.

'Are we all set?' asked Roy. He made it sound as if they were about to embark on a voyage of discovery, which in a way they were. 'Any mortuary virgins here?' He glanced sideways at Ffion.

The eyes of the young detective constable above her face mask gave nothing away. Either she was unaffected by the presence of death, or very good at hiding her feelings. 'This is my first post-mortem,' she said, 'but you don't need to worry. Blood doesn't bother me.'

'We'll be seeing a lot more than blood today,' said Roy, as if he relished the prospect.

Bridget had trained herself over the years to get used to post-mortems. She was better now than she had been, unless the victim was a child or a teenager. Every dead teenage girl laid out on a mortuary trolley reminded her of Abigail. In recent years, the corpses had started to look more and more like Chloe.

She nodded to Roy. 'Ready when you are.'

Ffion took out her notebook and pen, ready to take notes. The forensics men switched on their cameras.

'Is this thing on, Julie?' Roy pointed at a microphone hanging down from the ceiling above the slab. Julie gave him a thumbs up sign and he began his delivery. 'Forensic post-mortem of Miss Zara Hamilton, Saturday the eighth of June, conducted by Dr Roy Andrews in the presence of Julie Pearson, DI Bridget Hart and DC Ffion Hughes.' He waited for the forensics guys to speak their names too.

Then came the job of removing Zara's clothing and bagging it up for the forensics men to take back to the lab – a yellow summer dress and a matching bra and knickers in pale pink. Pretty but not overtly sexy, thought Bridget. Zara's taste had been good. She waited patiently while the forensics men got to work, cameras clicking, taking snapshots of the body. When they'd finished, Roy stepped back up to the slab as if for his starring role.

'Thank you, gentlemen,' he said, nodding as the forensics men moved aside. The warm-up act, thought Bridget. Now it was time for the main billing.

The pathologist cleared his throat. 'Preliminary findings first. I took the body's temperature when it was brought into the mortuary on Friday lunchtime. Temperature at midday on Friday was twenty degrees Celsius. Normal body temperature – as I'm sure you're aware' – he directed his attention to Bridget and Ffion – 'is thirty-seven degrees Celsius, and on average a dead body cools down at the rate of one degree per hour.'

'So can you give me a more accurate time of death?' asked Bridget hopefully.

'Hold your horses. It's not that simple.'

'I'd be surprised if it was.'

Roy's eyes smiled at her above his face mask. 'Her body temperature had dropped seventeen degrees which would put the time of death at seven o'clock on Thursday evening. But' – he held up a gloved finger – 'there are complicating factors. Firstly, thin people like Zara here cool more quickly than those of us with – how shall I put it? – more of nature's insulation.' He patted his own ample stomach.

Diplomatically put, thought Bridget.

'Secondly' – a second gloved finger shot up – 'she was sprawled on the floor and not curled up. And finally, she was wearing a thin summer dress. All three factors might well have resulted in more rapid cooling. Therefore the true time of death is likely to be later in the evening, perhaps around nine, ten or eleven, but probably not as late as midnight.'

Ffion made a careful note.

'That's very helpful to know,' said Bridget. It was becoming clear that a key question to establish was whether or not Zara was already dead when Zac was seen banging on her door.

'The other indicator of time of death is the state of rigor mortis,' continued Roy. 'Zara was completely rigid when she was brought in at midday on Friday, which is compatible with my earlier hypothesis that the time of death was somewhere between nine o'clock and eleven. It's now' – he glanced at the clock on the wall which read three o'clock – 'another twenty-seven hours since she was brought in and as you can see, the small muscles of the eyes and face have started to relax.'

He gently prodded the girl's eyelids, making Bridget wince. But at least the eyes stayed closed. There was nothing worse than a corpse that watched you throughout the proceedings.

'All clear so far?' asked Roy.

Bridget nodded.

'As to the actual cause of death, the primary cause would appear to be the blunt force trauma to the back of the victim's head. But we'll know more once we open her up.'

'Is there any possibility this could have been an accident?' asked Bridget. 'Might she have fallen and hit her head on some surface?'

'Patience, please, DI Hart. There is a procedure to be followed here, as I am sure you are well aware. Good things come to those who wait.'

Roy started with an external examination, commenting on every mark while the forensics men took more detailed photographs. Other than the wound to the head, there were no bruises on the body.

Next he took biological samples, plucking hairs from Zara's head, scraping her fingernails and swabbing her genital area.

'There's no obvious evidence of defensive wounds,' he said. 'And no evidence of sexual assault either.'

Bridget breathed a sigh of relief. At least that was one less thing to worry about.

'All right,' said Roy at last. 'Now we move on to the internal examination.'

Bridget glanced at Ffion. This was usually the point at which inexperienced detective constables had been known to pass out. Ffion's green eyes showed no sign of emotion, so Bridget guessed she was doing all right.

With practised strokes Roy drew a Y shape on Zara's torso from the shoulders down to the groin. Then he cut her open and removed the breastplate, revealing her heart and lungs.

Bridget swallowed, willing herself not to look away, but seeking instead to detach herself mentally from the process. As she had told Jake, Zara's body was now evidence in the investigation. The girl was dead, but she could still communicate with them from beyond the grave, revealing vital clues to how she died, and perhaps other secrets – things that Zara herself could no longer tell them. Things that no one else knew, except perhaps her killer.

Ffion leaned in closer, peering with interest at the space opening up in the corpse's chest.

Roy worked quickly and meticulously, lifting out the organs and inspecting them, then passing them to Julie who weighed them and sliced off samples for further analysis. Even though the cause of death was in all probability the trauma to the head, Home Office rules insisted on detailed examination of all the internal organs.

'Well there was nothing wrong with her innards,' said Roy. 'Now for the head.'

As he moved to stand behind Zara's body, Bridget found she was holding her breath. This part of the autopsy was going to tell them what they most needed to know. It was also the most difficult to watch.

Roy made an ear-to-ear incision over the top of the head and peeled back the scalp. Then he sawed away part of the skull to reveal the brain.

Bridget experienced a strange feeling of anti-climax, as if she'd been expecting the brain of this brilliant young student to be different somehow from the brains of ordinary mortals. As if all that studying of English literature and accumulated knowledge would have resulted in something more stellar. Zara's brain looked disappointingly like other brains. But still, a brain was a remarkable thing. What knowledge, thoughts and memories stored in the neural pathways of that lump of grey matter were now lost to the world forever? It wasn't as if you could download all that data onto a flash drive. Once it was gone, it was gone.

Roy and Julie carefully rolled Zara over so that they could examine the injury site in more detail.

'Hmm,' said Roy, peering at the wound to the back of the head. 'Tweezers please.'

Julie passed him a pair of fine-tipped tweezers. With care he pulled several fine white threads from Zara's blood-clotted hair. He held one up to the light for them all to see. 'These fibres may have come from a cloth or tissue used to try to stem the blood flow.' The forensics men were ready with their evidence bags.

'Probably from the blood-soaked towel,'

commented Ffion.

'This is interesting. Can you see what happened here?' Roy motioned for Bridget and Ffion to gather closer.

Bridget peered at the wound from where she was standing. She was quite close enough.

'A piece of bone has broken loose from the skull and been forced into the cranium, causing concentric fractures to occur.'

'Yes,' said Bridget. She didn't really understand what she was looking at and was happy to take Roy's word for it.

'It's a common enough outcome in this kind of injury. The shape of the bone matches the object that caused it. As you can see, the displaced bone is elliptical in shape and measures perhaps ten centimetres along its major axis. I'll be making a more detailed measurement later. But there's something else in here too.'

With extreme delicacy he extracted an object from Zara's skull and placed it on a glass dish that Julie held out for him.

'What is it?' asked Bridget.

'That,' said Roy, 'looks to me like a sliver of purple glass. I'd say it came from the murder weapon.'

Bridget stared at the glass fragment, the hairs on the back of her neck slowly rising. 'I know what this is,' she said. 'I know where to find the murder weapon.'

CHAPTER 12

'Harry,' said Jake to the young detective sitting at the desk facing his, 'any chance of a decent cup of coffee round here?'

'I was thinking the same thing,' said Ryan, the other sergeant. 'Caffeine boost needed, Harry.'

'But why do I have to get it?' moaned Harry.

'Because Jake and I are sergeants, and you are but a lowly constable,' said Ryan. 'Respect for authority is the foundation stone of human civilisation. I read that in a Christmas cracker once. Go on, off you go.'

'Yeah, all right,' agreed Harry. 'I could use a break anyway.'

The three of them had been trawling through the CCTV footage from the college entrances for hours. Ryan and Harry had taken the videos from Meadow Gate and Canterbury Gate, leaving Jake to study the footage from Tom Gate, the college's main entrance on St Aldate's.

Normally a Saturday afternoon would have found Jake in one of the pubs off Cowley Road, pint in hand, watching the football on a big TV. The season for his own team, Leeds United, was over, but a couple of international friendly matches were playing today. He would just have to catch up with them later.

Instead he stared at his computer screen, watching people enter and leave the college just as closely as he ever watched any game of football. Closer in fact because he was running the video at one and a half times normal speed. Otherwise he'd be here all night.

He watched as students and academic staff came and went through the big double gates that were kept open during daylight hours. Tourists crept inside in small groups, trying to get pictures of Tom Quad on their phones, but were never allowed more than a couple of feet inside the gates before being dismissed by the bowler-hatted custodians – the bulldogs, as Ryan called them. At one point a homeless man who appeared to be drunk staggered into the college and was sent on his way with a firm shove. The message was clear – undesirables were not welcome in these hallowed halls.

At just after half past six – six thirty-two to be precise – someone looking like Zara strode out through the college gates. Jake rewound thirty seconds and watched again to make sure it was definitely her. Yes, there was no mistaking that long blonde hair, nor the summer dress she was wearing when they found her yesterday. She walked with a natural grace and confidence that seemed effortless. She'd certainly have made Jake's head turn if he'd seen her in the street. She exited left out of the college, walking away from the city centre. Jake paused the video and made a note of what he'd seen with the relevant timings. Then he settled down for another session. Where had Harry got to with those coffees?

As if on cue the DC returned with three lattes from the Starbucks round the corner.

'Real coffee,' said Harry. 'Not like the dishwater that comes out of the machine here.'

'Cheers, mate,' said Jake, taking his coffee. Hot, milky and with two sugars – it would power him through the next few hours of tedium. He took a sip and returned to his screen.

Around eight o'clock there was a lot of coming and going from the main gate as the dean's guests arrived for the drinks reception, but Jake just managed to catch sight of Zara returning to college. He made a note of the time.

Fifteen minutes later, Zac's girlfriend, Verity, left with a couple of other students. They were all carrying folders. Jake had assumed that the ball committee meeting she'd chaired had taken place in the college, but maybe it was held somewhere else. Local pub? He made a note to check.

Ryan wandered over to peer at his screen. 'Found anything yet?'

'Yeah, a couple of relevant sightings.'

'That's good,' said Ryan, yawning. 'At Meadow Gate it's just a steady stream of tourists trooping in and out all day long. The college must milk a fortune out of them.'

As the evening progressed, the number of people coming and going through Tom Gate diminished, and Jake fast-forwarded the video to twice normal speed. He had to concentrate harder, but made quicker progress.

Half an hour after Verity had left, Zac himself was on his way out, dressed in formal black tie – black dinner jacket, white dress shirt and black bow tie. He looked immaculate and certainly hadn't been in a fight yet. He turned right on leaving the college and headed north up St Aldate's towards Carfax, presumably on his way to the Oxford Union.

At nine o'clock, Verity re-entered the college, this time alone. Just after nine o'clock, a custodian appeared and pulled the large double gates closed, leaving only a small pedestrian gate inside the main gate open, just wide enough for one person to step through at a time. The smaller gate appeared to be operated with a security pass.

Verity reappeared twenty minutes later, carrying more files. More stuff for the meeting? At five past ten, a very drunk-looking Adam stumbled out through the door and onto St Aldate's. For a moment he staggered around as if unsure of his direction. Then he seemed to come to a decision and headed north towards Carfax, the same direction Zac had taken earlier. Fists were about to start flying at the Oxford Union.

'Whoa,' said Ryan suddenly. 'Have you seen the score?'

'What?'

'South Korea beat Austria, three-nil.'

'Oh, cheers,' said Jake, who'd been planning on watching the match when he got home.

'Sorry. Did I spoil it for you?' asked Ryan, not sounding the least bit sorry. 'Who do you support, then?'

'Leeds.'

'Ha! You're a glutton for punishment.'

'Loyalty, I call it.'

'A fine quality,' said Ryan, 'both in life and in football. So what about your chances of scoring with the young and unattached DC Ffion Hughes?'

'What do you mean?' asked Jake, startled by the question.

'It's a football metaphor,' explained Ryan, deadpan. 'Scoring means –'

'I know what it means,' blurted Jake, turning red. 'Why do you think I'm interested in Ffion?'

'That would be my superior powers of observation, no doubt.'

'Well you got it wrong, mate.'

'Really? So you won't mind if I try my own luck?'

'Be my guest.'

'Right. I'll report back in due course.'

Jake returned to his task, rattled by Ryan's banter. He had no idea if the guy was serious, or if he was just winding him up. He wasn't entirely sure himself what he thought of Ffion. She was a real stunner, for sure, but rather strange and aloof. He did his best to dismiss all thoughts of her lithe, leather-clad form and concentrate on the video.

Zac returned at five past eleven, looking in no better state than the homeless man who'd tried his luck getting into college earlier in the evening. He carried his jacket in one hand, slung over his shoulder, his bow tie hanging loose, his collar undone. He walked with the traditional zig-zag gait of the severely inebriated. His hand kept going to the cut on his cheekbone. It took him a couple of goes to open the door to the college with his security pass.

There was no sign of Adam.

Suddenly Jake sat bolt upright. Verity and her co-committee members returned to college at close on midnight. According to Verity, she'd been waiting in Zac's room from eleven o'clock and had spent the rest of the evening with him. But Verity hadn't even been in the college during that time. She had lied, and Zac's alibi was blown. Result!

'Spotted something?' asked Ryan.

'Yeah,' said Jake. 'I think I may even have single-handedly solved this case.'

'Nice work. In that case, the beers are on you.'

CHAPTER 13

Chief Superintendent Grayson was waiting in his office, as patient as a spider, almost as if he'd been expecting to be told of a breakthrough. Whether this was some sixth sense honed by decades in the job, or just wishful thinking, Bridget was pleased not to disappoint him. She knocked on his glass door and entered. She didn't waste time taking a seat.

'Sir, I think we've got enough on Zac to make an arrest.'

Only the narrowing of his eyes told her that this was not the news he was hoping for.

'First, his alibi has been blown. The CCTV footage proves quite clearly that his girlfriend, Verity, wasn't in college until nearly an hour after she claimed. That leaves Zac without an alibi, and we know that he was in college during that time.'

'Circumstantial,' was all Grayson had to say to that.

'Secondly,' continued Bridget undaunted, 'Zac was seen banging on Zara's door at a time consistent with the time of death.'

Grayson swatted the fact away like a fly. 'Circumstantial again.'

'Thirdly, Zac's handprint was found on the wall of the seminar room immediately below Zara's. The wall had been freshly painted that afternoon. Next to it was a towel covered in Zara's blood.'

'Anything else?'

'I've just returned from the post-mortem. The pathologist confirmed that Zara was killed by a blow to the head from a blunt object. A fragment of purple glass was embedded in Zara's skull. In Roy Andrews' opinion, it most likely broke off the murder weapon on impact.'

'Yes?'

She delivered her coup-de-grace. 'When I was in Zac's room yesterday, I saw a glass paperweight on his desk. It's the same colour glass as the fragment found in Zara's skull.'

She waited for that to sink in. 'My theory is that Zac and Zara got into an argument. He was drunk. The argument turned violent and he struck her with the paperweight. Afterwards he tried to stop the bleeding with the towel, then ran off, dumping the towel on his way out. He and Verity concocted the alibi afterwards.'

The Chief Super was listening carefully, studying her through hooded eyes. He said nothing for a minute. Then, 'All right. Bring him in. I'll take the flack. But be discreet.'

★

Bridget followed the marked police car down Banbury Road as they battled through the late evening weekend traffic. Sitting next to her in the passenger seat was Jake, his long legs folded awkwardly like before, but obviously elated that they were acting on his discovery. 'We've got him, haven't we ma'am?' he pressed eagerly.

'One step at a time,' cautioned Bridget. The evidence was sufficient to justify an arrest, but they needed more to make a murder charge stick. She knew that Grayson had taken a bold decision in backing her. She prayed it wouldn't turn out to be a reckless one. 'We still need the forensic evidence to back us up.'

A quick phone call to Jim Turner in the porters' lodge before they left Kidlington HQ had confirmed that Zac had indeed returned to college from the Cotswolds. Bridget hoped they'd find him in his room in Peckwater Quad. She wasn't expecting him to cooperate meekly like a lamb, hence the presence of the two uniformed officers in the other car. Both were battle-hardened old-timers who wouldn't take any crap from an uppity rich kid. The two vehicles entered St Aldate's and pulled up near Christ Church.

The area in front of the college gates was packed with a bustling crowd. 'What's going on, ma'am?' asked Jake.

Bridget already knew what. Half of the people spilling onto the road in front of them were wielding cameras packing huge lenses and professional flashes. Press photographers. As Grayson had warned, the wolves had scented blood at last. The college had closed its gates to them and two grim-faced custodians were standing guard at the entrance, preventing anyone from approaching.

'Shit,' swore Bridget. 'Someone must have tipped off the press.'

'Not one of us?' asked Jake, sounding appalled.

She shook her head. 'It could have been anyone. A student, a member of staff at the college, a friend of the family. A tip like that can earn good money.'

The case had all the ingredients needed for a front-page story in tomorrow's Sunday papers. The violent murder of a beautiful young woman; an Oxford student and daughter of a titled businessman; and an opportunity to wheel out all the usual clichés and stereotypes of the British class system.

Up ahead, the two uniformed police officers emerged from their car and began pushing their way through the crowd. Cameras flashed. Journalists swarmed around them, clearly loving the action.

'Shit!' said Bridget again. 'Come on, let's get this done.'

She forced her way past the cameras and microphones, very glad of Jake's tall frame to plough a furrow in front of her. She kept her head down and said nothing in reply to the shouted questions. At Tom Gate, a bowler-hatted custodian held the narrow wooden door open for them to pass.

They made their way to Peckwater Quad, ignoring the stares of the handful of students who were milling excitedly around the quad.

When they arrived at Zac's room, they heard voices. Bridget rapped three times on the door and the voices fell silent. The door opened and Bridget was greeted by a scowling Verity. The girl's expression quickly changed from contempt to bewilderment when she noticed the two PCs hovering behind.

'Is Zac here?' asked Bridget.

'Yes.'

'Good. We'd like to speak to him please.' She walked into the room without waiting for a response. The three men followed.

Zac was sprawled on the sofa, drinking a glass of wine. An empty bottle lay on its side at his feet.

He raised his glass to her in mock salute. 'Well, if it isn't DI Smarty Pants and her trusty sidekick come to ask more of their tedious questions.' His expression darkened when he saw the two uniformed constables. 'I thought my father warned you not to come near me again.'

'Zachary Hamilton,' said Bridget, 'I am arresting you on suspicion of murder. You do not have to say anything. But, it may harm your defence if you do not mention when questioned something which you later rely on in court. Anything you do say may be given in evidence.'

Zac stared at her, dumbstruck, but Verity's response was instantaneous and vicious. 'This is ridiculous. Zac didn't kill his own sister. For God's sake!'

Bridget swivelled to face her. 'Miss Cunningham, one of the reasons I am arresting Zac is because we have evidence that the alibi you provided for him is false. Do you have anything to say to that?'

Verity's mouth fell open but no sound came out.

'No, I didn't think so.' Bridget signalled for the uniformed PCs to step in. They marched up to Zac and hauled him to his feet.

'Get your hands off me,' roared Zac. He struggled in the men's grip before allowing them to cuff him. 'You people have no goddamn manners.'

Bridget almost laughed at that.

'I'm entitled to one phone call, aren't I?' he demanded.

'You'll be able to make a phone call from the station. And then your phone will be confiscated as evidence.'

'Christ,' muttered Zac. 'It's like a bloody police state.'

As the two PCs led Zac from the room, Bridget moved over to the desk. Amongst the bottles of vodka and scotch and the used glasses was a purple glass paperweight. On one side the glass was clearly chipped.

'Bag that up and bring it in for evidence,'

Bridget told Jake.

Verity stared at them, horrified, then flew from the room.

CHAPTER 14

'When is his lawyer getting here?' asked Bridget, dumping her bag on her desk.

Jake had gone on ahead in the police car to drop the paperweight off before forensics all went home for the evening. The police car had made use of its blue flashing lights and siren to zoom past the traffic on the Banbury Road, but Bridget had got stuck behind a double decker bus and it had taken her an age to get back to HQ.

Jake checked his watch. 'Should be here within the hour. She's driving over from London.'

'London?' Bridget rolled her eyes.

'Zac used his one phone call to contact Daddy, who told him to say nothing until the family lawyer arrives. She's from some top-notch London law firm apparently.'

'Terrific.' Bridget was familiar with the type. This lawyer probably earned in a day what Bridget earned in a month. 'Where's Zac now?'

'Interview room two. He wanted to know if we had somewhere more comfortable he could wait. Duty officer told him it's not the bloody Ritz.'

'All right, it won't hurt him to stew for a while. Have we taken a DNA sample and fingerprinted him yet?'

'First thing we did, ma'am. The forensics team are working on it.'

'Okay.' Bridget knew that the case against Zac would stand or fall on the strength of the detailed forensic work that was now taking place behind the scenes. She had staked a lot on the evidence going her way. 'Good work,' she told Jake. 'Now see what you can get off his mobile phone.'

'Yes, ma'am.'

'DI Hart. My office now!' Detective Chief Superintendent Grayson's voice boomed across the CID suite.

'Oh Christ,' muttered Bridget.

'Good luck,' whispered Jake.

Bridget had barely closed the Chief Super's door before he began. 'Well, DI Hart, I don't need to ask you how the arrest went, because I've just watched it on the news. What did you not understand about the word discreet?'

'Sir –'

'Sit down and shut up. Now watch this.'

He turned his laptop screen so she could see, clicked his mouse and a video began to play. The footage was shot immediately outside Tom Gate. Bridget watched with dismay as the two PCs emerged from the gate, an aggrieved-looking Zachary Hamilton between them. His hands were clearly cuffed behind his back. Bridget and Jake followed a few paces behind, trying to avoid making eye contact with the cameras. The film tracked Zac as he was bundled into the car and driven away.

Grayson stopped the video. His mouth was drawn in a tight line and a vein pulsed in his right temple. 'How the hell did those vultures know what was happening?'

'I don't think they knew anything specific about the arrest, sir. But it's impossible to keep a murder like this a secret. It was bound to leak.'

'Was it strictly necessary to cuff him?'

'He resisted arrest, sir. The constables made the decision.'

'I see.'

Grayson sighed, pressing his forefinger and thumb into his eye sockets. 'So what's happening now?'

'We're waiting for his lawyer to arrive. She's on her way from London.'

'Oxford lawyers not good enough for the son of Sir Richard Hamilton, eh?' The remark was a concession that Bridget appreciated.

'It would appear not, sir.'

'Very well then. When she gets here let me know. I want to observe this interview from the other side of the glass.'

'Yes, sir.'

Bridget left Grayson's office with mixed feelings. She'd smoothed over his immediate fury, but she didn't much like the idea that her boss would be watching from behind the two-way mirror. As if she wasn't under enough pressure already.

She checked her watch. It was already nearly six o'clock and they were still waiting for the lawyer to make her grand entrance.

The phone rang and Jake picked up. 'Great. We'll be down straight away. Thanks for letting us know.' He put the phone down. 'That was the desk sergeant. She's just arrived.'

'About bloody time. Meet me downstairs. I'd like you to join me in the interview. You handled Zac well this morning.'

'Thanks, ma'am. I'll be with you in a minute.'

From the handful of people in the lobby, there was no mistaking the lawyer. Everything about her, from the salon-tinted hair and flawless make-up, to the well-cut designer suit, Mulberry handbag and briefcase, spoke of an eye-watering hourly rate. In her patent high-heeled shoes she towered over Bridget.

She held out a manicured hand. 'Caroline Butler, from the law firm Kingsley, Butler and Cooke.'

'DI Bridget Hart.'

'Are you the Senior Investigating Officer?' asked Caroline, looking surprised.

'Yes, why?'

'Oh, no reason. I was expecting to find someone more senior in charge, given the high profile of the case.'

Bridget bristled at that. 'Couldn't the family have found a lawyer closer to Oxford?' she asked pointedly. 'We do have them here, you know.'

163

'Kingsley, Butler and Cooke have been the Hamilton family's lawyers for years.'

Bridget forced a small smile. She mustn't allow this high-powered lawyer to rattle her. 'Well, let's not waste any more time, shall we? This way please.'

Behind Caroline's back Bridget thought she caught a glimmer of amusement on the desk sergeant's face.

She led the way down the corridor in a cloud of expensive perfume that she couldn't identify. They met Jake coming in the opposite direction and the lawyer accepted a quick handshake from him.

'Would you like a coffee?' asked Jake.

'A skinny latte, please,' said Caroline.

Dream on, thought Bridget. The canteen did black or white coffee. With sugar or without. They all tasted much the same.

'I'll see what I can do,' said Jake.

They stopped outside interview room two. 'Zac is in here,' said Bridget.

Caroline looked at her watch. 'We'll start the interview in one hour. I want to spend some time alone with my client first. I'm sure you understand.' She opened the door and disappeared inside.

'She's stalling,' said Bridget, fuming. 'We've wasted time already waiting for her to arrive, and now this.'

It was a standard technique of lawyers to delay the start of the interview. They only had twenty-four hours in which to question Zac before they had to either charge him or release him. The clock was ticking but there was nothing they could do.

'I'll get her that coffee,' said Jake.

'Okay. Tell them to use full fat milk if they've got it.'

Jake grinned.

Bridget returned to her desk and phoned Chloe. She braced herself for the familiar voicemail message to kick in, but instead Chloe answered on the seventh ring.

'Hi, Mum,'

'Hi, darling. Are you back home from Olivia's?'

'Yeah. Don't worry, everything's good.'

Bridget heard music playing in the background, and the chatter and giggle of other girls' voices. It was inevitable that Chloe would take her friends back to her empty house. Bridget wondered if there were any boys there. 'Listen, I'm sorry but I've got to work late tonight.'

'Sure, no problem.' Chloe sounded positively elated at the prospect of having the house to herself and her friends. A pause, then, 'Are you working on that dead student case?'

'Where did you hear about that?'

'Everyone in Oxford has heard about it.'

By everyone Chloe presumably meant her school friends. But she was right – now that the press had arrived in town, very soon literally everyone would know.

'Well, are you?' demanded Chloe.

'You know I can't discuss work with you.'

'You are, I knew it,' said Chloe with obvious glee.

'I think there's a pizza in the freezer if you want it tonight,' said Bridget.

'Don't try to change the subject. Anyway, we already got a bucket of KFC when we were in Oxford earlier.'

'Oh, right.' Bridget hated the thought of her daughter living off fast food. She'd wanted to be a better parent than that. But life just kept getting in the way. At least they'd be having vegetables at her sister's house on Sunday. 'Don't forget that you're going to lunch at Aunt Vanessa's tomorrow.'

'I haven't forgotten. Aren't you coming too?'

'It depends on how the case is going.'

'The dead student case?' probed Chloe.

'No comment.'

Chloe laughed at that.

Bridget savoured the shared moment. 'I'll see you later.'

'Yeah, bye Mum!' The phone went dead.

Jake waved her over.

'Look at this, ma'am.' He handed her Zac's mobile phone. 'Some very interesting texts between Zara and Zac over the last week.' He seemed buoyed up by what he'd found.

Bridget scrolled up and down the screen, reading and re-reading the exchange with mounting interest. 'Very good. Can you print

166

these out for me?'

'Sure.'

While he did that, Bridget grabbed herself a quick coffee from the machine (milk, one sugar, that unmistakable dishwater taste) and sat down to read once more through the case notes on Zac. Having all the facts at her fingertips was a habit that stretched back to her days as an Oxford undergraduate and the weekly one-on-one tutorial with her tutor, a woman possessed of unparalleled mental agility and wit. She had constantly challenged Bridget with probing questions and controversial hypotheses, forcing her to engage in arguments which she hadn't previously considered. Gruelling at the time, but a surprisingly good preparation for a police detective.

At seven o'clock on the dot Bridget decided she'd allowed the over-paid lawyer more than enough time with her client and told Jake it was time to go. She tapped on Grayson's door to let him know she was about to start the interview. Before heading downstairs she tasked Ffion with finding out how forensics were getting on. She needed fast results if she was going to nail Zac.

She knocked on the door of the interview room and entered without waiting for a reply. She was pleased to note that Caroline's mug of coffee was untouched and had gone cold. Zac had not been offered any. He sat slumped in his chair, looking tired. An hour alone with the London lawyer had obviously been an exhausting experience.

Good, thought Bridget. It shouldn't take him long to crack.

'I think we'll make a start,' she said briskly. She and Jake took seats opposite the lawyer and her client. 'Ms Butler has a long journey back to London.'

'I'll be staying at the Randolph Hotel until this matter is satisfactorily concluded,' said Caroline.

Of course, thought Bridget. Five-star luxury in Oxford's best hotel for the celebrity lawyer. Zac could expect the comfort of a police cell for the night.

She switched on the digital interview recorder. 'Is everyone ready?'

'Yes,' said Caroline curtly.

Zac just nodded.

'Good.' Bridget pressed the Record button on the machine. 'This interview is being recorded. This is an interview with' – she looked across at Zac – 'state your full name please.'

Zac said nothing, just stared at her with a look full of disdain.

'Your name please,' repeated Bridget patiently. If Zac was going to behave like a spoilt brat they could sit here all evening. She'd seen hardened criminals break after a few hours of waiting, and whatever Zac was, he certainly wasn't that.

'Zachary Hamilton,' he said eventually.

'And your address please?'

'Which one would you like?' He was playing with her, flaunting his wealth.

'The one where you reside during term time will be fine.'

'Christ Church, Oxford.'

For the sake of the recording Bridget identified herself and asked Jake and Caroline to do likewise. Once she'd stated the date and time, explained the procedure for accessing the tape afterwards and repeated the words of the caution, they were ready to start.

She began with some easy questions to loosen him up and get him talking.

'Zac, can you tell me about the early part of the evening of Thursday 13th June? Did you see your sister, Zara at any time during that evening?'

He delayed slightly before answering, as if probing the question for some kind of trap. 'No. The last time I saw her was earlier in the day, just after lunch.'

'Where did you see her?'

'In Tom Quad. She was on her way to the library. I was just returning from a tutorial.'

'What did you say to her?'

'Nothing much. I just asked her how she was.'

'And how was she?'

'Good.' A trace of a smile.

He was visibly relaxing as the questions flowed. Caroline, by contrast, was perched on her seat like a bird of prey.

'And how did you spend the rest of that afternoon?' asked Bridget.

'I was working in my room until dinner.'

Bridget found the idea of Zac doing much work hard to believe, but she let that pass. He may well have been in his room though with the delectable Verity.

'And what time was dinner?'

'Like I told you previously, I went to formal hall at seven twenty.'

'Alone?'

'With Verity.'

'That's Verity Cunningham, your girlfriend?'

'Of course.' The smile had gone. He was bored now.

'What did you do after eating?'

'I went to the Oxford Union, around nine o'clock.'

'In your initial statement to police,' said Bridget, 'you claimed that after visiting the Union, you returned to college at eleven o'clock and spent the rest of the night in your room in the company of Miss Verity Cunningham. Is that correct?'

Zac leaned back in his chair looking uncomfortable.

'Is that correct?'

Caroline gave him a nod and he answered. 'Yes.'

'Verity stated specifically that you were with her from 11:20. And yet CCTV footage supplied by the college indicates that although you returned to college at 11:05, Verity herself did not return until 11:55. Why did you and Verity lie when you told us you were in your room together during that time?'

'I didn't lie,' said Zac. 'I just didn't know exactly what time I got back.'

Caroline fixed Bridget with a steely gaze. 'Please do not accuse my client of lying, DI Hart, unless you have unequivocal evidence that he did so.'

'So, Zac,' continued Bridget, 'tell me precisely what you did after returning to college.'

'I don't remember. I'd been drinking.'

'You remember nothing about your movements?'

He shook his head.

'Interesting. At 11:30, Megan Jones, Zara's neighbour, reports seeing you banging on Zara's door. In her statement, she describes your mood as foul and states that you were hammering violently on the door. Do you remember that?'

'Like I said, I was drunk.'

'But surely you remember knocking on Zara's door?'

Zac looked to Caroline, who nodded.

'I may have gone there, but I didn't see her. There was no answer.'

'Why did you go?'

'I wanted to see my sister.'

'Why did you want to see her?'

Zac shrugged. 'I just did. Does it matter?'

Caroline shot him a warning look. 'I have advised my client not to comment on questions that have no relevance to the case.'

'Okay,' said Bridget. 'Let's take a step back.

Earlier that evening you were involved in a fight with Adam Brady, Zara's ex-boyfriend, at the Oxford Union. What was that about?'

'You'll have to ask Adam,' said Zac. 'He started it.'

'I think what my client means is no comment,' said Caroline.

'No comment,' said Zac with a smirk on his face.

'You're president of the Union, this term, aren't you?' enquired Bridget casually.

Zac's face brightened. 'Yes.'

'Enjoying that role?'

'Yes. Very much.'

'I fail to see how this is at all relevant,' interrupted Caroline.

Bridget studiously ignored her. 'Your invited speaker for the next debate is rather controversial, don't you think?'

A grin spread across Zac's face. 'Catriona Hodgson? I'd say that she's extremely controversial. That's why I invited her.'

'Some people aren't too happy with your choice.'

Zac shrugged. 'That's their problem.'

'There has, in fact, been a campaign on Twitter to stop her from speaking.'

'Yeah, well, those people need to learn to respect the right to freedom of speech.'

'And,' said Bridget, 'your own sister, Zara, was organising that campaign.'

She waited for her words to sink in.

Zac reacted as if she'd slapped his face. 'Zara? No… that's not true.'

'Here's the proof,' said Bridget, sliding the printouts from Zara's anonymous Twitter accounts across the desk.

Zac studied them, looking first mystified, then shocked, then angry.

'I fail to see what this has to do with anything,' said Caroline. 'Are you seriously suggesting that my client murdered his own sister because of some online messages about a debate?'

Bridget waited a beat before replying. 'Those aren't the only messages we found.' She paused again before elaborating. 'Do you have the printout, DS Derwent?'

Jake handed out copies of the texts he'd taken from Zac's phone. Bridget read through her own copy as she waited for Zac and Caroline to digest this latest piece of evidence.

'DS Jake Derwent has just passed me a piece of paper on which is printed out a text message thread between the suspect, Zachary Hamilton, and his sister, the late Zara Hamilton. The text messages are as follows.

Zara: When are you going to do it?
Zac: Never
Zara: You promised
Zac: Changed my mind
Zara: You've got 24 hours and then I'll tell everyone
Zac: If you tell anyone about this, I'll kill you

'The last text was sent on Thursday morning at 11:06,' said Bridget. 'It would appear to be a death threat.'

The interview room fell completely silent. Bridget let the silence grow before continuing her questioning. 'What is the "it" referred to in these texts?'

Zac shook his head. The colour had drained from his face, along with all traces of his earlier bravado. 'No comment.'

'When you knocked on Zara's door after returning from the Oxford Union, did you see your sister?'

'No.' It was barely a whisper.

'Did you see her?' pressed Bridget. 'Did she open her door to you?'

'No, she didn't. But I knew she was in there because her light was on.'

Bridget nodded to Jake. He leaned across the table towards Zac. 'Look mate, we've all been there. We've all had one too many as a student, and, well, sometimes things get a little out of hand. Sometimes you can't really explain why you did something. Hell, sometimes you don't even remember clearly what it was you did. So, you had a few drinks, got into a punch up with Adam. It wasn't your fault. You went to see your sister about it. You got angry, you hit her – you probably didn't ever mean to hurt her – and then you panicked.'

'No,' said Zac. 'It wasn't like that.'

'Tell me how it was,' said Bridget softly.

'You wouldn't understand. Do you have a sister, or a brother, DI Hart?'

Bridget held his gaze levelly. Two, she wanted to say. One living, one dead. She held her tongue.

Zac was in tears now. 'I loved Zara. That's what you can't seem to get. I would never have done anything to hurt her. Never, not even if I was drunk.'

'And yet you threatened to kill her.'

'That wasn't a threat. They were just words. They weren't even about... the debate, or Twitter, or anything like that.'

'What were they about?'

'They were private. No comment.' Bright spots of colour were highlighting his cheeks. He lapsed into sullen silence again.

Jake took up the thread once more. 'So, you had an argument, you hit her, and then afterwards you tried to stop the bleeding with a towel. But you couldn't. It was too late. You ran away, stopping in the seminar room below Zara's to be sick. You also dropped the bloody towel there and left a handprint on the wall.'

'No.'

'We matched the blood on the towel to Zara's,' said Bridget. 'Fibres from the towel were found in her hair, and we matched the handprint to yours.'

Zac clenched his fists and banged on the table. 'You've got it all wrong! Yes, all right, I threw up

175

in the stupid seminar room. I wasn't feeling well after Adam punched me. But I don't know anything about a bloody towel. I didn't hit Zara. I didn't even see her!'

Caroline's eyes had become cold. 'You don't have to say any more, Zac.'

Bridget pushed on. 'I think you should, Zac, because I don't believe your story. And I don't think that a jury will either. You see, the post-mortem revealed a sliver of purple glass in Zara's skull. It was an unusual type of glass. Very distinctive. And yet a purple glass paperweight with an identical design was found in your room in college. It even has a chip in it. What are the chances of that?'

Zac's eyes narrowed and he seemed to regain some of his composure. Then, slowly, he began to laugh.

Caroline glared at him.

'What's so funny, Zac?'

'You idiots, you don't have a clue.' He was grinning now, like a man led down from the gallows at the last possible moment. 'Zara and I owned identical paperweights. They were a gift from our godmother. Twin paperweights for twin brother and sister. Murano glass, from Venice. Mine got chipped, but Zara's was in perfect condition.'

There was a knock on the door and Bridget paused the interview to answer it.

Ffion was waiting in the corridor outside with a sheet of paper. Her face was grim.

Bridget closed the door to the interview room behind her. 'What is it?'

'The results on the paperweight have just come back from the lab.'

'Tell me the worst,' said Bridget.

'The paperweight in Zac's room was not the murder weapon. The sliver of glass found in Zara's skull doesn't match the chip in Zac's paperweight.' She handed Bridget the report from forensics. Bridget felt as if the ground was cracking under her.

She went back inside and resumed the recording. 'DC Ffion Hughes has just passed me the forensics report on the paperweight taken from the suspect's room. It confirms that this was not the same paperweight used to attack Zara. There will be no further questions relating to the paperweight.'

The look of smug satisfaction on Caroline's face was galling. 'DI Hart, I think you've just demonstrated that you have no substantive evidence against my client. I therefore insist that you bring this farce of an interview to a close.'

CHAPTER 15

Bridget woke early on Sunday morning feeling almost worse than when she had gone to bed. The spirit of Detective Chief Superintendent Grayson had haunted her dreams, rattling chains and bellowing, 'Find me evidence. Hard evidence. And when I say hard, I mean rock bloody solid.'

She hoped that Zac had fared no better. A night in the cells could be a sobering experience, especially for a young man accustomed to luxury and privilege. No doubt Caroline Butler of Kingsley, Butler and Cooke had enjoyed a more recuperative rest at the Randolph Hotel in her £300 a night room.

She showered and dressed and went downstairs to find Chloe still in her pyjamas, eating breakfast at the kitchen table. She watched her daughter for a second as she thumbed her mobile phone in one hand while spooning cereal with the other. Sometimes when Bridget studied her daughter's face, she saw Ben's staring back. Chloe certainly took after her father in many ways. She was already taller than

Bridget, with shiny black hair, and those mysterious dark eyes that promised so much. Bridget could only hope that Chloe had inherited Ben's best genes. With any luck, she'd got the best of Bridget too, the best of both parents. But somehow that seemed too much to hope for.

'Mum, have you seen my black top, you know, the off-the-shoulder one from Superdry?'

Bridget sighed. Here was a crisis of a more domestic variety than the one that had kept her awake half the night. 'Isn't it in your wardrobe?'

'I couldn't see it anywhere.'

'Well, why don't you wear the nice blouse with the polka dots.'

'Oh, Mum, that's so, like last year.'

Last year? If any of Bridget's clothes were only a year old, she considered them to be new.

'If you can't find it, then it's probably still in the laundry. I haven't had time to get round to it, these last few days.'

She was treated to a sour-faced scowl.

'You could always learn to use the washing machine yourself.' No response to that one.

Bridget flicked the switch on the kettle. 'Haven't you showered yet?' she asked Chloe. 'We'll be going to Aunt Vanessa's in an hour. I'll have to drop you there and get back to work.'

'Oh, Mum!'

'It can't be helped. I'm busy with that case. You know. The one I can't discuss.'

Chloe's face lifted from her phone. 'Go on, tell me about it. I heard that the murdered student's

179

incredibly rich.'

'So they say.'

'Have you arrested anyone yet?'

'I can't say.'

'Come on, Mum. Give me some gossip I can tell my friends.'

'Chloe, this is a murder case. A young woman was violently killed.' It came out as a rebuke.

The scowl returned to Chloe's face, and she flounced upstairs.

Oh God, thought Bridget. Give me a break. Just one.

An hour later they headed off to her sister Vanessa's house in North Oxford, the interior of the Mini filled with an uncomfortable silence.

Chloe had somehow managed to slide into a pair of skintight jeans that were more slashes than fabric. The nice polka dot blouse was nowhere to be seen, and instead she was wearing an enormous baggy Coldplay T-shirt. Bridget could imagine her sister's silent disapproval and the inevitable hushed comment when she thought Chloe was out of earshot – Doesn't she own any decent clothes?

Bridget put her foot down as they sped out of Wolvercote village, keen to drop off Chloe and get back to Kidlington. They could only hold Zac in custody without charge for another eight hours. The case depended now on whatever forensics had managed to find overnight. And also how cooperative Zac was feeling after his night in a police cell.

'I hope you don't mind spending a few hours with Aunt Vanessa,' said Bridget. She also hoped her sister wouldn't be too grumpy at the news that Bridget couldn't stay. She hadn't yet told her. Coward, she chided herself.

Beside her in the passenger seat Chloe fiddled with her phone. Shame the ban on using phones in cars didn't apply to passengers as well as drivers. Bridget tried again to start a conversation.

'Sorry I couldn't be with you for your birthday,' she said. 'I'll make it up to you, I promise.'

'It's all right,' said Chloe. 'I had a nice time with my friends.'

'What did you do?'

'Oh, you know, just hung out.'

'Right.' Bridget was only too aware that conversations with her daughter tended to be a bit like interviews with suspects – Bridget asking all the questions and getting minimal, evasive answers in return. Still, she persisted. It was good practice.

'Who were you hanging out with?'

'Just friends.'

Girls or boys, Bridget wanted to find out, but knew that some questions were best left unasked.

They were halfway down the Banbury Road when Chloe suddenly twisted round in her seat and said, 'That student at Christ Church, how did she die?'

'I can't tell you. We haven't released any

details to the public yet. Why do you want to know?'

'It's just that Olivia's sister is in her first year at Christ Church, and she told Olivia all about it. She said that the dead student was really popular. She was really upset about it.'

'Yes,' said Bridget gently. 'Murder is upsetting. It's more than just headlines in the newspapers. It leaves a mark behind that perhaps never heals.'

'I know.'

She turned to give Chloe a reassuring smile. Sometimes she was still just a child, and other times she was so grown up and independent.

'Do you think the killer was someone who knew her?'

'We're not sure at the moment.'

'But you'll catch whoever did it, won't you?'

'I'll do my best.'

They turned left into Belbroughton Road and then right into Charlbury Road. Immediately the bustle of the main thoroughfare gave way to the sort of peace and tranquillity that only money could buy. Large Edwardian detached houses were set back from the road behind clipped hedges and old stone walls. They had been built in a more genteel age, when ladies stayed at home and entertained their guests with afternoon tea, served by the maid. Bridget suspected that for Vanessa the house was a defence against the outside world – an imposing property of brick and stone, big enough to accommodate a huge family and their domestic entourage. Bridget's house would have squeezed into a quarter of the space, yet somehow her sister managed to occupy her vast home with just herself, her husband, two children and a dog.

Bridget pulled into the driveway and parked her Mini behind Vanessa's Range Rover, the de facto vehicle for ferrying small children to prep school with their sports bags and musical instruments.

'Are you coming in?' asked Chloe. 'You're not just going to leave me to explain that you're not staying for lunch, are you?'

'No. Of course not.' The thought had crossed her mind, if only for a second. She couldn't help it. Her sister had that effect on her.

Vanessa was two years older than Bridget, and taller and slimmer too. Bridget had always found that most unfair. Unlike Bridget, Vanessa had approached life's milestones in a sensible and correct order – a career first, then a husband, followed by children (one of each, to complete the set.) Bridget, by contrast had reached these three landmarks in reverse order – an early pregnancy, followed by a hurried marriage to an ultimately disappointing husband, and eventually a late career that was only now getting going.

'You ought to have been more careful,' Vanessa liked to tell her, seemingly at every opportunity.

And yet, while Bridget had some regrets – Ben,

183

for all his charm and good looks, had turned out to be an indifferent father and an unfaithful husband – she would never regret having Chloe, even though having a baby at a young age had shunted her career into the slow lane.

Besides, Vanessa too, had her sorrows and her remorse.

They never spoke about Abigail, the murdered sister who hadn't lived beyond the tender age of sixteen. But whenever Bridget was with Vanessa, the third sister was always at their side. Beautiful Abigail would forever be the barrier that kept the two surviving sisters apart. But she was also the glue that bound them together.

Each had coped with her loss in their own way.

Bridget had joined the police force. She had wondered about that decision often enough over the years. She must have imagined that she could solve every crime and lock every criminal behind bars. She must still have believed that now at some subconscious level, or else what kept her going, day after day?

Vanessa had taken on perhaps a greater challenge – to make her world perfect. Her marriage, her beautiful house, her two lovely children – even the dog – were all part of a vain bid to paper over the cracks, to undo the one outrageous wrong that could never be undone. Bridget was not so different to Vanessa, and she could never be angry with her. That would have been too cruel.

Chloe reached the door first and rang the bell.

The loud chime was followed immediately by the sound of a dog barking.

The door opened and a Golden Labrador bounded through.

'Rufus!' cried Chloe, laughing. The big dog jumped up and licked her face.

'Down, Rufus, down!' Vanessa was right behind. She kissed her niece and turned to welcome Bridget.

Bridget got her apologies in before Vanessa had time to say anything. 'Really sorry, but I can't stay. I have to get back to work.'

Her sister frowned. 'I saw you on the news.' It was said as a reproof.

Vanessa had always found Bridget's job slightly distasteful. Bridget didn't know why. It's not as if she worked in a strip club, although she had raided a few in her time as a uniformed constable.

'What am I going to say to Jonathan?'

Bridget had forgotten about the lunch guest Vanessa had invited. 'Just explain where I am,' she said. 'It's not as if this –'

'Jonathan.'

'– this Jonathan even knows who I am.'

'Yes he does. I told him all about you. Look, here he comes now.'

A man was walking up the path, past the Mini. He looked much younger than Vanessa had described, more like late-thirties than mid-forties. He was tall and had warm, intelligent eyes behind tortoiseshell glasses that gave him a quirky, boyish look. His navy open-necked shirt and smart designer jeans were casually understated.

'Vanessa,' he said, offering up a bottle of wine wrapped in tissue paper. 'And you must be Bridget.'

'Hi,' she said. 'Correct first time.' She shook his hand.

'Not exactly a great deduction,' he said. 'Your sister described you very well.'

'Oh,' said Bridget, wondering exactly how Vanessa had described her. 'I'm afraid I can't stay for lunch.' She was surprised to find that she was genuinely sorry.

Jonathan seemed so too. 'That's a shame. Perhaps some other time?'

'Yes. Perhaps.'

CHAPTER 16

Jake was enjoying his breakfast outside in the warm sunshine. A bacon roll and a coffee. Bliss. He looked up as a sleek green machine roared into the Kidlington HQ car park. Ffion brought her motorbike to a neat halt, jumped off, and removed her crash helmet, running her hand through her hair. 'Be with you in a mo,' she called to him.

'No worries,' said Jake, watching as she darted nimbly up the steps, her skintight green leathers squeaking as she moved. His suggestion that he pick her up from home had been politely but firmly rebuffed. He wondered if Ryan had made his move on her yet. He didn't rate the guy's chances highly. If he were a betting man, he'd put his money on 'no score'.

The previous night, after the interview with Zac had ended in a stalemate, Bridget had asked him and Ffion to go and have another try at coaxing the truth out of Adam. He was obviously still hiding something, and both he and Zac were refusing to discuss the fight at the Oxford Union.

Ffion appeared five minutes later dressed in

her work clothes. 'Ready?'

Jake tossed his empty coffee cup into the bin and led the way to the Subaru. This time, he'd remembered to clear the passenger seat of chocolate wrappers before leaving home.

They stopped at a newsagent's on the way to see what the Sunday papers were saying about the case. The headlines splashed across their pages spoke of murder, beauty, wealth and privilege. The articles that accompanied them seemed designed more to entertain than to inform. Jake bought a copy of each and Ffion read them aloud as they headed into the city centre.

When they arrived at the college gates the photographers and journalists standing outside seemed to have multiplied. Jake and Ffion pushed their way through, saying nothing.

Inside Christ Church, life looked to be continuing pretty much as it had done every Sunday for the past five hundred years. A line of choristers in red cassocks and white surplices were leaving the cathedral and trooping across Tom Quad. All male, they ranged from young men to boys of no more than seven or eight. Jake couldn't imagine life as a choirboy. At that age he'd spent his weekends kicking a football in the garden if it was dry, or watching cartoons on television if it was raining. He wondered what Ffion had been like as a child. Probably weird then as well.

Only one thing had changed since their

previous visit. All around the black and yellow tape that marked the perimeter of the crime scene, bouquets of flowers had been left. Dozens of them, of all colours and sizes, with personalised messages and cards attached, lay in tribute to the murdered student. A uniformed PC still stood guard at the foot of the staircase, surrounded now by the floral display. Jake nodded to him as they passed.

They found Adam in his room in Blue Boar Quad. Jake had to bang on the door three times before he appeared, unshaven and with a crumpled look about him as if he'd just got out of bed and thrown on the first thing that came to hand – grey jogging pants and a Christ Church rowing club sweatshirt. 'You again,' he said. 'What do you want now?'

'Can we come in?' asked Jake.

Adam shrugged and let them inside.

The floor of his room was still strewn with discarded rowing kit, tracksuits and muddy socks. An empty pizza box rested on the bed. The place looked like a pigsty even to Jake's undiscerning eye, and it didn't smell much better either. He wondered if Adam had been out of his room since they'd left him here the day before. He seemed to have given up on life. Ffion picked her way through the detritus and sat down on the window seat after shoving aside a damp bath towel.

'We want to talk to you about the argument with Zac at the Oxford Union,' said Jake.

'Oh God, not that again,' said Adam, collapsing onto the unmade bed and knocking the pizza box onto the floor.

Jake took the desk chair, removed a pile of clothes, and sat down. 'Yes, that. Talk us through that encounter. Why did you go to see Zac at all?'

Adam stretched out on the bed, staring up at the ceiling. 'I'd been thinking about what Zara said when she broke up with me, and I thought that maybe Zac might know something.'

'What exactly did Zara say?'

Adam pursed his lips, reluctant to speak. 'She told me there was someone else,' he said eventually, his voice full of bitterness.

So that was it. The truth was beginning to emerge, just as Jake had finally managed to drag the truth out of his own girlfriend, after so many tears and lies. 'Did she say who?' he asked gently.

'No. She wouldn't discuss it. I told her I would find out sooner or later and it was better if she told me herself, but she just didn't want to talk to me.'

'Did you have any ideas?' asked Ffion.

'None. I kept thinking about it afterwards, and it just didn't make any sense. I don't understand how she could have been seeing anyone else.'

Jake nodded. His own girlfriend had been seeing someone at work. It had been easy for her to hide her cheating from him, especially since he'd been so unwilling to see it for himself. All those mysterious texts, the times she'd arrived home late from work, the weekends she'd had to go into the office. He was a police detective. He ought to have been suspicious. But he had trusted her. He didn't know now if he'd ever be able to trust someone in the same way again.

'So you went to see Zac.'

'Yeah,' said Adam. 'I was sure he would know. He must have known all the time. She was his sister, for God's sake. But the bastard wouldn't talk about it. In fact he got really aggressive, started shouting at me. He even shoved me. That's when I snapped.'

'You punched him?'

'Yeah,' said Adam. 'Felt good at the time. Didn't get me anywhere though, except in a whole heap of trouble.'

'And did you ever find out who the other person was?'

Adam shook his head, defeated. 'If I knew I'd tell you.'

CHAPTER 17

'So who was Zara's new man?'

On Bridget's arrival at Kidlington, Jake and Ffion had quickly filled her in on what Adam had told them that morning. Adam's claim that Zara was seeing someone else was now the best lead she had. She'd also received news from forensics that had confirmed her worst fears – while the vomit in the seminar room was definitely Zac's, the bloodstained towel held no traces of his DNA. There was no hard evidence to link him with the murder.

But Zac didn't know that yet. He sat slumped in his chair in the interview room. All the arrogance and belligerence he had displayed yesterday had drained away overnight. He looked like a man who'd given up hope. His hair was dishevelled and there were black smudges under his bloodshot eyes. The man who aspired to be prime minister had been broken by a single night of discomfort.

By contrast, Caroline Butler appeared to have enjoyed a most refreshing stay at Oxford's five-star hotel. Her make-up was immaculate and she was wearing a fresh blouse and jacket. On the table in front of her stood a Starbucks coffee. She watched Bridget from across the table.

Bridget repeated the question to Zac, trying to inject some kindness into her voice. There was no need to push him now. He was a defeated man.

'I don't know,' he mumbled. 'She didn't tell me.'

'Were you close to your sister?'

'Yeah, but you know...we didn't discuss everything.'

'Is this line of questioning going anywhere?' asked Caroline impatiently.

Bridget took no notice of her. 'But you knew there was someone else?'

'No. Not until Adam told me.' He was staring at his hands, not looking her in the eye.

'At the Oxford Union?'

'Yeah.'

'Is that why he came to see you?'

'Yeah. He asked me if I knew who it was.'

'And what did you tell him?'

'That I didn't know.'

'Anything else?'

Zac shrugged. 'I told him a few home truths.'

'Such as?'

A faint smile of amusement twitched his mouth. 'That it was time Zara dumped him. That he wasn't good enough for her. That he was a nobody.'

'And what was his response?'

Zac touched the purple bruise on his face.

'He punched you. And then you went back to college to look for Zara.'

Zac ran a hand through his fair hair, making it stand up. 'I was angry, all right? I thought it was Zara's fault that Adam had come after me. I was mad at her, that happens with siblings, okay?' He put his head in his hands and let out a huge racking sob. 'But I would never have hurt her. I loved her.' He buried his head in his hands, in tears.

'Satisfied now?' demanded Caroline, her eyes blazing. 'Rest assured that Sir Richard will hear all about this.'

Bridget was out of ideas. She looked across at Jake who was sitting next to her. It was obvious he had none either.

'You're free to go,' she said to Zac. 'But stay around Oxford. We might need to speak to you again.'

★

Chief Superintendent Grayson's vast desk was littered with a selection of Sunday papers, mostly tabloids. Photographs of a smiling Zara Hamilton, her blonde hair like a halo, stared back at Bridget from their front pages. Lurid headlines seemed to accuse her. Oxford student in savage murder. Brutal killing of wealthy heiress. Golden girl murder.

'We let him go, sir,' she said. 'Zachary

Hamilton. There wasn't enough evidence to detain him.'

The lines etched into Grayson's forehead seemed deeper this morning. He ran a hand through his greying hair. 'I've already spoken to his lawyers. They're considering a civil action against the police.'

'We had reasonable grounds to arrest him, sir.'

'I know. And you sought my permission before making the arrest. There's no need for you to worry about your own career, Bridget.'

She nodded. She couldn't remember him using her first name before.

He swept the desk clean with his arm, depositing the newspapers into his waste paper bin. 'So where do we go from here? Do you have any leads?'

'Zac's in the clear, unless new evidence emerges. It's still possible that the murder was a burglary that went wrong – her wallet is missing, and also her mobile phone.'

'What about the murder weapon?'

'We still haven't found it. But it was almost certainly Zara's paperweight.'

'That suggests the killing may not have been premeditated, perhaps not even deliberate. It adds weight to the burglary scenario.'

'Yes, sir. The murderer may simply have grabbed the nearest heavy object.'

'But you don't believe that the killer was unknown to the victim.' It was a statement, not a question.

'No. The ex-boyfriend, Adam, now claims that Zara split up with him because she was seeing someone else.'

'Who?'

'We don't know. No one we've interviewed so far has mentioned another boyfriend. But if there was someone, then we need to find out who he was and talk to him.'

'Do you think Adam's telling the truth?'

'I think so, sir. Zac confirmed that's what their argument was about. Adam went to him demanding to know who the other person was. The only question is whether Zara was telling Adam the truth when she said there was someone else. Zac maintains that he had no idea she was seeing someone.'

'Well, this gives us a new line of enquiry to follow. What about call records from Zara's phone?'

'That's got to be our top priority, but the phone company's dragging its feet because it's a weekend. We should get her call records tomorrow, and we'll be interviewing all of Zara's friends again to ask about this other boyfriend.'

'Good. Take the rest of the day off.'

'Sir?'

'It's Sunday afternoon. Your team deserves a few hours of rest. Next week isn't going to be easy, for any of us.'

★

Despite the Chief Super's instruction to take the rest of the day off, Bridget spent a couple of hours sorting through her emails and her overflowing inbox. By the time she arrived to collect Chloe, the family lunch was long over.

'Sorry,' said Bridget as Vanessa let her into the house.

'Jonathan's already gone,' Vanessa told her in a tone of voice which was half scolding and half despairing. 'And I so wanted you to meet him.'

'I did briefly,' said Bridget, giving her sister a kiss on each cheek. 'He seemed nice. Maybe I'll get to meet him another time.'

She did feel bad about letting her sister down. She knew how much effort Vanessa put into preparing these lunchtime gatherings. And however irritating she might be as a matchmaker, she was a superb cook. No ready-made microwave meals for Vanessa's family. Her kitchen boasted a library's worth of cookbooks. A Sunday roast would have been far preferable to the slightly stale sandwiches that Bridget had salvaged from the office vending machine.

Chloe was sitting on the floor playing a board game with her younger cousins, eight-year-old Florence and six-year-old Toby (Vanessa disapproved of electronic devices and video games). Beside them, the dog was asleep in front of the fireplace. It opened one eye as Bridget entered.

'What have you all been up to?' she asked.

'We had an ace time in the garden with Rufus,'

said Chloe. 'And Jonathan was fun too.'

'Good.'

James, Vanessa's husband, wandered into the room wearing a blue and white striped apron over his shirt and jeans. 'Just been loading the dishwasher,' he said. He greeted Bridget with a peck on the cheek.

Bridget smiled. James was a successful businessman running his own IT company (hence the house worth millions) but still managed to find time for family and home. Her own ex-, Ben, had hardly known one end of a dishwasher from the other. How had Vanessa succeeded in bagging such a man? The difference between the two could not be marked down to bad luck, but poor planning. Bridget had jumped at the first handsome man to flatter her with his attention, while Vanessa had stalked potential partners for a decade before finally pouncing on her prey.

'Solved your golden girl murder, yet?' he enquired.

'Don't tell me you read that kind of newspaper, James.'

'Only the headlines. They make a change from the Weekend Financial Times.'

'I'm sure they do.'

She turned to her daughter. 'Come on, then. Say goodbye to everyone.'

On the drive home, Chloe seemed more relaxed than when Bridget had dropped her off.

'You really did have a nice time?' Bridget

asked. 'I'm sorry I had to leave you on your own.'

'No worries.'

'I know that the children are only small, and that Aunt Vanessa can go on a bit.'

'Honestly, Mum, it wasn't a problem.'

'Okay.'

A minute passed.

'Jonathan was really nice,' said Chloe.

'Oh?'

'Yeah.' A short silence. 'He kept asking all about you.'

'Did he?' Another beat passed. 'What did you tell him?'

Chloe laughed. 'Only the good bits. You should ask him out on a date.'

'What?' Bridget felt herself blushing.

'Before you get too old,' added Chloe.

'Cheers. Thanks for that.'

'You know what I mean.'

Did she? At thirty-eight, she must seem ancient to Chloe. Too old to go on a date? Apparently not.

But since when had her teenage daughter offered her dating advice? Wasn't it supposed to be the other way around? Not that Bridget had much advice to give other than don't do what I did.

'Oh, and by the way,' Chloe continued, seamlessly transitioning to a different topic, 'Dad called to say he's going to drop in tomorrow with a birthday present for me.'

'Oh. Is he?' Bridget's world came crashing

down once again. That was so like Ben. He paid his daughter no attention for months, then flew in from nowhere bearing expensive gifts.

'And I've been thinking,' added Chloe. 'I'd like to go and visit Dad in London.'

'What?' Bridget was caught off guard by the twist in the conversation. 'Did he suggest that?'

'Yeah, he did. He said I could go and stay with him for a few days over the summer.'

'Did he now?' The anger was rising up inside Bridget. How dare Ben suggest that! And to go behind her back, speaking directly to Chloe. He had never shown any interest in having her to stay before. He'd been too busy chasing women to show any concern for his daughter. But now he had settled down with this latest girlfriend, he was trying to have it all. Well, it was Bridget who had done all the hard work, bringing up Chloe single-handed, sacrificing her own career, going without –

'Don't be like that, Mum. You know I don't get to see him very often. It would only be for a few days. It's no big deal.'

The years of contained anger and resentment boiled over and Bridget was yelling before she realised it. 'No! Absolutely not. I won't allow it.'

CHAPTER 18

Bridget was still fuming when she rose on Monday morning. But now the anger was directed at herself. She had allowed Ben's behaviour to rattle her again, this time turning her against her own daughter. Chloe had hardly spoken a word to her after their row yesterday, and Bridget could scarcely blame her.

She popped her head around Chloe's bedroom door before leaving to see if the dark clouds had blown over, but the stormy weather seemed to have intensified.

'I'm just getting ready for school,' snapped Chloe, still clearly resentful.

'I'll see you this evening,' said Bridget, 'although I might be late. I'll leave some money in the kitchen in case you want to buy yourself a takeaway.'

This wasn't how she'd intended to bring up her daughter. Today of all days she should be spending time with Chloe, patching up the mess she'd made yesterday. When she'd first had Chloe, she'd imagined an idyllic future in which she would always cook proper meals for her family. They'd sit around the dining table enjoying their evening meal together. But those dreams had come to nothing. How could she do that and pursue her career too? She hadn't even managed to hold her family together. A career, a husband and a daughter – was it too much to want all three? She didn't think so.

'No need,' said Chloe with a shrug. 'I'm meeting Dad this evening, remember? He said he'd pick me up from school and take me out to dinner.'

'Oh.' Bridget held her tongue. The less she said on the subject the better. 'I'll catch you later, then. Have a nice time.'

For once she was grateful to be distracted by her work. As soon as she arrived at the office she grabbed herself a coffee and settled down to read through Zac and Adam's statements again. Zara had told Adam there was someone else, but refused to say who. If Zac was to be believed, she had never mentioned another relationship to him. None of the students who'd been interviewed had suggested that Zara was seeing someone else. Who could it be? Someone from outside the university? Someone inappropriate? Certainly no one had come forward to volunteer for the role.

As soon as the rest of the team arrived and got themselves some coffee (green tea for Ffion), she called a briefing. Everyone already knew of Zac's release, and the mood in the room was downbeat. Bridget's first job was to rally her troops.

'The case against Zac has crumbled. But we have a new lead. Zara finished her relationship with Adam for someone else. What we need to establish now is, who was the other man? Zara was protecting him for some reason. Why?'

She scanned the sea of faces before her. Mostly blank. That Monday morning feeling.

Ffion raised a hand. 'Why do you say a man? It might have been a woman.'

Ryan chuckled, but Bridget glared at him and he tried to turn his snigger into a cough. 'Good point. Zara kept the identity of this other person a secret. She must have had a reason for that. I want to know who it was and why she was so secretive about it. That could be the key to solving the case.

'Jake, Ffion, Ryan, I want you three to go back to Christ Church and get alongside the students. Talk to them. Someone must know something. Andy, Harry, you go through the statements we've already taken with a fine comb. Re-read everything in the light of this new information. Someone might have let something slip. What's happening with Zara's phone records, anyone?'

'Still nothing, ma'am,' said Ffion. 'I called again this morning. Some kind of technical glitch is holding them up, but they promised to get them across by the end of today.'

'They can do better than that,' said Bridget crossly. 'I'll speak to them myself and put a rocket under them. Come on then people, let's get moving.'

She was rewarded by a flurry of activity as they scrambled to their feet. Coffee mugs clattered on desks. Chairs scraped against the floor. Doors opened and closed. They were moving forward again.

★

Jake was pleased when Ffion joined him in his car. 'You're not taking your bike to the college, then?' he asked.

She shook her head. 'It makes more sense to come with you than bring two vehicles.'

'Yeah. I suppose it does. You wouldn't rather go with Ryan instead?'

'No. Why would I?'

'Good point.' He waved at Ryan, who was stalking across the car park, his hands in his pockets, trying hard not to look at Ffion in Jake's car. It was hard not to smirk at him. 'Did Ryan say anything to you?'

'No. What about?'

The guy hadn't made his move then. Perhaps he never would. Guys like Ryan were all talk. 'I don't know. He just mentioned you the other day.'

'Did he? So you two talk about me behind my back, do you?'

'No,' he blurted. Why couldn't he talk to Ffion without always saying the wrong thing?

He turned to her and was relieved to find a

mischievous grin on her face.

'I expect you just talk about beer and football,' she said.

'You're not too far wrong there.'

A disgruntled Ryan caught up with them in Tom Quad where they found the porter, Jim Turner, re-arranging the growing carpet of flowers outside the staircase to Zara's room. He was clearing a path so that people could still walk past without having to descend to the lower level of the quad.

'That's quite a display,' said Jake, glancing at the bouquets and handwritten messages. Hearts and kisses and a small teddy bear in a Christ Church jumper with a single rose between his paws. We will miss you, Zara. Heaven has another angel. Rest in peace. He wondered how well any of these people had really known Zara. Perhaps her death had somehow made people think they knew her, the way Princess Diana's death had affected millions who'd never even met her.

'It is that,' said Jim Turner, straightening up. 'Zara is greatly missed. Anyway, how can I help you?'

'We just want to chat to as many people as possible. Anyone who knew Zara.'

Jim gestured with his arm. 'Everyone knew her. I suggest you start knocking on doors. Although you might find that people are at lectures or in tutorials this morning. It's the exam season too. But perhaps you could go along to the dining hall at lunchtime.' He pointed to the opposite side of the quad. 'Through that archway and up the stairs. Can't miss it.'

'Good idea,' said Jake, wondering if you had to be a member of college to eat there. He wouldn't say no to a plate of something tasty for lunch. It would surely be better than the police canteen back at Kidlington.

'We'll get round more people if we split up,' said Ffion.

'Just like in Scooby-Doo,' grinned Jake. 'But remember, don't go down into the cellar on your own.'

Ffion rolled her eyes, but he thought he detected a hint of amusement, even in those cool, emerald orbs. Ryan looked miffed that he hadn't thought of anything witty to say.

Ryan agreed to take Tom Quad and the Meadow Building while Ffion headed off to Peckwater Quad. Jake made for Blue Boar Quad. Despite his initial shock at the modern architecture planted so brazenly next to the sixteenth- and eighteenth-century buildings, he'd come to like the straight lines and right angles of Blue Boar's utilitarian architecture. He hoped the students living there would be straight-talkers too.

★

In a high-ceilinged room in Peckwater Quad, Sophie Hinton sat opposite Dr Claiborne, feeling

206

ill at ease in the unfamiliar surroundings. This room belonged to a maths tutor, and on one wall was a whiteboard covered with incomprehensible equations. Dr Claiborne had rescheduled Friday's missed tutorial, asking her to come and see him today instead. She supposed he felt obliged to fulfil his teaching commitments but she wished he'd simply cancelled. It felt wrong being here on her own, without Zara by her side.

She stumbled her way through her essay, reading it aloud, doubting the strength of her own literary analysis. Lust and ambition are the driving forces of tragedy. Discuss. What she'd written seemed trite compared to the real-life events of the last few days. Her mind was so numbed by horror that there was no capacity left for thoughts of English literature. She wondered if Dr Claiborne felt the same. He sat with his head tilted back, his eyes half closed. Was he even listening to a word she was saying?

She ploughed on to the last sentence of her essay, and silence filled the room. Dr Claiborne seemed unaware that she had finished. She knew where his thoughts were directed. Zara Hamilton.

It was impossible to think of Zara now without picturing her as Sophie had last seen her, prostrate on the floor, the carpet spattered with blood. She could not scrub that image from her mind. But when she tried to guess at the identity of Zara's killer, a shadowy form without features was all that she could conjure. Yet someone here must know who had murdered Zara. Sophie was sure of it.

The college was very claustrophobic to her now. The ancient walls seemed to be closing in on her, shutting her into a dark, enclosed world. This place was full of secrets. Old secrets, accumulated over the centuries, like dust in the library. New secrets, hidden cunningly away by clever people, stacked as thick as the stone walls that enclosed them. Even eagle-eyed Val, the scout, with her network of spies did not know them all.

Dr Claiborne removed his glasses and rubbed his eyes. She waited patiently for him to question her about her essay, to challenge her arguments so that she could defend them, arguing her case with more clarity. That was how a tutorial was supposed to work. But Dr Claiborne seemed too distracted. It suddenly occurred to her that, maybe for once, the tables had turned and it was now her tutor who was under scrutiny.

He certainly had plenty to hide, and Sophie had no wish for him to guess how much she knew. But perhaps she had been wrong to keep his secrets hidden.

The truth was a mosaic, a pattern that emerged when all the facts were placed together in the right way. The police were searching for that pattern, but they didn't yet have all the facts. She wondered if she should have told them more when they had interviewed her.

But she was not the only one with secrets. Zara had kept her own secrets too, perhaps more than any of them.

'Sophie?' Dr Claiborne's voice broke through her thoughts. 'I think we'll wrap up. The maths tutor will be wanting his room back.'

She was glad to get away. She ran through the college to her room in the Meadow Building. The familiar rooms and buildings felt very threatening now and she couldn't wait for the end of term when she could return home to where she belonged.

CHAPTER 19

The huge stone staircase that led up to the dining hall at Christ Church looked like something out of a medieval castle. Jake was reminded of school trips to stately homes as a kid. Those places had always had a dead feel to them, the great rooms roped off, their inhabitants long dead and buried. But these walls reverberated with life, footsteps echoing on the stone steps, voices magnified by the cathedral-like acoustic. A women's rowing crew, not bothering to change out of their kit for lunch, overtook him, taking the stairs two at a time. They were probably starving after their training. Jake, too, was ravenous after a frustrating morning of interviews.

No one he'd spoken to had told him anything he didn't already know. Just as Jim Turner had said, a lot of the students were out at lectures or tutorials. He'd barged into one room where a small group of students were having their essays scrutinised by their tutor. The process seemed unduly harsh and adversarial to Jake. He'd seen suspects treated better back at the interview rooms in Kidlington, and none of the students here even had a lawyer to defend them. Except that it turned out they were all law students. No wonder lawyers always turned out to be such hard-nosed bastards. Jake's sympathy for them had waned at that point. The tutor had glared at him over his half-moon spectacles while he questioned the students about Zara. But even though they'd seemed glad of the interruption, none of them could tell him anything useful. He was really starting to wonder if he was on a wild goose chase. It was definitely time for a break.

The dining hall itself was one of the grandest rooms he'd ever seen. He gazed up at the wooden beams in the ceiling, feeling as if he really had just entered the Great Hall of Hogwarts. Centre-stage on the wall behind high table, a portrait of Henry VIII in his familiar wide-legged stance presided over the clatter of serving spoons and the babble of a couple of hundred chattering students. They queued up to collect their food from a row of mobile, stainless steel hotplates which looked oddly out of place next to the stained glass windows, the wood panelling and the vaulted ceiling. Three long wooden tables adorned with table lamps ran the full length of the hall, with a fourth table, at the far end, running perpendicular.

Ffion was waiting for him near the entrance. 'Made any progress?' she asked.

'Not really. You?'

She shook her head. 'Maybe we'll have better

luck here.'

He sniffed at the smells rising from the hotplates. 'Do you think we could grab a bite to eat first?'

'We're supposed to be working. Come on. I'll start on high table.'

'Okay.' Jake's stomach grumbled.

He saw Ryan wander into the hall.

'Fancy a bite to eat?' asked Jake.

'Good idea,' said Ryan. 'Let's grab a tray before it all goes.'

★

Ffion moved around the dining hall, chatting to different groups of students. She'd spoken to some of them before, but they were all happy to talk again. It seemed they welcomed the opportunity to talk about Zara, and what she meant to them. No one had a bad word to say about the murdered student. However much Ffion probed, the answers were always the same. Zara was adored by everyone, and no one could imagine who might have wanted to kill her, or why. As for the possibility of an unidentified lover, Ffion got the impression that any number of the men she talked to – and perhaps a few of the women – would have been delighted to have taken that role, but none of them had.

She came to the shorter table that ran perpendicular to the others at the top end of the hall. High table. At formal dinner in the evening,

212

high table would be reserved for the dean, the dons and any visiting dignitaries, but at lunchtime students were allowed to occupy it just like any other table. Verity, Zac's girlfriend, was sitting with a couple of other students, deep in conversation. One was a young man in a buttoned-down shirt and tweed jacket. He looked as if he bought all his clothes from Shepherd & Woodward, the old-fashioned gentleman's outfitters on the High Street. The other was a girl with blonde hair cascading down her back. They appeared to be discussing the menu for the upcoming summer ball. Ffion distinctly overheard the words Jerusalem artichokes.

'Sounds absolutely delicious,' trilled the long-haired girl.

Pretending to examine the portraits of Elizabeth I, Henry VIII and Cardinal Wolsey, Ffion hovered behind them, listening in.

Verity was clearly in charge of the meeting. 'What about the choice of wines?' she asked. If she'd noticed Ffion lurking, she was deliberately ignoring her.

'The butler gave me a tour of the wine cellar,' replied Mr Shepherd & Woodward. 'He suggests a 2009 Alsace for the starter and fish course, and for the main course, a rather fine Burgundy. They've got gallons of it in the cellar. For dessert I've chosen a sweet Bordeaux from 2014. Obviously there'll be port served with the coffee.'

Obviously, thought Ffion.

'Super!' squealed the excitable girl.

The girl didn't strike Ffion as particularly intelligent, and yet here she was at Oxford University. She didn't appear to be much of an asset to the ball committee either, although she must have been elected to her position on the ball committee, whatever it was. Or had she? Maybe she had simply volunteered to do a job no one else wanted. Ffion had no idea. Balls, and their committees, had never interested her.

She'd heard enough of fancy menu planning. She pulled up a chair and sat down opposite, bringing the discussion to an abrupt end. 'DC Ffion Hughes of Thames Valley Police.' She flashed her warrant card at them.

The group fell silent. Ffion said nothing more, waiting as the silence stretched out uncomfortably. The blonde student flicked her long hair nervously. Mr Shepherd & Woodward fidgeted with the buttons on his tweed jacket. He might know his wines, but his taste in fashion was abysmal. Only Verity kept her cool, regarding Ffion with a look of disdain.

'Um,' said the blonde girl at last. 'I expect you're here to ask about Zara. Absolutely shocking what happened. We thought of cancelling the ball, but Zara always wanted the best for everyone, so we decided to go ahead, and hold the ball in her honour.' She smiled, revealing a mouthful of pretty, white teeth.

'I'm sure Zara would be delighted,' said Ffion.

The girl's smile wavered.

'Are you here just to talk about the ball?' said Verity. 'Or is there something you want to ask?'

'Yes. The day Zara was killed, she split up with Adam. Was she seeing someone else?'

The blonde girl shrugged and looked around the group for support.

'No, there was no one else,' said Verity with emphasis. 'I expect that she simply grew tired of Adam. I was surprised she endured him for so long. He's such a boor.'

There was a general nodding of agreement around the table. 'Adam gave Zac an awful black eye,' exclaimed the blonde girl. 'We think the dean will have him sent down.'

Verity looked pointedly at her watch. 'I'm sorry, but is there something else you want to ask? We have a meeting in five minutes with the bursar about the ball.'

'No,' said Ffion. 'You can go.'

She was wondering who to speak to next when she noticed Sophie, Zara's tutorial partner, holding a tray of food and looking for a place to sit. Ffion waved her over. 'Hi,' she called, giving the girl a welcoming smile. 'Come and join me.'

Sophie seemed nervous and reluctant to sit with Ffion. 'You don't mind?' she asked.

'Not at all.'

She hesitated a moment before sitting down in the chair that Verity had vacated. 'How's the investigation going?' she asked.

'Slowly,' admitted Ffion.

'You released Zac.'

'Yes.' No doubt everyone in the college knew about Zac's arrest and subsequent release. 'We're exploring other avenues now.'

'I see.' Sophie stared at her plate of pasta, leaving it untouched.

'Talk to me about Zara,' said Ffion. 'You must have known her well.'

'Oh, yes,' said Sophie. 'I first met her when we came up for interview. I knew at once that she would be offered a place here. She was so bright and intelligent. She was very kind to me, too. I was rather shy in those days, you see.' Ffion smiled at the thought that Sophie had been even shyer than she was now. 'We became tutorial partners at the start of our first year, and we've been friends ever since. I mean, we were, until her death.' Her eyes welled with tears and she bowed her head over her uneaten plate of food.

Sophie's claim to know Zara felt much more convincing than that of most of the students she'd interviewed. Ffion remembered the close relationship she had developed with her own tutorial partner at college. When there were just two of you facing the tutor for the weekly tutorial you forged a strong bond, even if you socialised with other people the rest of the time. If anyone could give them some insight into Zara's personal life, it was surely Sophie. She waited patiently for the girl to compose herself.

'Is there anything particular you want to know?' asked Sophie eventually.

'Did she ever talk to you about her love life?'

probed Ffion. She watched as Sophie bit her lip, shaking her head a tiny fraction, saying nothing. It was obvious that the girl knew something.

'What we'd really like to know,' said Ffion, 'is why Zara split up with Adam. We've been told that there was someone else in her life, but we don't know who. Any ideas?'

Sophie stared at her pasta and shook her head. Then she looked around the hall. It was beginning to empty but there were still groups of people dotted around. 'We can't talk here,' she said. 'Let's go outside.'

CHAPTER 20

'I don't know if I should be telling you this,' began Sophie. 'It's probably nothing.'

'This is a murder enquiry,' said Ffion. 'If you have any information, no matter how insignificant you think it is, you must tell me.'

Sophie had left her lunch uneaten back in the hall. The stairway leading from the hall was busy, as was Tom Quad. Walking with her head bowed and her arms folded, Sophie led the way out through the Meadow Gate to the Broad Walk at the top of Christ Church Meadow. They walked some distance from the college buildings before she said anything again.

She checked to make sure no one was near, then continued. 'A couple of weeks ago there was a faculty dinner.'

'English faculty?' Ffion knew the kind of thing. She had been to faculty dinners at Jesus College as an undergraduate. They were an opportunity for students and tutors to meet in an informal setting. Informal by Oxford standards, at least. Typically they involved a posh dinner in a private room in college, often followed by copious quantities of alcohol in one of the larger student rooms.

Sophie nodded. 'Yes, undergraduates from all three years, plus post-graduates and tutors. About thirty people in total. It was quite an evening. Champagne aperitifs, a four-course dinner with a different wine at every course, followed by port.'

And that's even before you moved on to the after-dinner piss-up, thought Ffion.

'Did something happen at the dinner?'

'Not during dinner. But most people were pretty drunk after the meal. We were all mingling and talking, which is the whole point I suppose. And then a few of us went to have more drinks in Zara's room.'

'How many of you?'

'Perhaps eight in all. I didn't want to go, but Zara insisted. Everyone was really pissed by then. One of the first years threw up all over the carpet and had to be carried back to his room. Some people got a bit too friendly with each other.'

'Including Zara?'

Sophie looked uncomfortable. 'The thing is, our tutor was there and, well, he'd had loads to drink and he and Zara... they got rather companionable. I think he might have been the last to leave her room.' She looked away as if regretting she'd said so much.

'When you say our tutor, do you mean Dr Claiborne?'

'Yes.' Sophie grimaced.

Was this the elusive other man? 'You're saying that he and Zara had an affair?'

'I don't know if you could call it an affair,' said Sophie quickly. 'I didn't see them together again, apart from during tutorials, of course. It was probably just a one-night stand. Dr Claiborne is very young and good looking, but he is married and I think he and his wife have recently had a baby.'

'Do you think Zara might have left Adam because of her relationship with Dr Claiborne?'

'I couldn't say. I don't really know what went on with Adam. He seems like a decent guy. Zara cared for him. I can't believe she didn't wake up the next morning and regret what had happened between her and Dr Claiborne.' She took a deep breath as if making up her mind to continue. 'But there's something else.'

'What?'

'On Thursday night I was walking past Zara's staircase in Tom Quad and I distinctly heard raised voices coming from Dr Claiborne's room on the ground floor. I think one of the windows must have been slightly open, it had been such a hot day.'

'This was the evening that Zara was killed?'

Sophie nodded.

'What time was this?'

'About half past eight.'

'The voices were raised?'

'They weren't shouting exactly, but they were

definitely angry.'

'And whose voices were they?'

'Well, it was Dr Claiborne and a woman.'

'Did you catch any of the argument?'

'No. I didn't want to be found eavesdropping outside the window. Besides, I had an essay to finish.'

Ffion stared at the timid girl in front of her. 'Why didn't you mention this earlier?' she demanded. 'This might be crucial.'

Sophie looked aghast. 'I didn't want to betray Zara.'

★

'Zara slept with who?' asked Bridget in astonishment.

After a morning with little progress to show, she'd driven to Christ Church to find out how Jake, Ffion and Ryan had got on interviewing the students. With nowhere in college to talk in private, they'd decamped across the road to St Aldates Tavern. The traditional Victorian pub was the sort of place that could get very crowded and noisy if there was a football match playing on the large wall-mounted television, but this afternoon there were just a handful of students grabbing a late lunch, some regulars nursing pints at the bar, and an American family trying to decide whether to go for Ale Battered Haddock or Cumberland Sausage. She found a quiet corner where she could talk with her team without being overheard. The four of them huddled around a circular wooden table, perched on the sort of high bar stools that Bridget always had trouble getting on and off.

'Dr Claiborne,' repeated Ffion. 'Her English tutor.'

Bridget pictured the man in her mind's eye. The young tutor with his stylish dress sense, designer glasses and trendy haircut might well have held appeal to his female students. 'You think Sophie was telling the truth?'

'I think so. She said she didn't tell us earlier because she was worried about the damage it might do to Zara's reputation.'

'Or she was afraid of getting her tutor into trouble?' suggested Bridget.

'Quite possibly that too.'

Bridget waited as the waitress arrived with their food order, putting out a bowl of soup for herself, some pitta bread with houmous for Ffion, and sausage and onion sandwiches for Jake and Ryan.

'I thought you two already ate lunch at Christ Church,' Ffion remarked to the boys.

'Only a small one,' said Ryan, the grease from the sausage running down his chin as he took a large bite. Ffion pulled a face and looked away.

Jake wiped his own mouth with a paper napkin. 'On the CCTV I don't remember seeing Dr Claiborne leaving college the night of the murder.'

Bridget frowned. 'What, not at all? He said he

went to the drinks reception in the dean's lodgings. But where did he go after that? Did he stay overnight in the college? We need to find out.'

'With Dr Claiborne's room immediately below Zara's, it would have been very easy for him to have visited her,' said Ryan.

'And there were the raised voices coming from Dr Claiborne's room at eight thirty on Thursday night,' said Ffion. 'Was Claiborne having a row with Zara?'

Bridget made another note. Then she checked her watch. 'We need to talk to Dr Claiborne, but first I have a meeting with the dean.' She had been summoned for an update on the case and Bridget was not looking forward to it. But if they were to continue having smooth access to the college, its grounds and its members, then keeping the dean happy was part of her job description. Besides, this information about Dr Claiborne shed a new light on things. She wondered if the dean had any idea what his staff got up to out of hours.

'Jake, Ffion, you head back to Kidlington. Zara's phone records should have arrived by now. Ffion, can you go through them please? Jake, double-check Dr Claiborne's movements on Thursday. Brief the team on what you've found this morning, and look again at every witness statement that references Dr Claiborne. By the time I get back, I want to see a detailed time-line of every move he made the day of the murder. Ryan, I'd like you to go back to college and see if you can catch anyone who was out doing exams this morning. See if they know anything.'

A look passed between Jake and Ryan as if to say, 'Jake one, Ryan nil.' Bridget wondered what was going on with her team and whether the enigmatic Ffion Hughes had anything to do with it.

★

Situated in the college grounds next to the cathedral, the deanery was an elegant building with Georgian windows looking out onto a mature, well-tended garden blooming with summer flowers.

'I thought we would sit in the garden,' said Dr Reid, indicating the open French windows. 'I've asked the housekeeper to bring tea.' His manner was charming, not rude like the first time she'd met him. Still, Bridget was on her guard.

She followed him outside to a wooden bench in the shade of a sprawling horse chestnut tree. It was a beautiful day and in other circumstances she would gladly have whiled away the whole afternoon in this idyllic garden, preferably with a good book for company rather than the dean.

'You'll notice the green door in the north wall,' he said, pointing to an arched doorway that looked as if it might lead to a secret garden.

'Oh, yes?'

'It's featured in Alice's Adventures in Wonderland. In the story the door is kept locked and Alice is forbidden from using it. It leads to the cathedral garden.'

'Fascinating.' Bridget remembered that Charles Dodgson, better known as Lewis Carroll, had been a mathematics tutor at Christ Church in the nineteenth century. Alice Liddell was the daughter of the dean at the time.

'Indeed,' said the dean, warming to his subject. 'The Mad Hatter's tea parties were based on Alice's own birthday parties held in the garden. And this horse chestnut tree is the one in which the Cheshire Cat sat.'

'Is that so?' Bridget gazed up at the leafy branches of the ancient tree overhead, through which the sun cast a dappled light.

Interesting as it was to be surrounded by such iconic literary features, Bridget had the feeling that the dean had chosen to hold their meeting in the garden so that he could impress her with cultural references. No doubt he was used to entertaining visiting academics and basking in the reflected glow of five hundred years of history. This was his territory and he was sending a message that she was merely a visiting guest, here at his largesse. She should probably have insisted on holding the meeting at Thames Valley HQ in Kidlington. But she was not going to let the hospitality deflect her from raising the thorny question of Dr Claiborne and his inappropriate relationship with one of his students. She imagined the Queen of Hearts shouting, 'Off with his head!'

The housekeeper arrived carrying a tray with a tea pot, cups and saucers and a plate of shortbread. She set the tray down on a wooden table.

'Thank you, Margaret,' said the dean. 'I'll take it from here.' Margaret bowed her head and returned to the house. 'How do you like your tea, Inspector?'

'Milk, no sugar please.'

The dean poured two cups of tea into the fine bone china cups and handed one to her.

'Can I tempt you?' He offered her the plate of shortbread. 'It's Margaret's homemade recipe.'

She was growing tired of his perfect host act. 'Thank you,' she said, taking a small piece and putting it on the edge of her saucer.

The dean smiled. 'Perhaps we can get down to business. I was dismayed to read the newspapers this Sunday. It was precisely the kind of bad publicity I feared. I can't imagine how upsetting it must have been for Sir Richard and Lady Hamilton.' It was a relief to hear him finally express his reason for summoning her here.

'The newspapers didn't receive a tip-off from us, if that's what you're concerned about,' said Bridget. 'And I'm sure that Zara's parents have more to be upset about than newspaper gossip.'

'Quite. I hope that now poor Zachary has been found innocent, you will soon be arresting the actual murderer?'

'Zachary has been released without charge,' said Bridget carefully, 'and we are following up fresh leads.'

The dean raised an eyebrow. 'Can you share those leads with me?'

'No, but I would like to talk to you about one of your academic staff, Dr Claiborne.'

'Dr Claiborne?' The smile vanished from his thin lips. 'What is it you would like to know?' he asked stiffly.

'Have any students or members of staff ever raised any concerns or made a complaint against him?'

'Certainly not. Dr Claiborne holds an exemplary record.'

'So you're not aware that he may have had an inappropriate relationship with one of his students?'

'Dear Lord, what on earth are you referring to?'

Bridget found his tone disingenuous. 'I'm referring to the fact that he may have slept with Zara Hamilton two weeks ago on the night of the English faculty dinner.'

The dean took a sip of his tea before replying. When he spoke again his voice was icy. 'One hears idle gossip in the Senior Common Room. I assume that is all you have. Idle gossip.'

'Is there a possibility it could be true?'

'I think that you should tread very carefully before making any allegations. You have already dragged the good name of Oxford University and

Sir Richard Hamilton through the mud, not to mention making your own investigation look ridiculous by arresting an innocent man. If you have nothing of substance to implicate Dr Claiborne in this investigation I demand that you desist this line of enquiry.'

'My duty is to follow up all possible lines of enquiry.' She tried a different angle. 'On the night of the murder you hosted a drinks reception in your lodgings.'

'That's correct.' A note of wariness had crept into his voice.

'Dr Claiborne told us that he attended the drinks reception.'

'Did he?' said the dean. His face brightened again, the Cheshire Cat smile returning. 'Why yes, I do believe he did.'

'In your initial statement you claimed that you had spoken to him yourself at the reception.'

'Did I? Well then, I must have done.'

'And yet none of the other guests recall seeing him there.'

The smile disappeared as quickly as it had come. 'Perhaps I was mistaken then. I assumed he was there, as he had been invited.'

'But he wasn't invited,' said Bridget. 'His name didn't appear on the guest list we obtained from your secretary.'

'Well, now you come to mention it, I can't be absolutely certain. I was busy most of the evening with George Romano, the head of Oxford City Council. Most members of the

Senior Common Room were there, so I assumed Dr Claiborne was too. I can't be held responsible for knowing the whereabouts of my staff at all hours of the day and night!'

'No,' said Bridget calmly. 'No one expects you to. But they do expect you to tell the truth.'

The dean's mouth twisted unpleasantly. He looked ostentatiously at his watch. 'Is there anything else I can help you with?'

Bridget treated him to a smile of her own. 'No, I think that's all for now.' She took a bite of the shortbread. The buttery biscuit melted in her mouth. 'This really is very good,' she said, standing up. 'Please do tell Margaret.'

★

On the way out of college Bridget called in at the porters' lodge to see Jim Turner. His face brightened when he saw her.

'How can I help you, Inspector?'

'I was just wondering how common it is for tutors to stay in college overnight, and would there be a written record of them staying?'

'You mean to sleep in a guest room? It's not common, but it does happen. Do you have anyone particular in mind?'

'Dr Claiborne, for example?'

The porter nodded his head and leaned confidentially over the counter. 'I'm not one to gossip, but as this is a murder enquiry...'

'Go on,' said Bridget.

With her encouragement, the porter quickly overcame any reluctance to gossip. He leaned further forward and lowered his voice to a hoarse whisper. 'Rumour has it that he's been sleeping in college for some time. And I don't mean in a guest room either.'

'Where then?' asked Bridget.

'In his own room, where he holds his tutorials. Those rooms are really small suites, you know, with a study area and an adjoining bedroom. I expect you've seen them. Now, you'll be wondering how I know such a thing. My wife, Val, who cleans the rooms on that staircase, saw his pyjamas in the bedroom. Not once or twice, but every night for a couple of weeks. And on one occasion she went in early and found him brushing his teeth in the sink. And him being married, with two little'uns, a toddler and a baby. Very peculiar. That's the reason she mentioned it to me. Like I said, I don't normally gossip.'

'I see. That does seem strange, doesn't it? I don't suppose you've heard any more rumours?'

The porter peered around the corner to make sure they were still alone. 'Not rumours, as such, but I can tell you that his wife came to visit him on Thursday evening.'

'You mean the evening Zara was murdered? What time would that have been?'

'Let me check the visitors' book,' said Jim.

He flipped back a few pages and ran his finger down the list of names. 'Yes, here it is. His wife,

Helen Claiborne, signed in at five past eight. But she didn't sign out. That doesn't mean she didn't leave, of course. She might have forgotten to sign out.'

'Would she have been able to leave the college without signing?'

'Oh yes.'

'Thank you very much,' said Bridget. 'You've been most helpful.'

Jim beamed back at her. 'Always a pleasure to be of assistance.'

CHAPTER 21

Bridget was eager to speak to Dr Claiborne, but wanted to gather as much information as she could about his movements before interviewing him.

She returned to her car and headed west along the Botley Road. It was late in the afternoon and more people were heading out of Oxford now than coming in. The traffic was crawling and she found herself stuck behind one of the purple Park & Ride buses as she crossed the bridge at Osney Island, a small community of houses surrounded by the River Thames on one side and the Osney Ditch backwater on the other. Osney came from the old English word for river, so the name meant River Island, Bridget supposed. The terraced cottages were charming, and she imagined it would be a nice place to live if you didn't mind occasional flooding. She didn't think she would mind all that much. That damned romantic streak of hers was always getting her into trouble.

The Claibornes didn't live on the island, but just beyond, in a modest 1930s semi near the retail parks on the edge of town. Handy for shopping at the DIY superstores and PC World, but the view of a permanent traffic jam on the Botley Road was less appealing. So this was what a junior lecturer's salary bought you in Oxford. Not exactly in the same league as the dean of Christ Church's private lodgings.

Bridget parked on the rough grass verge that separated the pavement from the main road and walked up the short drive to the front door. A Volkswagen Polo was parked in front of a small garage that looked as if it had been added later, perhaps in the 1960s. It was certainly too small to hold any modern car, even the Polo. The back seat of the car was fitted with two car seats, one for a toddler and the other for a baby.

Bridget rang the bell. A minute later the door was opened by a woman in her early thirties, her shoulder-length hair tied up in a loose ponytail with strands escaping around her neck. She was pretty, with intense dark eyes beneath deep lashes, but wore no makeup and was dressed in baggy grey jogging pants and a stripy top with milk stains on one shoulder. The daily attire of mothers with babies, thought Bridget. She herself had spent months smelling of formula milk, baby sick and nappy cream after Chloe was born. After a while you stopped noticing. A little girl of about two years old clung tightly to the woman's leg and eyed Bridget with suspicion.

'Mrs Helen Claiborne?' asked Bridget.

'Yes,' said Helen, warily. 'What is it?' The wail

of a baby came from inside the house. Helen looked over her shoulder. 'Mummy's coming, sweetie.'

'Sorry to bother you, but I'm DI Bridget Hart of Thames Valley Police.' She showed her warrant card. 'Do you have a minute?'

'I'm just giving the children their tea, what's this about?'

'It's about the death of Zara Hamilton at Christ Church. I expect you've heard about it.'

Helen nodded, biting her lip.

'This won't take long,' said Bridget. 'We can talk while you feed the children.'

Helen was clearly reluctant to let her in, but nodded. 'All right. As long as you don't mind the mess.'

'Not at all,' said Bridget. Her own house was hardly a show home.

She followed Helen and the little girl to the kitchen, squeezing past the double buggy that filled half the space in the hallway. The wailing was coming from a red-faced little boy of about six months who was strapped into a high chair and banging his fists on the plastic tray in front of him as if he was trying to break it. The kitchen surfaces were cluttered with baby equipment – steriliser, bottle warmer, tins of formula, baby wipes, bottles and teats. Bridget remembered all too well the chaos a baby brought to a household. The little girl went back to playing with her building blocks which were scattered all over the kitchen floor, waiting to be tripped over.

'Just let me sort the children out,' said Helen. She took a bottle of milk out of the bottle warmer, tested its temperature on her wrist then gave it to the baby who grabbed it with both hands and started guzzling it greedily. The wailing ceased. Then Helen warmed a tin of baked beans in the microwave and put them on a plate for the little girl.

'Sit down and have your tea, Ellie,' said Helen.

'Don't want to,' said Ellie, continuing to play on the floor.

Helen leaned against the kitchen counter, her arms folded defensively. 'What was it you wanted to talk to me about? If this is about the murder, I don't know anything, other than what I've read in the papers.'

'I was actually more interested in talking about your husband.'

'My husband? What does Anthony have to do with anything?'

'Well, he was the tutor of the dead student, Zara Hamilton. We need to establish the whereabouts of everyone who was close to Zara.'

'I see,' said Helen guardedly.

'How long have you been married?'

'Three years now. And we lived together for five years before that.'

Bridget had the impression that Helen was firmly staking her claim to her husband, just in case there was any doubt.

'Happily married?'

'I'd say so.' Helen brushed a strand of hair

235

from her eyes and turned to check that the children were okay. 'Come and eat your food,' she said to Ellie.

'No!' shouted the little girl.

'How long have you lived here?' asked Bridget.

'Since we got married.' Bridget waited to see if Helen would volunteer any further information. After a moment she continued. 'We lived in Cambridge before. That's where we both studied for our doctorates.'

'I see. And do you work now?'

'Huh,' said Helen. 'No, I look after the children. When Anthony was offered the job at Christ Church, we decided to move to Oxford and put my career on hold. It seemed like a great time to start a family. Lectureships at Oxford don't come up very often. It would have been foolish for him to turn it down.'

'And you enjoy being a full-time mum?'

Helen turned her gaze to the little girl, who was pushing over the block tower she had just built. The baby boy dropped his milk onto the floor and began to wail. Helen retrieved it for him. 'When they're a little older I'll start looking for work again. It won't be easy though, having had a career break. And arranging good childcare isn't easy either.'

Tell me about it, thought Bridget, thinking of her own long battle to return to work after having Chloe. 'Your husband, Anthony, has been sleeping in college recently.'

She wondered if Helen would try to deny it,

but instead she snorted with nervous laughter. 'That's because I threw him out.'

'Do you mind me asking why that was?'

Helen turned her back to the children and lowered her voice. 'Because I found out about him and that girl.'

'Zara Hamilton?'

Helen nodded. She pursed her lips and looked out of the window, struggling to keep her emotions in check.

'But you went to the college on Thursday night. Why was that?'

She turned back to face Bridget. 'He'd been sleeping in college for a couple of weeks by then. I wanted to see if we could talk things over, patch them up even. I thought that perhaps he'd had enough of the cold shoulder treatment. To be honest, I'd had enough. It's bloody hard on my own with these two.'

'I can imagine,' said Bridget. The baby was now hammering the empty bottle against the tray. Ellie was still ignoring her food and regarding Bridget with suspicion. 'So what happened that night?'

'I went to his room in Tom Quad, but he wasn't there.'

'What time was this?'

'I think it was just after eight. I had to sign in at the lodge.'

'What did you do when you couldn't find him?'

'I tried the Senior Common Room. The

academics often hang out there after dinner. But that night the SCR was virtually deserted. I was going to give up and leave, but I thought I'd just try his room once more in case he'd returned and we'd missed each other. So I went back to the staircase in Tom Quad and that was when I found him.'

'In his room?'

Helen shook her head vehemently. 'No. Not in his room. He was coming down the stairs. From her room.'

'And then what happened?'

Helen sighed. 'I was furious. We went into his room and had a blazing row. I challenged him and he said he'd been up to see Zara to tell her to stop sending him texts, but that she wasn't in her room.'

'Did you believe him?'

'I told him he was a liar. He claimed he'd only slept with her once, but ever since then she'd been harassing him, sending him texts and begging to see him again. I didn't know what to think. I could tell he was still infatuated. That girl had some kind of hold over him.'

'How long did you spend with him?'

'About half an hour, I guess. I stormed out and we haven't spoken since.'

'There's no record of you signing out of college.'

'I was upset and in a hurry. I wanted to get home to the children. I just forgot to sign out, that's all.'

'Mummy! Mummy! Mummy!' shouted Ellie, who had now moved to the table and was prodding at her food. 'I hate baked beans!' In response, the baby began to wail again.

'I'll let myself out,' said Bridget. 'Thanks for your help.'

★

Bridget didn't envy Helen Claiborne. Stuck at home with two small children, and with an errant husband who couldn't be trusted with his young, nubile students. She wondered if there had been other infidelities before Zara or if she was the first.

Her phone rang as she was walking back to her car. Ffion. She picked up on the first ring.

'Ma'am, Zara's mobile provider has sent us a list of calls and text messages to and from her phone as promised.'

At last, thought Bridget. 'Anything interesting?'

'Very,' said Ffion, drawing out the two syllables with her musical voice. 'In the two weeks prior to the murder, there were dozens of incoming calls and texts from one particular number. That number is registered to Dr Anthony Claiborne.'

'Those were sent to Zara's phone? Did she reply?'

'No. The messages were all from Claiborne to Zara. Looks like he was obsessed with her.'

'Good work,' said Bridget. 'Anything else?'

'Nothing that stands out. There were exchanges between Zara and Zac, and with Adam too, and Zara did make one outgoing call to her sister on the afternoon of the murder.'

'Her sister?'

'That's right. There's a younger sister, Zoe, aged seventeen, currently studying for her A-levels at Cheltenham Ladies' College.'

Bridget remembered the girl she'd seen at the top of the stairs when she and Jake visited the Hamiltons' house in the Cotswolds. It would be interesting to know what the two sisters talked about just hours before Zara was murdered. But right now the priority was Dr Claiborne and his fixation with his student.

'All right,' said Bridget, 'I'm going to bring Claiborne into the station. Could you make sure there's a room available for us, please?'

'I'm on it,' said Ffion.

Bridget arranged for a patrol car to meet her at Christ Church. 'Use an unmarked car,' she told Dispatch, 'and send it around to Canterbury Gate at the back of the college. There's no need to feed the media circus any more than necessary.'

She started her car and headed back into the centre of Oxford. The case was moving forwards again.

★

Mercifully there were no press photographers outside the Canterbury Gate in Oriel Square when Bridget pulled up there twenty minutes later. Dr Claiborne should have finished his tutorials by now, and with any luck they'd catch him alone in his room.

Two uniformed officers on loan from the St Aldate's police station were waiting for her in an unmarked patrol car. The young female PC and her male colleague came over to meet her.

Bridget greeted them. 'We're here to bring in a suspect for questioning. Let's keep a low profile. I'm not expecting any trouble.'

As they climbed the stairs to Dr Claiborne's new room in Peckwater Quad, the door opened and two female students appeared, clutching folders and books to their chests. They stared wide-eyed at Bridget and the two police officers. She stood aside and waved them past with irritation. How long would it take for the news to spread around college that she had come to speak to Dr Claiborne? It was impossible to do anything in this environment without everyone knowing about it. Which made it all the more frustrating that no one seemed to know what had happened to Zara. She knocked on Dr Claiborne's door.

'Come in.' The voice was bright and cheerful. It must have been a good tutorial.

Bridget pushed open the door and entered, the two police officers at her heel. Claiborne was standing at the desk with his back to her, stuffing papers into his old briefcase.

'Dr Claiborne?'

He turned around and the smile slid from his face like melting snow slipping off a roof. 'Oh,' he said, his eyes flicking nervously from Bridget to the police officers and back to her. 'I thought it was one of my students coming back to ask me something.'

'I'm afraid not,' said Bridget.

★

As Bridget had expected, Dr Claiborne had come quietly enough and was now waiting in an interview room with a mug of weak tea supplied by Ffion. When given the chance to make a phone call, he hadn't called his wife. Instead he'd spoken to the dean of Christ Church who had arranged for a lawyer to be sent.

She wondered if Claiborne had made a wise move. The college might well be able to afford the best legal advice, but their lawyer would inevitably by more interested in protecting the reputation of the college than defending the best interests of the suspect. At least this time it would be someone local. She had no wish for another encounter with the smooth-talking Caroline Butler of Kingsley, Butler and Cooke.

While they waited, she tapped out a quick message to Chloe to let her know she'd be late back again this evening. She wasn't expecting a response, but a minute later her phone buzzed with an incoming text.

No worries. Dad picked me up from school and gave me an awesome birthday present. Going out later for a slap up meal. Chloe x

Bridget was grateful for the reply but wondered what the awesome present might be. Some expensive gift to win over her daughter's affections, no doubt. Being a parent was easy for Ben, dropping in now and again to visit his daughter, never having to deal with problems at school, arguments about rules and boundaries, and all the myriad practicalities of daily family life. Her thoughts drifted back to Helen Claiborne, stuck in her cheerless house with a baby and a toddler demanding her attention, her dreams of a career on hold while her husband enjoyed a cushy academic post, picking up attractive young students, free of the burdens of childcare. However difficult raising a teenager might be, it was nothing compared with looking after a baby and a toddler.

She realised that her fists were clenched tight. Her shoulders had tensed too. She breathed deeply and tried to calm herself down. Whatever her own problems might be, and her personal feelings about Dr Claiborne, she couldn't afford to take them into the interview room with her. She needed to keep a clear mind.

Her phone buzzed with another incoming text, this one from a number she didn't recognise.

Frowning, she tapped the message.

Sorry you couldn't stay for lunch on Sunday. Vanessa does an excellent roast. I'm hosting an exhibition over the summer for some local artists and tomorrow is the opening night. Champagne and canapés. Doors open at 7pm. Hope you can come. Jonathan.

Jonathan. The man her sister had tried to fix her up with. Ordinarily her sister's choice of potential partners was dreadful. But Jonathan seemed different. Not dull like the other men Vanessa had paraded before her. She'd enjoyed their brief meeting, even though they'd only exchanged a handful of words. And what had Chloe said about him? Jonathan was really nice. You should ask him out on a date. Was this a date? Should she accept his invitation? Her thumb hovered over the Reply button.

'The lawyer's here,' said Jake, interrupting her thoughts.

She slipped the phone back into her bag, pushing Jonathan from her mind. 'Right, let's see what our Oxford academic has got to say for himself.'

CHAPTER 22

Dr Claiborne sat bolt upright at the table, his fingers interlaced, the knuckles showing white. The young tutor looked more like a nervous student up for interview than a fully-fledged academic with publications to his name. Good. With any luck it wouldn't take much pressure to prise information out of him.

His solicitor, a neat man in a dark grey three-piece suit with a silver tie pin in his silk tie and matching cufflinks in his crisp white shirt, rose to his feet as Bridget entered. He held out a hand and introduced himself as Mr Raworth, lawyer to the college. He passed her an ornate business card. His firm was an old established outfit on the High Street with impeccable credentials and a history dating back to Victorian times. It was the sort of place where the partners sat at mahogany desks in wood-panelled offices. Bridget imagined that they regarded the decline of wax seals as a sign of how standards had slipped. Raworth withdrew a leather-bound notebook from his briefcase, turned to a fresh page and unscrewed the lid on a gold-nibbed fountain pen.

Bridget introduced herself and Jake, then pressed Record on the interview recorder and asked Dr Claiborne to confirm his name and address. He hesitated slightly over the address and Bridget wondered for a moment if he was going to give Christ Church as his place of residence, but in the end he opted for the house on Botley Road. Presumably he still hoped to move back there at some point.

With the preliminaries out of the way, Bridget kicked off the interview with some easy questions.

'How long have you been a tutor at Christ Church, Dr Claiborne?'

The tutor looked to his lawyer, who nodded his head. 'Almost three years.'

'You were at Cambridge before. Is that correct?'

'Yes. My wife and I studied there and held temporary teaching positions.'

'Why did you move to Oxford?'

'I was offered a lectureship. A permanent faculty position at Oxford is like gold dust.'

'And how long had you taught Zara Hamilton?'

'Since she started her course at Oxford. That was two academic years ago.'

'What was Zara like as a student?'

'One of the best I've ever had.'

'In what way?'

'The clarity of her thought. She always wrote

such articulate, well-argued essays. She would invariably bring a new insight into whatever topic we were studying. That's quite rare, even amongst Oxford undergraduates.'

The tutor was beginning to relax and talk freely now. It was time to turn up the heat.

'So Zara was a good student,' said Bridget. 'What about her other attributes?'

Claiborne blinked at her from behind his glasses. 'What do you mean?'

'I'm referring to her personal attributes.'

'Well...'

'Would you say she was attractive?'

Bridget detected a faint blush creeping up the tutor's neck. She decided to take advantage of his discomfort. 'Dr Claiborne, are you in the habit of sleeping with your students?'

The blush reached right to the tips of his ears. Claiborne shifted in his seat and looked down at his interlocked hands.

'My client has no comment,' said Mr Raworth without batting an eyelid.

'Did you have sex with Zara Hamilton?' asked Bridget.

The solicitor made eye contact with his client and gave the faintest shake of his head.

'No comment,' mumbled Dr Claiborne.

Bridget wasn't surprised by the lack of cooperation. As she'd suspected, the lawyer had more interest in sweeping unsavoury allegations under the carpet than obtaining justice for his client. She almost felt a stirring of sympathy for the handsome young tutor. But then she remembered the battered skull of Zara Hamilton, her golden hair streaked with blood.

'There's no point denying it,' she said sternly. 'Everyone knew. Your wife, other students, your colleagues. Even the scout who cleans your room told the porter that you've been sleeping in your room in college for the past two weeks.'

'No comment.' Claiborne's gaze was fixed resolutely on his clasped hands.

'This is nothing but tittle-tattle,' interjected the lawyer.

'I spoke to your wife earlier today,' said Bridget.

Dr Claiborne looked up sharply and the colour drained from his face. 'You spoke to Helen? What did she say?'

'We'll come to that.' Bridget opened a manila folder and pulled out the list of calls that Ffion had retrieved from Zara's mobile provider. 'You were certainly very busy sending Zara lots of messages in the two weeks before she was murdered. Let me see' – she ran her pen quickly down the list – 'there must be at least fifty text messages from your number to hers, as well as numerous voice calls. So what were those messages about, Dr Claiborne? Surely they weren't all discussions of English literature?'

'My client has no –'

'Actually,' said Dr Claiborne, interrupting the lawyer, 'I admit that I did have a... a brief fling with Zara.' He turned to his lawyer. 'There's no point denying it. My wife knows about it already. I expect that gossip is circulating around college too.' He looked back at Bridget. 'But you have to believe me when I say it was just a one-night stand when we'd both had too much to drink. There was nothing more than that, I swear. I couldn't say anything to you earlier. I was scared of losing my job. My family depend on my income. My wife and children… they'd be in dire straits if the university dismissed me.'

'Dr Claiborne, there is more at stake here than just your job. This is a murder enquiry. I think that you should focus on the bigger picture.'

Her words brought him up as sharply as if she'd slapped his face. 'I…'

'What about the text messages and calls?' Bridget continued. 'Can you explain those, if it was just a one-night stand?'

'I… I may have behaved somewhat foolishly. But there was nothing sinister about them.'

'In that case, I'm sure you won't have any objection if we examine your mobile phone?'

'My phone?' His right hand went protectively to the breast pocket of his jacket.

'Yes, your phone.'

'My client is not under arrest,' insisted the lawyer. 'He's free to go at any time.'

'But we would like to eliminate him from our enquiries, if at all possible,' said Bridget. 'So, I'll ask once again, do you mind if we take a look at your phone?'

Claiborne's fingers continued to rest over his

jacket pocket. 'My mobile phone,' he repeated. 'Yes, of course.' Reluctantly, he reached inside and produced his phone. He passed it across the table.

'Take it to Ffion,' Bridget told Jake.

The DS picked up the phone and left the room.

'We're going to take a short break,' said Bridget, 'but before we do, I'd like to take your fingerprints.'

'For elimination purposes?' asked Claiborne wearily.

'Precisely.'

Half an hour later Bridget was back in the interview room and this time she was ready to apply some real pressure.

'You see, this is how the situation looks to me. Your fingerprints are consistent with prints found in Zara's room. You have no alibi for the time of the murder. You claimed to be at the drinks reception in the dean's lodgings, but it seems that no one saw you there that evening. You weren't even on the guest list.'

Claiborne said nothing, but nodded miserably.

'You admit that you gave a false alibi?'

'Yes.' His voice was barely a whisper now.

'Please repeat that again, loud enough for the voice recorder.'

'Yes!'

'So,' said Bridget. 'Here's what I think happened that evening. You had been pursuing Zara for almost two weeks since your one-night stand, but she ignored you. Instead of leaving her alone, you became obsessed, bombarding her with more and more texts and calls. That evening you went up to Zara's room and confronted her.'

'No, that's not what happened.'

'Your wife says that she visited you in college on the evening of the murder and found you coming down the stairs from Zara's room.'

He shook his head, a tear running down one cheek. The solicitor was now regarding his client with a look of distaste.

'You and your wife then had an argument in your room. Would you care to elaborate?'

Claiborne began to sob. He put his head in his hands. 'Helen came to see me in my room. She wanted to try and reconcile our differences. But when she saw me coming down the stairs, she lost it. She assumed I'd just been in bed with Zara.'

'And had you?'

'No, absolutely not.'

'Perhaps not,' said Bridget. 'Zara had already made clear her desire not to continue the relationship by ignoring all of your attempts to contact her. But you weren't willing to take no for an answer. You pleaded with her. Emotions were running high, things got out of control and you struck her.'

'No!'

Bridget continued relentlessly. 'You didn't mean to kill her. You even tried to stop the bleeding with a towel. But it was too late. She was dead.'

'No!'

'Zara's phone is still missing. Did you take it?'

'No!'

'I think you did. I think that after you killed her, you took her phone away in order to hide evidence of the incriminating texts you sent. We're currently conducting a search of your room in college. Perhaps we'll find her phone there.'

'No! No! You're twisting everything. It wasn't like that.'

'So, what was it like?'

'Careful,' warned Raworth. 'I would advise you to think very carefully before you speak.'

'What happened then, Dr Claiborne?' persisted Bridget.

'I went up to her room,' blurted Claiborne. 'I know I shouldn't have done. It was a stupid mistake. We talked. But I didn't hit her. I couldn't ever do that! I adored Zara. Perhaps I even loved her. I was a fool, I see that now. But she was alive and well when I left her, I swear. I didn't kill her.'

★

'You think he's lying?' Bridget asked Jake after leaving Dr Claiborne to stew in the interview room.

'I think so. In fact, I think he's just about ready

to confess. Why don't we go back in again and push him?'

'I'd like to see if we can find any more evidence first.'

They went back to the incident room to check on the progress of the rest of the team.

Ryan had just returned from Christ Church. He seemed very excited.

'You have some news?' asked Bridget.

'Big news. I spoke to some English finalists who'd just finished their exams and were still just about sober enough to string a sentence together. They confirmed Sophie's story about the after-dinner drinks in Zara's room. I managed to get several statements from people saying they saw Claiborne snogging Zara on the sofa.' He smirked.

'Actually,' said Bridget, 'we already know that.'

Ryan's face fell.

'That's old news, mate,' said Jake, rubbing it in. 'Claiborne's admitted sleeping with Zara. He's been stalking her ever since. He even admits to being in her room just before she died.'

'Oh,' said Ryan, crestfallen.

Bridget turned to see what Ffion was up to. 'Any luck with his phone?'

'He deleted all the texts between himself and Zara, but I'm working to recover them now. It shouldn't take long.'

'Good.'

'A warrant has come through for us to search

his room in college,' said Andy, 'and his wife has agreed to come in and give a formal statement. A car's bringing her here now.'

Excellent,' said Bridget. 'You arrange the search. I'll go and speak to Helen myself.'

★

Helen Claiborne sat across the table from Bridget, looking pale and nervous, her hands wrapped around a cup of coffee from the vending machine. She was still wearing her milk-spattered top and jogging pants, and the lingering smell of babies had followed her into the police station. Andy had told Bridget she'd been reluctant to come to Kidlington at all, but had finally agreed after arranging for her sister to take care of the children.

She seemed distracted, perhaps overwhelmed by the situation. 'I hope you're not going to keep me here for long. I have to get back home.'

'I'll try to keep it short,' Bridget assured her. 'I'd just like to go over what you told me this afternoon. Just to clarify a few points.'

'I've already told you everything,' said Helen, her voice sounding weary.

'There are some details I'd like to check.'

'Okay.'

'Can you tell me how you found out about the affair,' said Bridget. 'Is this the first time you've suspected your husband of being unfaithful?'

Helen's shoulders slumped. 'It's happened a

254

few times before, I think, although I couldn't ever be certain.' She looked up earnestly at Bridget, as if appealing for her understanding. 'You must realise that Anthony is a young and exceptionally good-looking man, unlike most Oxford academics. He's also quite brilliant. He's bound to attract the attentions of impressionable young women. It's not his fault.'

'I see,' said Bridget. 'That doesn't excuse his behaviour.'

'No, but it does help to explain it.'

Bridget wasn't sure who Helen was trying to convince – Bridget or herself. 'How did you find out, this time?'

Helen paused, seeming to wrestle with her emotions as she composed her answer. 'It was the day after the English faculty dinner. When he came home the next morning, he seemed very preoccupied. He didn't want to talk to me or spend time with the children. He started acting secretively. A couple of days later, when he was in the shower, I checked his phone.' She hesitated. 'You mustn't think badly of me. I was scared about what was happening to our relationship.'

She stopped again, as if waiting for Bridget's permission to continue, to tell her that she'd done the right thing.

'Go on,' said Bridget.

'That's when I found the text messages from him to Zara. I felt sickened. I confronted him about it and he admitted that he'd slept with her.' A tear formed in her eye and ran down her cheek. 'So I asked him to leave. I was angry. I wasn't thinking straight. Previously, when I suspected he was having an affair, it never lasted long. He always came back to me. But this time I sent him away.'

Her tears began to fall freely. 'It was all my fault. I shouldn't have confronted him. I never wanted him to leave me.' She pulled a paper tissue from her pocket and blew her nose. 'So that's why I went into the college to see him. I wanted to let him know that I forgave him and that he could come home.'

'But it didn't work out that way?'

'No,' she said bitterly.

'Tell me again exactly what happened that evening,' said Bridget gently. 'You told me that you signed into college just after eight o'clock. Your entry in the visitors' book in the porters' lodge was at five past eight.'

'That sounds about right.'

'And then?'

'I went to Anthony's room but he wasn't in. I tried looking for him in the Senior Common Room but I couldn't find him. However I did bump into the biology tutor, Liz, who said that some people were at a drinks reception in the dean's lodgings. I looked, but Anthony wasn't there either. Nobody had seen him anywhere. So I decided to try his room one last time.' Her expression was calm now as she recalled the events. 'And that was when I saw him coming down the stairs.'

'From Zara's room,' prompted Bridget.

'Yes.'

'And how would you describe your husband at that time?'

'What do you mean?'

'What sort of state was he in?'

Helen gave a rueful smile. 'He was certainly surprised to see me there.'

'And what time was that?'

Helen shrugged. 'I don't wear a watch these days. My last one got covered in baby sick. I guess I spent about fifteen minutes looking for him around college, so it must have been about twenty past eight when I eventually found him.'

Bridget made a note of the times. 'And then what happened?'

'It's like I told you this afternoon. We went into his room and had a row. He was trying to tell me the affair was over, but I didn't believe him. I'd just seen him coming downstairs from her room. What was I supposed to think?'

'And what time did you leave your husband's room?'

For once Helen didn't hesitate before replying. 'At nine o'clock precisely.'

'How can you be so sure about that, since you don't wear a watch?'

'The bell in Tom Tower was chiming,' said Helen. 'My sister had come round to babysit the children and I'd promised her I wouldn't be late back. When I heard the clock chime the hour, I knew I had to hurry home.'

'Like Cinderella,' said Bridget.

'I suppose so.'

Bridget studied the woman carefully. She felt a strong sympathetic bond with Helen over her husband's infidelities. But at the same time, she was frustrated to hear how in thrall she was to her husband. She had tried to justify and excuse his behaviour. Was she even now still protecting him in some way?

She let the silence stretch out and Helen began to look agitated. Bridget knew there was something she wasn't telling her. 'What really happened?' she asked. Her voice was quiet but insistent.

Helen looked up at the ceiling, biting her lip. She slowly crumpled under Bridget's steady gaze. 'Oh God, this is all such a bloody mess.'

Bridget waited patiently for her to continue.

After a moment Helen recovered her composure. 'When I left Anthony's room, I went upstairs.'

'To Zara's room?'

She nodded. 'I wanted to see her for myself, I suppose. I wanted to find out what he saw in her. Perhaps I even hoped that I could persuade her to leave him alone.'

'For Zara to leave him alone?'

'Yes. She kept chasing him, you see. She kept coming to his room at all hours. She just wouldn't leave him alone, he told me that.'

Bridget said nothing. It wasn't her job to tell

Helen that her husband had been lying to her. 'So you went up to Zara's room, and then what?'

'The door to her room was ajar. I pushed it open with my foot and I saw…'

'What did you see?'

'I saw her lying there in a pool of blood.' The tears were streaming down her face again. 'I waited and watched, but she didn't move. She was dead, I was sure of it. And – this sounds horrible – I was glad. I knew that it was over and that Anthony could come home again.'

'What did you do then?'

'I ran out of college.'

'You didn't speak to your husband again before leaving?'

'No. I just wanted to get away.'

'And you didn't raise the alarm?'

'No,' said Helen quietly.

'Did it occur to you that your husband might have killed her?'

She looked shocked at the prospect. 'No! Of course not! Anthony might have been unfaithful, but he's a gentle man. He couldn't possibly have killed that girl. He just couldn't.' She began to sob.

Poor Helen. Was that what people had thought of Bridget while Ben had been off having his affairs? Like Helen, she'd been blind to his adultery at first, then pathetic when confronted with the reality of her wrecked marriage – too worried about what would happen to Chloe to think of herself. She was well past that stage now.

She'd picked herself up and rebuilt her life, and was leading a murder enquiry. And she was going to nail the man who'd killed Zara Hamilton. She was damn well going to nail him.

'Thanks for your help,' she said to Helen. 'I'll fetch a car to take you home.'

CHAPTER 23

The interview with Helen had saddened Bridget, but also made her more determined than ever to bring the case to a close. It seemed that there were more victims here than just Zara Hamilton, but there was nothing Bridget could do to protect Helen Claiborne from the consequences of her husband's infidelity. Some battles, it seemed, simply couldn't be won.

She went back to the CID suite. Ffion was at her desk, a mug of herbal tea cooling beside her computer while she tapped with lightning speed on her keyboard. Whatever the young DC might lack in social skills, she certainly made up for in technical ability.

'Did you retrieve the deleted texts from Dr Claiborne's phone?' asked Bridget.

'I certainly did,' said Ffion, 'and most entertaining they are too.'

'Oh?'

She read from her screen. '"My bounty is as boundless as the sea, My love as deep; the more I give to thee, The more I have, for both are infinite."'

'Shakespeare?' guessed Bridget.

'Romeo and Juliet. It seems that our tutor is quite the Romeo himself. Try this one. "Doubt thou the stars are fire; Doubt that the sun doth move; Doubt truth to be a liar; But never doubt I love."'

'Hamlet.'

'Very good. What about this? "Love looks not with the eyes, but with the mind; And therefore is winged Cupid painted blind."'

Bridget shrugged. 'You've got me there.'

'A Midsummer Night's Dream.'

'It's not exactly Roses are red, violets are blue, is it?'

'Do you want to hear any more? I've printed them off for you. They go on for pages.' Ffion passed Bridget the sheets of paper.

Bridget glanced down the list. The bard certainly had plenty to say on the subject of love, but she could only identify a handful of the quotes. 'Claiborne was completely smitten, wasn't he?'

'Like a lovesick teenager.'

'Did Zara ever reply to any of these?'

'She appears to have ignored all his texts,' said Ffion, 'right up until Thursday morning, when she texted back to say that she would make a formal complaint to the college if he didn't stop pestering her. His response was interesting.'

Bridget read out the last but one message from the list. 'I must see you one more time, just to talk.' The very last message was Zara's response.

'I'll be in my room tonight at eight.'

★

When Bridget returned to the interview room, she found Claiborne showing signs of strain. His foppish hair was a mess from running his fingers through it repeatedly, and he had bitten his nails, making him look even more like a student than a tutor. As Jake had said earlier, he looked ready to break.

He gazed miserably at her as she sat down. 'What's been going on?' he asked. 'Why did you leave me here?'

The whining in his voice generated no sympathy from her. She placed the printed text messages on the table for him to read. 'Do you recognise these? We recovered them from your phone.'

'Oh God,' said Claiborne, slumping back in his seat.

Raworth picked up the list, scanning it with raised eyebrows. 'And what does this prove exactly? That my client has an extensive knowledge of England's greatest playwright. It hardly proves he committed a murder.' He tossed the piece of paper onto the table. 'Since we're quoting Shakespeare here, your evidence is hardly lapped in proof.' He smiled as if pleased with himself.

'What these texts demonstrate,' said Bridget, 'is your client's obsession with the murder victim. And when people become obsessed with another person, they sometimes do things they later regret.'

'Such as?' asked Raworth.

'Perhaps Dr Claiborne can tell us,' said Bridget, fixing the tutor with her gaze. 'What precisely happened when you went up to Zara's room on Thursday night?'

'My client has no comment,' said Raworth.

'What happened?'

'I saw her,' said Claiborne before his lawyer could intervene again. 'She let me into her room. I wanted to apologise for my behaviour.'

'You were worried she was going to make a formal complaint about sexual harassment?'

'No. Yes. I mean, I just wanted to talk to her, that was all. After she sent me that text about making a complaint, I realised what a fool I'd been. I'd ruined my marriage because of her, and all I'd done was cause her pain and distress. I wanted to apologise for all the trouble I'd caused.'

'Or perhaps you wanted to stop her making a complaint against you. You would probably have lost your position as a university lecturer, wouldn't you?'

He ran his fingers through his matted hair again. 'That wasn't my primary concern. I wanted to say I was sorry. I wanted to put things right.'

'Did putting things right involve making certain that Zara Hamilton never talked to anyone again?'

'No!'

'Then tell me exactly what happened in her room. Don't leave anything out.'

'Remember what I told you earlier,' cautioned Raworth.

'Oh, shut up!' snapped Claiborne at the lawyer. 'Stop telling me what to do! I only want to tell the truth.'

'Go on, then,' urged Bridget.

Claiborne chewed at his nails, glancing furtively at his lawyer, who had fallen silent. 'I went to Zara's room at eight o'clock, just as she'd asked. She let me into her sitting room and sat down on her sofa, while I stood. I told her I was sorry, and that I realised now that my behaviour had been inappropriate. I apologised unreservedly for any embarrassment or distress that I had caused.'

'What did she say to that?'

'That she understood. She was very mature about it. We agreed that I would stop sending her messages and that she would take the matter no further. Then she asked me if I would go back to my wife, and I told her that I didn't know. I didn't know if Helen would take me back.'

'Anything else?'

'No. We parted on amicable terms.'

'And how long did you spend in Zara's room altogether?'

'Not long. Just five minutes.'

'And you went to her room at exactly eight

265

o'clock?'

'Yes. That was the time she'd requested.'

'And yet,' said Bridget, 'your wife met you returning from Zara's room at' – she checked her notes – 'approximately twenty past eight. That's a discrepancy of fifteen minutes. Time enough for you to have killed Zara.'

Claiborne gave her an agonised look. 'Perhaps I was with her for longer than five minutes. Yes, I must have been.'

Bridget leaned forward. 'So why don't you tell me what actually happened in her room? What did you really say to Zara?'

Claiborne tugged at his hair so hard Bridget thought he was going to pull it out. 'All right!' he yelled. 'This is the truth. I told her I loved her. I said I would leave Helen. I begged her to continue seeing me. I said I would do anything to be with her. But she wouldn't have it. She just kept on saying no.'

'You were angry with her?'

His face was red now. 'Yes, I was angry. I'd left my wife to be with her, and this was how she treated me. I was going to lose everything – my family, my job, my home. And she just sat there, with that butter wouldn't melt look on her face.' He stopped for breath. 'Of course I was angry. But I didn't kill her. She was alive and well when I left her.'

'Nevertheless,' said Bridget calmly, 'you were the last known person to see her alive, and just over half an hour later she was dead. In fact, your own wife discovered her body.'

'She did what?'

'After leaving your room, Helen went up to Zara's room. She hoped to talk to her. Instead she found Zara lying on the floor in a pool of blood.'

Claiborne's face had blanched white. 'I don't... no... I don't...'

'Dr Claiborne, I am arresting you on suspicion of murdering Zara Hamil...'

'No, wait!' Claiborne held up a hand. 'There's one more thing I have to tell you.' He leaned across the table in his eagerness, the words spilling from him. 'When I went up to Zara's room she invited me into her sitting room. The door to the bedroom was ajar, and before sitting down she pulled it closed. I've been thinking about this ever since. I'm certain that there was someone in there, someone she didn't want me to see.'

Bridget cast a sideways glance at Jake, who merely raised a sceptical eyebrow.

'It's the truth,' blurted Claiborne. 'You have to believe me. The murderer must already have been in her room.'

★

Superintendent Grayson was waiting for Bridget by her desk. 'I've been watching the interview on the video link. The man's a terrible liar. The prosecution barrister will make mincemeat of

267

him.'

'You think we've got enough to charge him, sir?'

'Certainly. Don't you?'

Bridget hesitated. 'I'm not sure. That last part about someone being in the bedroom while he was with Zara in her sitting room…'

'Humph!' said Grayson 'You don't believe that? How many times did he change his story under pressure?'

'A few times, sir.'

'He'll say whatever comes into his head to try to get himself off the hook. It's not your job to find holes in the case. Leave that to his defence lawyer.' He thumbed in the direction of the interview room. 'Our friend Raworth looks like he's ready to wash his hands clean of Claiborne. I don't envy his job. You've done well, DI Hart.'

'Right, sir. Thank you, sir.' She watched him return to his glass fishbowl.

Jake was still at her side. 'You don't believe there really was someone in Zara's bedroom, do you, ma'am? Who could that possibly have been? And why didn't he mention that at the start?'

'I don't know, Jake. But I don't like loose ends.'

'I agree with the Super, ma'am. We've got him. Job done!'

'Maybe,' said Bridget. 'Maybe. Let's see what the search team comes up with.'

★

An envelope was waiting for Bridget on her desk. The final post-mortem report. She pulled the piece of paper out of the envelope and scanned it quickly. The cause of death was confirmed as blunt force trauma to the head resulting in a hemorrhage, just as Roy Andrews had said during the PM. Toxicology tests had come back negative, indicating that Zara had not been taking drugs or drinking. But there was one interesting piece of data that caught Bridget's attention. The analysis of Zara's stomach contents showed that she had eaten lamb, most probably in the form of a doner kebab, shortly before she died. Megan had said that Zara ate dinner in college at six twenty, but Bridget was fairly certain that doner kebab was not on the menu of Oxford's grandest dining hall, even at the informal setting.

'Andy?' she called across the room. 'What were they serving in the dining hall on the evening of Zara's death?'

'Just a moment.' He was back with a sheet of paper a few minutes later. Bridget scanned it quickly. Mushroom tagliatelle; fried chicken; a selection of vegetables and potatoes. Lamb was not on the menu, not in kebab form, nor any other.

However, the popular snack was easy enough to obtain in Oxford each evening when mobile fast-food vans moved in to occupy their reserved spaces in the city centre. They were a magnet for students, especially late at night.

Roy had attached a handwritten note to the report.

If you can find out what time she ate the kebab, it would help to pin down the time of death more accurately.

Bridget scanned the office for likely volunteers. She didn't need to look far. Jake was already back at his desk munching a chocolate bar. That man was permanently hungry. She remembered his fondness for sausage sandwiches and burgers. No doubt his enthusiasm for meat-based snacks wrapped in bread stretched to kebabs too.

'Jake?'

'Yes, ma'am?'

'Fancy a bit of overtime?'

CHAPTER 24

Jake nudged his car into a spot on St Giles' close to where he'd parked when he and Ffion had visited the Oxford Union. Hassan's Kebabs was pitched opposite, in front of the Taylor Institute for Medieval and Modern Languages. He got into line behind a group of boisterous students, his mouth watering at the smell of roast lamb slowly turning on the vertical rotisserie. The lads in front of him were probably taking a brief food break during an evening of beers. In a city with over twenty thousand students, running a mobile kebab van wasn't a bad business to be in. Jake waited patiently for his turn.

'What can I get you, mate?' asked Hassan, a Turkish man in his early twenties.

It would have been rude of Jake not to buy something. A lamb kebab in a wrap would do very nicely.

While Hassan shaved off slivers of seasoned meat, Jake fished in his jacket pocket for the photograph of Zara.

'Were you here on Thursday night?' he asked.

'I'm here every night, mate,' replied Hassan.

'D'you want salad with this?'

'Just a bit of onion, please, and some ketchup.'

Hassan worked quickly, folding the corners of the wrap into a neat package.

Jake held out the photograph. 'Did you see this girl by any chance on Thursday night?'

Hassan peered briefly at Zara's picture. 'Nah, sorry, mate. Can't help you.'

'Are you sure? Take a good look.'

'I'd remember if I had. She's that murdered student, isn't she? She's quite a stunner. That'll be six fifty, please.'

Jake handed over the right change and took the kebab. 'Cheers. Thanks for your help.'

'No worries,' said Hassan. 'Next please.'

Jake headed into town, munching on the kebab. It was just as he liked it, the meat tender and juicy, the red onions tangy and sharp. He could easily get to like this assignment.

The next van he found was on Broad Street. 'Hi,' he said. 'A chicken kebab and a bag of chips, please, mate. Oh, and a bottle of Coke too.' The first kebab had left him quite thirsty. He held out his photograph. 'Have you seen this girl before?'

Three vans later, Jake approached a van on St Ebbe's, by the side of the Westgate shopping centre, not too far from Christ Church. Radio Four was playing quietly on a portable radio at the back of the van. Jake really didn't think he could eat another thing. He took out the now rather greasy photograph of Zara and showed it to the van owner, Kemal, according to the sign on his van.

'Yeah, I saw her,' said Kemal without any hesitation. 'When was it? Let me think, must have been last week, on Thursday night.'

'That sounds right,' said Jake, relieved to have hit the bull's eye at last.

'She bought two kebabs, one for herself and one for her friend.'

'Her friend? Can you describe her friend for me?'

'Well, here's the thing,' said Kemal, leaning through the window of his van. 'She was one of them homeless kids you see on the street, innit? She looked like a druggie to me, all hollow-eyed, straggly hair, filthy clothes, you know what I mean?'

Jake took out his notebook. 'Could you be a bit more specific?'

'Nah, mate. I'm not good with faces. The only reason I remember the girl in the picture so clearly is because she was obviously a posh girl. She was nice looking and well spoken and all that. But the other girl she was with, well she was from the wrong side of the tracks, you know what I mean? I thought at the time they made an odd couple.'

'Can you remember what time they were here?'

Kemal thought for a moment. 'Yeah, it was quarter to eight. I say that because I had the radio on and Front Row was just finishing.' Jake looked at him blankly. 'You know, mate. The arts and culture show on the radio, innit. Now, can I get you anything to eat?'

'A hot dog and a coffee, please.' Jake gave them to an old bloke huddled in a sleeping bag in a shop doorway. He looked like he might welcome something hot.

★

'Spare any change?'

The cries followed Jake all the way up Cornmarket as he hurried back to his car. Oxford's homeless problem was dire, with lost souls huddled in shop doorways and outside the gates of the colleges. The man he'd given his hot dog and coffee to had been surprised but grateful.

From what Kemal had told him, it sounded as if Zara had done the same, buying food for this girl, whoever she was. But had Zara done more than that? Had she offered the girl a place to stay for the night? Could she even have been in Zara's bedroom when Claiborne went up to see her?

'Any luck?' asked Bridget when he returned to the office.

'Yeah,' said Jake. 'Your hunch proved right. Zara bought a kebab for herself from a van on St Ebbe's at a quarter to eight on Thursday night. But there's more to it. She also bought one for a homeless girl who was with her. The van owner couldn't describe the girl in any detail, but I want to watch the CCTV again and see if Zara was with anyone when she got back to college.'

'You think she might have taken this homeless girl back to her room?'

'Who knows? It's worth a shot.'

'I want to see this,' said Bridget, pulling up a chair.

Jake fast-forwarded the footage to the time stamped seven forty-five and together he and Bridget watched the comings and goings from Tom Gate. He paused the video at eight o'clock.

'There she is.'

Zara's long blonde hair was just visible in the freeze frame, but there were quite a few people coming and going at the same time. Most of them looked like guests for the dean's drinks reception.

'Rewind it a minute and play that again,' said Bridget.

Jake did as she asked.

'Stop!' said Bridget, leaning forwards and pointing a finger at a figure close to Zara. 'Who's that?'

Jake rewound the video again and advanced it frame by frame as Zara appeared in the doorway and stepped through. There was definitely a girl right behind her, but she was partially hidden by Zara.

'When I watched the first time, I didn't notice her,' he explained to Bridget. 'I was expecting Zara to be alone.'

'Did you see what Zara was doing as she

stepped through the doorway?' asked Bridget. 'She was licking her fingers as if she'd just finished eating something.'

'So the owner of the kebab van was right. She bought the kebab at quarter to eight and ate it on the walk back to college, finishing it just as she arrived. And this girl must have gone back to Zara's room in college.'

'I need to phone the pathologist,' said Bridget, reaching for her phone.

'It's a bit late in the evening, isn't it?'

'Roy will probably still be at work.'

She was right about that. Jake listened as she explained to Dr Roy Andrews what they'd found. When she put the phone down she looked thoughtful.

'Roy estimates that the food was in her stomach for one hour before she died. That would put the time of death at around nine o'clock.'

Jake picked up her train of thought. 'Which means that Zara must still have been alive at twenty past eight when Helen Claiborne saw her husband coming downstairs from Zara's room.'

'I knew something didn't add up,' said Bridget.

'So when Claiborne said there was someone else in Zara's bedroom, you think it was this homeless girl?'

'Yes. And the reason Zara closed the bedroom door was because she didn't want the other girl to be discovered,' said Bridget.

The case was crumbling again. 'What now, ma'am?'

'This changes everything. If Zara died at around nine o'clock, Claiborne couldn't have been the murderer. Helen discovered the body at nine o'clock precisely. Our top suspect now has to be this homeless girl.'

'You think that she attacked Zara, then stole her phone and wallet?'

'It fits the facts. The search of Claiborne's room didn't find her phone or wallet.' Bridget looked unhappy. 'We'll have to release Claiborne now. We can't hold him after this.'

'I'll carry on watching the CCTV,' said Jake, 'and see if I can spot this homeless girl leaving the college. I'll find out what time she left, and see if I can get a decent image of her.'

'Thanks,' said Bridget. 'I'll go and tell Claiborne he's free to go.'

While Bridget went to convey the news to Claiborne, Jake carried on watching the CCTV. There had been a lot of activity between eight and nine that evening – the arrival of guests for the dean's drinks, students coming and going, Zac leaving the college dressed in black tie, his girlfriend Verity popping in and out on ball committee matters, the bowler-hatted custodians going about their business. It's no wonder he hadn't spotted Zara's homeless friend among the crowds. And yes, there she was again.

He paused the video and checked the time. The girl went out through the gates at nine fifteen precisely. He watched and re-watched the scene several times. It was hard to get a good image of her from this angle, but it was definitely her. And one other thing was very clear – wherever she was going, she was in a big hurry to get there.

★

Bridget drove home in a morose mood. For once, the bravura and virtuosity of Cecilia Bartoli singing Rossini could do nothing to lift her mood, and she turned the music off. Two strong leads had led to nothing. At this rate, her first murder case might well turn out to be her last. Would Grayson be willing to cut her enough slack to see the case through to completion?

Davis and Baxter were both available again. Either one could be assigned to take over the case.

But at least she had a new lead. A good one. She'd fight her corner to be allowed to continue heading up the investigation.

She'd only been home for a minute when she heard the key turn in the front door and Chloe entered, greeted her with a quick, 'Hello!' and went upstairs.

Her ex-husband, Ben, was leaning nonchalantly on the doorstep, almost as tall as Jake Derwent, the street lamp outside illuminating him from behind like a celestial light. He grinned broadly. 'Hey, Bridget.

Looking good.'

She wasn't sure if he was referring to her or to himself. Ben had always looked good, and still did. He was wearing a dark navy suit with a loose tie and casually unbuttoned collar. His waxed black hair was styled differently to how she'd last seen it – longer, with a side parting, and a few grey strands beginning to show. He had aged noticeably since she'd first laid eyes on him more than fifteen years ago, but that intense, direct gaze and charming, open face still had the power to bewitch her. The only difference now was that she knew all too well the unscrupulous rogue that hid behind them. Perhaps she had always known.

If he had come yesterday, she would have launched into open warfare over his underhand invitation to Chloe, but the day's events had left her with no appetite for a blazing row. Besides, that would do nothing to smooth her relationship with Chloe. She regarded him in silence, wishing him gone.

But Ben showed no desire to leave. 'How are you doing?'

'Good,' she told him. 'I'm all good.'

Better without you.

The deep hostility she had felt towards him seemed to have evaporated now he was here, but she would never make the mistake of trusting him again. He'd given her some good years, a few not so good, and some that were absolutely the worst. What had he left her with at the end of it all? A daughter, some hard-earned life lessons,

279

and a new surname. She had kept the name Hart. It made things simpler. And just because it belonged to him, didn't mean she couldn't have it too. It suited her better than him. And besides, it was Chloe's surname.

'Are you going to invite me in for a coffee?' he asked.

'No. I don't think so. It's been a long day.'

He grinned again, undaunted. 'I hear you're heading up your first murder case.'

'Yeah,' said Bridget. 'It's going well.'

'Really? That's not what I read in the papers.'

'You shouldn't believe everything you read.'

He shrugged and raised an eyebrow as if to say, 'No smoke without fire.'

'Goodnight, Ben.' She closed the door and waited until the click of his heels had disappeared down the garden path. At least he hadn't mentioned his new girlfriend. The tall blonde. If he'd spoken her name, she might have hit him.

She went upstairs to look for Chloe. 'So, how was your evening with Dad?'

'Ace,' said Chloe, sitting on her bed. 'He took me out to dinner at Brown's. And even better, look what he gave me for my birthday!'

She held up a box.

'A new iPhone,' said Bridget, trying but failing to mask her dismay. 'Nice.' How typical of Ben to buy his daughter's affections. He had always been the same. She had fallen for the same trick herself, over and over again.

Chloe pulled a face at her. 'Why are you so

cross?'

'I'm not cross. I said it was "nice."'

'Yeah, but you said it like you meant the opposite.'

What could she say? She wanted to protect her daughter, but some lessons could only be learned by making mistakes. She bent down and gave the girl a hug. 'I'm glad you like it,' she said. 'And I'm sorry about what I said yesterday. I'm glad that you had a nice evening with Dad.'

'So does that mean I can visit him in London?' asked Chloe. 'Just for a weekend?'

Bridget swallowed. She wanted nothing more than to keep Chloe all to herself, forever. But her daughter was growing up quickly. One day she would want to fly away, and Bridget knew she would have to let her go, however much it hurt. 'Just for a weekend.'

Chloe leaned forward and gave her a hug.

If you love someone, set them free. She thought again of Abigail. Her sister had always craved freedom. That freedom had been taken from her in the most brutal way possible. You could say that her freedom had been her downfall. Yet still Bridget knew that a life in captivity was a life hardly worth living.

'I'll talk to him and arrange for you to visit.'

CHAPTER 25

When Bridget arrived at Kidlington the next morning she didn't wait to be summoned into the Chief Superintendent's office. She went straight there and rapped on his glass door.

Grayson wasted no time making it clear that he didn't think much of her team's progress so far. 'You've questioned two suspects, and let both of them go.' He spread his hands wide across the desk. 'What the hell's going on?'

Bridget was ready with her reply. 'Sir, we made a breakthrough last night, and we used new evidence obtained from questioning Dr Claiborne to make it.'

'What new evidence?' demanded Grayson. 'What breakthrough?'

'Zara took a homeless girl back to college with her on Thursday night,' explained Bridget. 'This girl was, we now believe, the last person to see Zara alive.'

'The murderer?'

'It's possible. At the very least, a key witness. We obviously need to follow this lead urgently.' And the sooner you let me out of your office, the sooner we can get to work on it.

'Why would Zara take a homeless girl back to college with her?'

'She took a strong interest in social issues. She was a supporter of the homeless charity, Shelter. The simplest explanation might be that Zara had a social conscience.'

Grayson grunted as if he thought that unlikely. To Bridget's relief, he dismissed her with a wave of his hand. 'Get results and get them quickly.'

'Yes, sir.'

She escaped from the glass office as quickly as she could and went to meet the team. She hoped she didn't look as rattled as she felt. She needed to get things moving fast. Fortunately the mood in the briefing room was upbeat. Everyone seemed to know the latest news, and was ready to move forward.

Jake raised his hand and Bridget invited him to speak. 'I watched more of the CCTV footage last night, and I believe the homeless girl left the college at quarter past nine. I got this still picture of her. It's not very clear, but it's the best I could manage.'

He handed around a grainy photograph of a girl exiting Tom Gate. Her head was down but she wore her hair in distinctive braids which looked matted and straggly. Her hands were thrust into the pockets of her combat trousers.

'She was running out of the college like she couldn't get away fast enough,' said Jake.

Ffion put her hand up next. 'When I went

through Zara's emails, there was an exchange with the dean about the homeless shelter. Zara was unhappy that the college had been given planning permission to knock it down and build new student accommodation. Perhaps the most likely place to find this homeless girl is at the shelter.'

'I agree,' said Bridget. 'And I hate to say this, but given that Zara's phone and wallet are missing, it's quite possible that we're looking at a simple robbery – an act of charity gone badly wrong. Jake, Ffion, can I ask you two to go and check out the shelter? Find out if Zara had any connection there and see if they can identify the girl in the picture.'

She gave her orders to the rest of the team. 'Ryan, search the witness statements for any references to Zara's work with homeless charities. And Andy, you take a team of constables and show this photo around college to as many people as you can find. See if anyone recognises the girl. Let's find her, and quickly. No more mistakes.'

They were on their feet as soon as she'd finished, chairs scraping and mugs of tea being drained. It would surely not take long to track down the mysterious girl.

★

Jake pulled up at the end of a cul-de-sac of council accommodation. This was a side of

Oxford that tourists never got to see, even though it was just a stone's throw from Christ Church and the swanky new Westgate shopping centre. Jake's orange Subaru was the only splash of colour in the street, apart from a yellow sign advising that 24 hour security cameras were in operation. He wondered if he ought to leave the car somewhere where it would attract less attention, but Ffion was opening the door and getting out before he could voice his concern. Hopefully the brightly coloured car would be so conspicuous that no one would dare to steal it.

The shelter itself was a brick building with aluminium windows. Two men and a woman sat cross-legged on the pavement outside the hostel, smoking and looking bored. They offered Jake and Ffion sullen stares as they passed. 'Spare any change?' asked the woman without much optimism.

The door to the hostel was painted an ugly shade of green. Ffion pressed the buzzer and when the door clicked open they entered a reception area furnished with cheap plastic chairs. A bolted-down table was covered with leaflets about HIV and drug rehabilitation programmes.

A young man with dreadlocks sat behind a counter, thumbing through a copy of the Oxford Mail and drinking tea from a Homer Simpson mug. He looked up at them without much interest. 'Can I help you?'

Jake introduced himself and Ffion.

As soon as Jake showed his warrant card the man became more alert, but seemed wary. He pushed the newspaper to one side. 'What's this about, then?'

'Can we have a word with whoever's in charge?'

'For the moment, that's me,' said the man. 'Kyle's the name.'

Jake showed him the photos of Zara and of the unknown girl. 'Do you recognise either of these women?'

Kyle didn't need to study them for long. 'Yeah, I know them,' he said gloomily. 'The first one's Zara Hamilton. Is that why you're here?'

'We're investigating her death,' said Jake. 'We'd like to know if she worked as a volunteer here.'

'Yeah, she did. She was one of the regulars, she showed up every week. We all had a soft spot for Zara. Everyone here was gutted when we heard about her murder on the news. So sad. Zara was always so full of life. She'd talk to anyone, didn't matter who you were. She made you feel special, somehow.'

'How long had she worked here?'

'About a year, I suppose.'

'And what kind of work did she do?'

'She'd turn her hand to anything. Chopping vegetables, cleaning pots and pans. I only found out after she died how rich she was. She never mentioned her family once.'

'Was she here last Thursday night?'

'Thursday? That's the day she was killed, yeah?' He nodded. 'Let me check in the logbook. Everyone who comes here signs in and out.'

He rummaged beneath the counter and withdrew a hardback notebook. Flicking through the pages he ran his finger down the list of handwritten names. 'Let me see. Yeah, here it is. Zara arrived at six forty and left just under an hour later.'

'That doesn't seem like long,' said Ffion.

Kyle agreed that it was odd. He pushed the book towards them so that they could see for themselves. 'God, I still can't believe she's dead,' he added.

'Can I get a copy of this?' asked Jake.

'Sure, I'll make you a copy before you go.'

Jake pushed the second photo along the counter. 'What about this other woman? You said you recognised her. Who is she?'

'Yeah, that's Shannon, one of the regulars here. A resident, I mean, not a volunteer.'

Jake exchanged glances with Ffion. 'Is Shannon here now?' he asked.

'Nah,' said Kyle. 'Everyone's out during the day.'

'Do you know where we might find her?'

Kyle shrugged his shoulders. 'Not really.'

Jake searched for Shannon's name in the logbook, but there was no record of her entering or leaving on the Thursday evening. 'Do you remember if she was here the day Zara was last here?'

'Dunno,' said Kyle. 'I clocked off early that night. Kat'll know though. Hang on a minute.' He left the reception for a moment and returned with a young woman wearing a pair of purple dungarees.

'What is it?' asked Kat nervously. 'Are they coppers?'

'Don't worry,' said Kyle, laying a hand on Kat's shoulder. 'They're here about Zara.'

Jake showed her the photograph of Shannon. 'This woman. Do you know who she is?'

Kat seemed reluctant to talk. 'Why do you want to know? Is she in trouble?'

'We only want to find out what happened to Zara,' said Jake.

Kat seemed to be weighing up whether or not to say anything. Kyle nodded encouragingly and she relaxed a little. 'Yeah. Shannon Lewis. Unmistakable hair. She's one of the women we help here. She's only nineteen but she's had a hard life. Abusive father, alcoholic mother. Usual stuff.'

'Was she here on Thursday night?'

Kat sighed. 'When Shannon showed up that evening she was really drunk and behaving badly.'

'Bad? In what way?' asked Jake.

'Oh you know, being violent. Threatening people. We couldn't let her in in that state. She was a danger to the other residents.'

'So what happened then?'

'Zara said she'd take Shannon away, get her

something to eat. Get her sobered up. That seemed to calm Shannon down a bit. They left together.'

'And have you seen Shannon since then?'

'No.'

'Do you have any idea where we might find her?'

Kat's face was suddenly angry and defiant. 'Any of the places where homeless people usually hang out in the city centre.'

Jake nodded. He'd often seen homeless people sitting on pavements, some with mangy-looking dogs for company. 'Can you help us look?' he asked gently. 'It's really important that we find Shannon.'

Kat looked to Kyle for guidance. 'It's for Zara,' he reminded her.

'Okay,' agreed Kat at last. 'I'll come with you.'

★

Kat still seemed unsure about the search. 'Why is it you want to find Shannon?' she asked.

Jake weighed up how much to tell her. He couldn't lie, but he didn't want to divulge the fact that Shannon was now their prime suspect. 'We believe she was the last person to see Zara alive.'

It seemed enough to satisfy Kat. 'I guessed as much. Volunteers aren't supposed to take people home with them, but Zara and Shannon got on well so I guessed that Zara was going to let

Shannon sleep on her bedroom floor or something like that.'

The people hanging around outside the homeless shelter hadn't seen Shannon for days, so Kat led them out of the cul-de-sac towards St Aldate's.

Jake checked the Subaru anxiously as they walked past, but it hadn't come to any damage so far.

'It's still got four wheels,' remarked Ffion. 'If you're lucky, someone might give it a more tasteful paint job by the time we get back.'

The city centre shop doorways that had provided shelter for the homeless the previous night had been swept clean ready for the day's business. Already the streets were filling up with early-morning shoppers, tourists, street-sellers and buskers. Outside McDonald's a large group of French school children with identical baseball caps and matching rucksacks were absorbed with their mobile phones, completely indifferent to Oxford's history, culture and architecture. A tightly-packed group of elderly Japanese tourists were being herded around by an officious-looking tour guide holding a closed umbrella high above her head and delivering a potted history of the university at breakneck speed.

As they walked up Cornmarket, Kat told them how Zara had helped out at the shelter and how she'd been trying to fight the threat of closure. 'If they shut us down it'll be impossible to find another location in the city centre,' said Kat.

'Rents in Oxford are just so high.'

Yeah, thought Jake. He knew a thing or two about high Oxford rents himself. His mates back in Leeds had laughed at him when he'd told them how much he paid each month for his tiny flat down the Cowley Road. The run-down area where the shelter was located, so close to the city centre, looked ripe for redevelopment.

They searched for Shannon in all the places the homeless tended to hang out: outside the banks, chain stores and mobile phone shops on Cornmarket; in the walkways of the Covered Market; in the fair trade café at the church of St Michael at the North Gate; around the foot of Martyrs' Memorial on St Giles' and up the Woodstock Road as far as Little Clarendon Street.

Kat knew a lot of the people on the streets and did most of the talking, asking if any of them had seen Shannon. Most of the people she spoke to eyed Jake and Ffion with suspicion. Even in plain clothes they seemed to exude an air of officialdom that put the wind up people who were living outside mainstream society. Without Kat to help, they would have got very little cooperation. But even so, none of them had seen Shannon recently.

The last place they tried was Broad Street. A Big Issue magazine seller was standing outside the Oxfam shop, in his distinctive hi-vis jacket. He didn't seem to be selling many copies of his magazines to the busy passers-by.

'Hey, Stu, how's it going?' asked Kat.

'Yeah, not bad,' said Stu, grinning broadly and revealing a wide gap where his two front teeth were missing.

Kat stared meaningfully at Jake, who reached into his pocket and handed the seller some coins in return for a copy of the magazine.

'Got a question for you,' said Kat.

'Oh aye?'

'We're looking for Shannon. Seen her around recently?'

Stu cast a suspicious look at Jake and Ffion. 'Who wants to know?'

'I do,' said Kat. 'I'm worried about her. I haven't seen her since Thursday.'

Stu scratched the stubble on his thin face. 'I saw 'er yesterday morning. She was acting a bit funny though.'

'In what way?'

Stu rubbed his thumb and forefinger together. 'She had some dosh on 'er. Shannon never has money usually. Wouldn't say where she'd got it. But she said there was lots more where that came from.'

'Do you know where she is now, mate?' asked Jake.

Stu shook his head. 'Nah, she buggered off.'

'Thanks, Stu,' said Kat. 'You look after yourself now.'

They walked back to the homeless shelter so Jake could retrieve his car. Fortunately it was still there, and undamaged. One of the men who'd been sitting outside the shelter earlier sloped over. 'Some kids were looking at it,' he informed Jake, 'but I scared them off.' He held out his palm. 'Reckon you owe me something for that.'

Reluctantly Jake handed over his last few coins. What with the Big Issue magazine and last night's kebabs, his wallet was looking decidedly empty.

Before leaving he handed Kat his card. 'Could you give us a call if Shannon turns up?'

'Sure,' said Kat. 'You don't think anything bad can have happened to her, do you?'

'I honestly don't know.'

★

Bridget's morning was going well. First Jake had called in with a positive ID on the girl who'd been captured on CCTV with Zara. Now she'd received an email from forensics. Two samples of DNA recovered from the crime scene had been analysed and checked against the National DNA Database. In both cases a positive match for Shannon Lewis had been found.

'We've got her!' said Ryan.

Bridget was reluctant to get her hopes up too much. She read from the email. 'Shannon Lewis, nineteen years old, of no known address. Convictions for possession and supply of drugs, common assault and robbery. The first sample was obtained from saliva in a glass of water in Zara's room; the second from sweat found on the

293

blood-stained towel downstairs.'

'So,' said Ryan, 'we know that she went back to Zara's room in college. The saliva in the glass proves she was in the room. The sweat on the towel means she was the one who tried to stop the bleeding after Zara was attacked. She threw it away when she realised Zara was dead and there was nothing more she could do.'

Bridget pored over the email again, searching for anything that might indicate doubt. She couldn't afford another mistake. 'The chance of getting a false match between two DNA profiles is one billion to one,' she read aloud.

'In other words, non-existent,' said Ryan. 'No jury is going to have doubts on that score.'

'But why would she do it?' mused Bridget. 'Zara was just showing her some kindness.'

'You know why, ma'am. Drugs. A druggie like Shannon needs money to feed her habit. She probably didn't plan to hurt Zara at all. She just saw a chance to grab her purse. There's a struggle. It ends badly. The fact that she tried to stop the bleeding with the towel proves that she didn't really intend to kill Zara. But when she realised she couldn't save her, she legged it with the money and the phone. It must have all happened while Claiborne was arguing with his wife downstairs. They were so busy shouting at each other, they didn't hear a thing.'

Bridget nodded slowly. 'Get an arrest warrant for Shannon Lewis. Put her photo out to all the local stations. Let's find her and bring her in.'

★

Shannon Lewis prowled along the back streets of Oxford, her black hood pulled tightly over her face. Stu had tipped her off that Kat was looking for her, and she was keeping well clear of Cornmarket and anywhere else she might be spotted. There were cameras all over the place and you couldn't be too careful.

She knew why they were after her. She'd got herself tangled in some serious shit this time. She turned her head to check no one was following her and bumped into some old woman coming in the other direction.

'Sorry,' said the old cow.

Shannon flew into a rage. 'Yeah? Watch where you're fucking going!' The old bitch scurried off looking terrified.

Now Shannon was angry with herself. She mustn't attract attention. The last thing she needed was a trail of witnesses blabbing their stories to the cops. She glared at some bystanders, and they turned away quickly and vanished.

At least she had cash in her pocket. She'd need it. No way was she going back to that crappy hostel. The sooner she was out of Oxford the better. Wherever she went next, she'd be sleeping out on the streets until things calmed down, but that didn't worry her. She'd slept out in the middle of winter before now, and that was when sleeping rough really got to you. Summertime was easy. And soon she'd have more money. Enough to last her a long time.

Someone else knocked her arm and her mouth was open before she'd had time to think. 'Watch where you're fucking going!' Biting her lip, she turned down a side alley and was gone.

CHAPTER 26

Bridget left the office with growing confidence that the case would soon be solved. It was only a matter of time before Shannon Lewis was picked up. Ryan and his team were trawling through CCTV footage from the bus and train stations in case Shannon had tried to travel to London or elsewhere. Her description had been passed to British Transport Police. But if the Big Issue seller that Jake and Ffion had spoken to could be believed, Shannon was most likely still in Oxford.

It was as Bridget was getting into her car that she remembered the invitation from Jonathan to attend the exhibition at his gallery. She hadn't replied to his text, but hopefully that wouldn't matter. He hadn't asked her for a response, just hoped she could make it. He was obviously doing his best to make the invitation casual. He certainly hadn't asked her out on a date, just drinks and canapés. Was she reading too much into it?

Driving back to Wolvercote, she wondered what to do. She felt guilty about going out and enjoying herself when members of her team were still hunting for Shannon. But she'd put in plenty of long hours recently herself. She'd even missed Chloe's birthday because of the case. She deserved some time out, and this was a low key way to meet Jonathan. Besides, she couldn't remember the last time she'd been to an art gallery.

She would go. She would forget about the case for one evening, and try to have fun.

'Hello,' she called as she arrived home. No response.

She climbed the stairs and knocked on Chloe's door. Still nothing. She turned the handle and opened the door, worried about what she might find.

Chloe was sitting at her desk, headphones on, doing her homework. Bridget breathed a sigh of relief and tapped her on the shoulder.

'God, Mum, you frightened the life out of me.' Chloe took her headphones off.

'How can you concentrate on your work listening to music?'

'It's not that hard.'

'You didn't hear me come in with those things on. A burglar could have got in and you wouldn't have known.'

'Stop nagging, Mum.'

'Anyway,' said Bridget, aware that the conversation had got off to a more confrontational start than she would have liked. 'Would you mind if I went out this evening?'

'You don't need my permission to go out,' said Chloe. 'Where to?'

'I've been invited to an exhibition at a gallery.'

'Jonathan's art gallery?' asked Chloe, her eyes lighting up. 'Then you've totally got to go.'

'I won't be long. I'll just call in for a quick –'

'But you can't go in your work clothes,' interrupted Chloe, standing up and walking towards the door. 'They're far too boring. Let's find something more suitable.'

Oh God, thought Bridget. Fashion advice from my teenage daughter.

Chloe was already in Bridget's room pulling things out of the wardrobe unenthusiastically. 'These are all so dull, Mum,' she said, dumping trousers and shirts onto the bed.

'What about this?' said Bridget hopefully, pulling out the outfit she had intended to wear – a navy sheath dress with three-quarter length sleeves.

Chloe shook her head. 'It's a party, not a business meeting.' She held up a maxi dress covered in yellow and orange swirls that Bridget had bought in Spain when the hot Mediterranean sun must have addled her colour sense.

Bridget shook her head. 'Too summery.'

'It is summer,' said Chloe, rolling her eyes. 'What about this then?' She held up a black lace top.

'Far too skimpy.'

'This then?' A green dress that Bridget rather

liked.

'Too tight. Last time I tried it I nearly burst the zip trying to do it up.'

'There must be something nice you can wear,' said Chloe, rummaging amongst the hangers.

Bridget doubted it. She had been quite slender in her student days, but being pregnant with Chloe had increased her girth by several dress sizes, and subsequent breastfeeding had only helped to reclaim a little of the lost territory. Over the years, the weight had steadily crept up, advancing on a wave of creamy carbonara and rich chocolate gateaux, aided and abetted by regular glasses of Pinot Noir – not to mention occasional whole bottles. Her only protection against the rising tide was restraint, which had proved to be an unreliable defence, and exercise, which was vulnerable to long working hours and the demands of single parenthood.

Chloe reached far into the dark recesses of the wardrobe and triumphantly pulled out a slinky burgundy dress. 'This!'

Bridget eyed the dress warily. She seemed to recall that it had been a struggle to coax her curves into it the last time she'd worn it, and that was over a year ago. But still…

She took it from Chloe and held it by its thin straps before clambering into it cautiously, squeezing her widest parts inside its cocooning fabric. She was dismayed to find that it hugged her relentlessly, making her feel quite breathless.

But there was some compensation. Her bust

size had expanded in line with her dress size, and she eyed her cleavage in the mirror with a sense of satisfaction. Perhaps there was some justice in this world, after all.

'Wear these with it.' Chloe handed her a pair of sandals with wedge heels that gave her a much needed extra two inches. 'Wow,' she said when Bridget had squeezed her feet into the sandals and done up the straps. 'It's perfect for a date.'

'This isn't a date. It's a cultural event.'

'Yeah, right. Now go, before you change your mind. If you get back early, I'll be cross.'

Driving into Oxford, Bridget tried to remember the last time she'd been out in the evening, just for fun. It must have been the Christmas concert she'd attended in the Sheldonian theatre. But that was six months ago. She loved going to concerts and plays and art galleries, but she just never seemed to find the time these days.

It was after six thirty, so cars were allowed on the High Street. She slipped the Mini into a tiny space just outside the University Church of St Mary the Virgin and crossed the road to the gallery.

She must have walked past the gallery many times but had never gone in. The paintings were out of her price range, but that wasn't the real reason she'd never been inside. As a young woman she'd popped into galleries and exhibitions all the time. But at some point in her life she'd simply forgotten how to enjoy herself.

Well, it was time to start again.

Tonight the gallery was full of people and their chatter, laughter, and the clink of wine glasses. She hovered just inside the door, wary of pushing into the crowded space. People were clustered in groups, talking together, looking at the pictures. She skirted around them to a table draped in a white linen cloth and groaning with pre-filled glasses of wine. She grabbed a glass of white and took a swallow.

'Bridget, I'm so glad you could come.' Jonathan weaved his way through the crowd towards her, smiling. He wore an open-necked purple shirt which perfectly complemented his strawberry blond hair. When he reached her he kissed her lightly on each cheek. 'You look wonderful.'

'I'm afraid I've been rather busy. That's why I forgot to reply to your text.' She could hear Chloe's voice inside her head, telling her off. Don't apologise to people all the time, Mum. Just be yourself. She took another swig of wine.

'No problem,' said Jonathan. 'You're here now, that's what matters. Let me show you the paintings.'

She felt a tingle as his fingertips touched the small of her back, guiding her towards the main section of the gallery. Although the shop front was narrow, the space opened out at the back to reveal high white walls, perfect for hanging large works of art. Jonathan walked her through the exhibition, explaining that he was showcasing the work of a group of artists who had graduated from the Ruskin School of Art in Oxford five years ago. He pointed to the paintings, telling her about each artist and explaining the inspirations behind individual paintings. His voice was easy to listen to, his words bewitching, his passion for the exhibits contagious. It was like a private showing for just the two of them.

'You must go and talk to your other guests,' said Bridget, aware that she was monopolising her host.

'Must I?' His eyes sparkled mischievously. 'I enjoy talking to you. Can I get you another glass of wine?'

She was surprised to find that her glass was empty. How long had she been here already? She heard her phone ringing in her bag. 'Sorry, I ought to answer that. It might be Chloe.'

'Of course.' He took her empty glass and moved away.

She fished the phone out of her bag. Not Chloe, but Jake. 'Hello?' she said. It was difficult to hear over the hubbub of conversation. She moved into a less crowded corner.

'Ma'am? Sorry to bother you, but you said to call if anything happened.'

'Have you found Shannon?'

'Yes.'

She breathed a sigh of relief. 'Well done. That's great.'

'Not exactly,' said Jake. 'She's dead.'

The pleasant haze that had briefly enveloped

her lifted, and Bridget suddenly felt stone-cold sober. She listened with a sinking feeling as Jake explained how a rowing crew had discovered the body floating in the river. He was there now at the boathouses with the scene of crime officers and a team of police divers.

'I'm on my way,' said Bridget, ending the call.

Jonathan returned with two glasses of wine. 'We should be finished here in thirty or forty minutes. I was wondering if afterwards you'd like to –' He stopped when he saw the expression on her face.

'I'm really sorry,' she said, 'but something urgent has come up at work. I'm going to have to leave.'

'Your murder case. Of course, you must go.'

'I'm sorry. But thank you for inviting me to your gallery. It's been a lovely evening.'

He nodded. 'It was my pleasure.'

She wondered if she should kiss his cheek before leaving, but Jake's phone call had conjured an image of Shannon's corpse floating face-down in the River Thames and it seemed to come between them.

'I'll see you again,' she said, then squeezed her way through the crowd of people to the exit, leaving him standing there with the two glasses of wine.

CHAPTER 27

A uniformed officer met Bridget at the gate that led to Christ Church Meadow and informed her that the college had granted permission for them to drive down the sandy path normally reserved for walkers. With the summer solstice three days away, the sun was only just dipping below the line of trees that bordered the meadow's western edge.

Bridget drove as far as she could, then left the car by the riverside, proceeding on foot across a narrow hump-back bridge that spanned a small tributary of the Thames, or the Isis as the locals called it.

As the boathouses came into view, Bridget recalled standing on the rooftop balcony of Merton College's boathouse one hot weekend during the annual Eights Week regatta, cheering for her team, a glass of Pimm's in hand. It had been a summer not unlike this one.

Christ Church boathouse, an older, red brick building, stood at the very end of the main row of twelve boathouses. It was the furthest point that could be reached on foot. Beyond it, the

Cherwell flowed languidly into the Isis. A ribbon of black and yellow tape fluttered in the evening breeze, cutting the crime scene off from the neighbouring boathouses.

On the opposite bank, joggers and dog walkers paused to stare across at the white-suited crime scene investigators and police divers bobbing in and out of the water in their wet suits and oxygen masks. The setting sun lent a blood-red glow to the sky behind them, and cast long rippling shadows across the quiet water.

A posh dress and high heels didn't make the ideal outfit for a crime scene. By the time Bridget reached it her feet were killing her. She would have loved to kick off her sandals and go barefoot. Jake, in a white coverall and rubber boots, met her at the cordon. She appreciated the fact that he didn't comment on her outfit.

'Fill me in,' she said.

'We had a call from the rowing team just after seven o'clock. They were finishing a training session when the cox spotted something floating in the Cherwell, over there by those tree roots.' He pointed to a spot where the mud bank had eroded, exposing a tangle of roots from an overhanging willow. 'The water level is low at this time of year. If the body hadn't caught on the tree roots, it would have washed into the Thames and been carried downstream. A couple of the biggest lads in the boat pulled her out, but she was already dead.'

A group of young men in Lycra rowing suits

were gathered in front of the boathouse. The cox and several of the rowers were giving statements to uniformed officers. She recognised the tallest. Adam. He stood watching her, his face in shadow, his coal-black hair messy and dishevelled.

Jake followed her gaze. 'Adam was one of the men who pulled the body from the river.'

'Coincidence?'

Jake just shrugged.

'And are we sure it's Shannon's body?' she asked him.

'I've arranged for Kat from the shelter to come and make a formal identification, but it looks like her. She didn't have any ID on her, however she was carrying Zara's wallet.'

'Let me guess. The wallet still had money in it?'

'Yeah. About fifty quid. So it doesn't look like she was killed for it.'

'Okay,' said Bridget. 'Let me take a look at her.' She removed her sandals and struggled into a white coverall, not an easy feat in her dress. She bunched the skirt up around her middle, abandoning any hope of retaining her dignity. Together they ducked under the crime scene tape and went over to the bank of the Cherwell where the body was stretched out on the grassy slope.

The girl was still fully dressed in combat trousers and a black hooded top. Bits of green duckweed were tangled in her matted braids. A forensic medical examiner was kneeling by the body. The examiner stood up as Bridget approached, and she recognised Dr Sarah Walker, a Cambridge-educated local doctor who was often called in to help the police.

'Hi,' said Bridget. 'What can you tell me?'

Dr Walker looked grim. She was a similar age to Bridget, but single, and had a dedication to her career that Bridget admired. 'A young woman, probably around eighteen or nineteen. She shows obvious signs of malnutrition. My guess is she's been sleeping rough. There are needle marks in her arm. Your sergeant here already seems to know who she is.'

'We think so. When did she die?'

'I wouldn't try to estimate a time of death. That's for the pathologist to determine during the post-mortem. It isn't easy to judge it accurately after a body's been submerged for any length of time. The temperature doesn't follow the normal rules. But she can't have been dead for too long. Rigor mortis is still only partial, and I don't think she's been in the water for more than a couple of hours. The skin is soft, and has a slightly whitish appearance, but there's no sign of the skin maceration or wrinkling you'd expect after prolonged hydration.'

'I see. So did she drown?'

Dr Walker shook her head. She knelt down and tilted the body carefully onto its side, revealing a gash to the back of the victim's head, about four inches in length. 'The post-mortem will reveal whether she was still alive when she entered the water, but with a gash of this size it's probable that she was already unconscious.'

'So she was hit over the head before she went into the water,' said Bridget.

'It would appear so.'

A small blessing, thought Bridget. The thought of drowning had always terrified her, even though she was a keen and strong swimmer herself. Perhaps because of that.

'What kind of weapon do you think caused that injury?'

'Something heavy, and sharp. A considerable amount of force must have been used.'

'I don't think we have to look too far for the murder weapon, ma'am,' said Jake.

She looked where he was pointing. One of the police divers was pulling a rowing oar out of the water where it had jammed against some reeds. The blade was painted the deep royal blue of Christ Church.

★

Bridget paced the floor of the incident room, still wearing her cocktail dress. The brief interlude with Jonathan at the art gallery seemed like a lifetime ago. Two murders now, and still no one charged. Two young women, closely connected. One rich, one poor, but both killed by the same method, even if a different weapon was used in each case. 'How soon will we know for certain if the oar was used as the murder weapon?' she demanded.

She was too impatient to wait for a reply, and answered her own question. 'We'll need the post-mortem results to confirm that the blade of the oar matches the head wound. I'll get onto Roy Andrews first thing in the morning. The oar was dumped in the water, but perhaps forensics will be able to find a trace of blood, or something else that we can use. Where is the damn thing now?'

'It's been logged with the other items recovered, ma'am,' replied Jake. 'The exhibits officer was moaning that he didn't know what to do about it, it was so long. He doesn't have any exhibit bags big enough.' He trailed off under her gaze.

'I'll bloody well tell him what he can do with it,' said Bridget. She took a deep breath. 'Sorry. I didn't mean to snap.'

'No worries.'

She turned to her team. She needed them all behind her now, more than ever. 'Any ideas? Let's hear what everyone thinks.'

Ffion raised a hand. 'I have a theory.'

'Go on,' said Bridget. She was happy to hear all theories. With their latest prime suspect dead, they needed to take stock and find a new direction yet again.

Ffion continued. 'So here's our picture of events so far. We know that Zara took Shannon back to her room in college. Dr Claiborne claims there was someone in Zara's bedroom when he went to see her. We don't know for certain if he was telling the truth, but it does seem likely that Shannon was there, given that she didn't leave the college until later. We know that Shannon took Zara's wallet, and quite possibly her phone too, when she left. But we shouldn't assume that she killed Zara. She might have just taken the valuables as an afterthought. She needed cash to feed her drugs habit. It's more likely that whoever killed Shannon also murdered Zara. But Shannon may have witnessed the murder, or at least been present in the bedroom when it happened.'

'Okay,' said Bridget. 'Let's go with that, for the moment. What are the implications?'

Jake took up the thread. 'If Shannon knew the identity of the murderer, she may have tried to blackmail them. Stu, the Big Issue guy, said that she'd come into money and was expecting more. So what if the murderer arranged to meet her at the river and then killed her?'

'Precisely,' said Ffion. Jake beamed.

'If only we'd been able to get to Shannon first,' mused Bridget. But she couldn't blame herself for that. She'd done everything she could to locate Shannon. Or had she? She didn't think she'd ever be able to forgive herself for being at an art exhibition while Shannon's dead body was being pulled from the river.

But she liked Ffion's theory. She had arrived at the same conclusion herself, but it was good

311

to hear that others thought the same. 'So the murderer must have gone to Zara's room while Helen Claiborne was with her husband. Helen found Zara's body when she went back up to see Zara, then left the college at exactly nine o'clock. Who was in college at that time?'

'Let me check my notes.' Jake turned the pages of his notebook carefully, squinting hard as he decrypted the scrawled writing. He looked up. 'Adam. He was seen leaving the college through Tom Gate at five past ten. Before then he'd been drinking in the college bar. But we can't confirm he was in the bar the whole time.'

'And who's most likely to have chosen the boathouse as a location to meet Shannon?'

'Adam,' said Jake and Ffion in unison.

'Coincidence?' It was the second time she'd asked the question that evening. Coincidences happened, but not that often. She checked her watch. It was getting late, already nearly ten o'clock.

Chloe wasn't expecting her back early – had even said she'd be cross if Bridget came back too soon – but even so she couldn't leave her daughter alone all night. And the team had been working all day long. They needed some rest. 'Arrange for Adam to be picked up first thing in the morning,' she said. 'I'll want everyone back in at seven. We'll search his room thoroughly. We're looking for a glass paperweight, and we still haven't found Zara's phone.'

As she left she overheard Ffion whispering to

Jake. 'I hope she doesn't get us to do the search. Not with that smelly sports kit all over the floor.' The sound of his chuckling followed her out through the door.

CHAPTER 28

On her way into work the next morning, Bridget wondered if she should call Jonathan to apologise for having rushed off the previous evening. She hadn't texted him when she'd got home because it had been late and Chloe had bombarded her with questions about her date, as she insisted on calling it. Her daughter had been suitably dismayed to learn that Bridget had left the gallery early to attend a murder scene. ('Honestly Mum, your first date in years and you didn't even see it through!') Bridget hadn't liked to enquire what Chloe had meant by see it through. Where would it have ended if she had seen it through? But if she did call to apologise, would she be obliged to suggest a second date? She still wasn't even certain that it had been a first date.

Her immediate dilemma was solved as soon as she entered Police HQ. The duty sergeant informed her that Mr Adam Brady had been brought in half an hour earlier and was waiting in interview room two. There was no time to call Jonathan now.

She got herself a quick coffee from the machine while Jake and Ffion brought her up to speed on the morning's events. There had been no problem bringing Adam in for questioning, and apparently it hadn't taken long to find Zara's mobile phone beneath a pile of dirty rowing kit. Unfortunately it had been wiped clean of prints – 'Not with that kit,' Ffion commented, wrinkling her nose – but it did contain the texts that Dr Claiborne had sent to Zara. Texts which would no doubt have enraged a jealous boyfriend, and Adam seemed to Bridget to be constantly on the brink of rage.

'What about the paperweight?' asked Bridget.

Ffion shook her head. 'No trace of it in his room.'

'He refused the offer to make a phone call when we brought him in,' said Jake. 'He's got a police-assigned lawyer with him.'

'Okay,' said Bridget. 'I'm going to speak to him now. Jake, you come with me. Ffion, see what else you can get off Zara's phone.'

★

The atmosphere in the interview room was charged, and Bridget was glad she'd brought Jake in with her. Adam sat behind the table, bristling with anger. His large, muscular frame made the tiny room feel claustrophobic.

Next to him sat Cameron Davies, his police-assigned lawyer. Unlike Zac and Dr Claiborne, who had been represented by highly-paid members of the legal profession, Adam was reliant on a duty solicitor for his defence. Mr Davies was recently qualified, with little experience of sitting in on police interviews. Dwarfed by his client, Davies appeared nervous, compulsively thumbing through his notes and fiddling with the top of his ballpoint pen.

Adam glared at Bridget as she sat down opposite, clenching and unclenching his fists. The cuts on his knuckles where he had punched Zac were still clearly visible.

Bridget didn't think there was anything to be gained by a softly-softly approach. With the preliminaries out of the way, she launched straight into the attack. 'Tell me how you felt when Zara finished your relationship.'

Adam stared right back at her. 'Angry. Confused. Jealous.'

'Angry enough to start a fight with her brother?'

'Sure.'

'Angry enough to start a fight with Zara?'

'I didn't even see her that night. I already told you.'

'I think you did though, Adam. In fact I think you killed Zara in a jealous rage and then killed Shannon Lewis when you found out that she had witnessed the murder.'

'Bollocks.'

Davies flinched and cleared his throat. 'You should say, no comment.'

Adam turned his sullen glare on his lawyer and said nothing.

'Let's talk about what happened yesterday. Where were you in the hours before Shannon Lewis's body was found in the water?'

'I think –' began Davies.

'In the college dining hall,' said Adam, cutting the lawyer off. 'Then rowing. Ask my teammates if you don't believe me. They'll vouch for me.' He sat back in his chair, crossing his arms over his broad torso.

'Tell me about the training session and the discovery of the body.'

'I've already said all this when I gave a statement yesterday.'

'But I'd like to hear it in your own words.'

Adam let out a long sigh. Then, grudgingly and haltingly at first, he began to explain how the team had run down to the boathouse, launched the boat and set off downstream, practising their racing starts. Before long, he seemed to forget he was in a police interview room, and his account became vivid and articulate. It was obvious that rowing was his passion. The team had done a long stretch, rowing as far as Donnington Bridge before turning the boat around and heading back to the boathouse. It was as they were passing the point where the Cherwell flowed into the Thames that the cox had seen something floating in the water. He'd yelled the command to stop the boat – Hold it hard! – and the rowers had done the equivalent of an emergency stop, digging their blades into the water, until they came to a standstill. By this time they'd drifted past the mouth of the tributary so the cox instructed them to back up. Two of the rowers – one of them Adam – had jumped into the water and swum over to the floating body. But they'd been too late.

'I'd never seen the girl before in my life, and I didn't bloody well kill her!' he concluded.

'So maybe you'd like to explain what Zara's phone was doing in your room?' said Bridget.

'How the hell should I know? I didn't put it there.'

'So who did?'

'You don't have to answer that,' said Davies.

Adam ignored him. 'Anyone could have planted it. I often leave my door unlocked.'

'That phone contained dozens of love messages from Dr Claiborne to your girlfriend.' Bridget slid the printout of Shakespeare quotes across the table. 'Are you telling me that you've never seen these before?'

Adam studied them briefly, then pushed the paper away, looking as if he would like to hit someone. Davies shifted slightly to the left, away from his client.

'I've never seen them before,' said Adam.

Bridget paused the recording. She now had a post-mortem to attend. Adam would have to wait.

CHAPTER 29

Bridget was met at the door of the morgue by Dr Roy Andrews himself. Today's bow tie showed yellow and black striped fish swimming in an aquamarine ocean. The bow tie functioned as a protective amulet, she supposed. An insanely cheerful display to ward off the madness of death. 'Back so soon,' he said sadly, shaking her hand. 'Let's hope this is your last visit, for a while at least.'

Bridget gave him a rueful smile. 'Let's hope so.'

She changed into a set of green scrubs then went into the theatre. She had decided to attend this second post-mortem on her own. Roy's assistant Julie was busy uncovering Shannon's emaciated body. The duckweed had been removed from the girl's hair, but otherwise she looked the same as when she'd been laid out at the riverside. Bridget winced at the thinness of her arms and legs and the way her ribs stuck out.

There were no known relatives to contact. According to her criminal record, Shannon had been brought up in a children's home. Earlier that morning, Ryan had brought Kyle and Kat from the homeless shelter to formally identify the body. They'd been upset to learn about the circumstances of her death, even though the girl had been 'a bit of a handful' and had caused them more than a few problems at the shelter. Ffion had cross-checked the girl's fingerprints against the National Criminal Database too. Everything confirmed the facts they already knew.

Shannon Lewis, nineteen years old, of no fixed address. A drug user and a petty criminal. The girl had managed to fit a surprisingly long string of convictions into her short life. It wasn't much of a biography, but according to Kat, Zara had begun to make a difference, helping Shannon to change her habits. A small flame of hope had been kindled all too briefly. Now both women were dead.

'Right then,' said Roy, breaking into Bridget's thoughts. 'Let's get started, shall we?'

He conducted the autopsy with the same due care and diligence that he'd shown to Zara. We are all equal in death, thought Bridget gloomily, and Roy was a professional, treating every corpse with the same dignity and respect. Bridget liked him all the more for that.

He found old needle marks on her arms, but no recent ones. It looked as if Shannon might really have been starting to turn her life around, before it was brought to such a brutal end.

'Time of death is always tricky to pin down

when a body's been recovered from a river or lake,' Roy remarked.

'Because of the water temperature,' said Bridget, trying to appear knowledgeable.

'That's right,' said Roy, nodding his approval. 'But first we must determine the cause of death. You will no doubt appreciate that not all persons found in water have drowned. Especially if, as in this case, they have obviously been very severely injured.'

He drew her attention to the wound on Shannon's head. Bridget looked on gingerly. The blade of the oar had delivered far more damage than the paperweight that had been used to kill Zara. Shannon's skull had been split almost in half. Bridget looked away.

Roy was peering closely at the shattered bone. 'Yes, I think it is very clear what the cause of death was in this case.'

'Blunt force trauma?'

'Indeed. There are no signs of the dilution of blood that would follow classic drowning in fresh water. This injury occurred before the victim entered the water. The subsequent examination of the organs will confirm that, I'm sure. As for the time of death, we are fortunate that the body was discovered so soon. The longer a corpse spends in the water, the harder my job becomes.'

'We're pretty certain that she was killed yesterday.'

'Indeed she was. You will want to know precisely when, naturally.' He moved around the table to consult his notes. 'The body cools much more rapidly in water, especially in flowing water, whereas the onset of rigor mortis is delayed. Therefore the usual indicators have to be modified. However, immersion in water does provide us with additional information to determine time of death.'

'Wrinkling of the skin?' suggested Bridget, repeating what she remembered from Dr Sarah Walker's assessment at the boathouse.

'That, and also lividity, maceration, and so on. You don't want to know all the details. Suffice to say, I can narrow the time of death to between five and seven yesterday evening. Is that good enough for you?'

Bridget nodded, relieved. In a way, the fact that Shannon had already been dead by the time Bridget had arrived at Jonathan's art gallery seemed to let her off the hook. There really was nothing more she could have done to prevent the young woman's death.

Roy's summary conclusion at the end of the post-mortem added little more to what had already been said. A blunt force trauma injury to the head resulting in very severe bleeding and immediate loss of consciousness. According to Roy she was likely to have died almost instantly, if that was any comfort. He promised to send his full report in a couple of days, once the organs had been analysed in the lab, but the conclusions seemed clear enough.

Julie covered the body again and prepared to

wheel the gurney back into the cooler. It was a sad end to a tragic life and Bridget felt thoroughly depressed as she changed back into her own clothes and left the hospital. In the open air, the bright sun shining down on her seemed almost to be in bad taste. She drove back to Kidlington with her music switched off.

★

Ffion flagged Bridget down eagerly as soon as she returned to the office. 'You have to see this ma'am.'

'What is it?'

'I've been pulling all the data from Zara's phone. I found this text message.'

She handed Bridget a printout of a text.

As Bridget read the words, a chill went through her. 'This message was sent to Zara?'

Ffion nodded. 'It was sent the morning of her murder.'

'Who sent it?'

'It's from a number registered to Dr Claiborne,' said Ffion. 'But it's not the one we examined when we brought him in for questioning. That's why it was overlooked. I've already contacted Dr Claiborne and asked him about the number. He says it's registered in his name, but it's his wife's phone.'

'Send a car to bring her in,' said Bridget, feeling a sudden surge of excitement at this turn of events. 'Let's see what the harassed mother

323

has to say for herself now.'

CHAPTER 30

This time Helen Claiborne presented Bridget with a rather different image. She'd changed from her stressed-out mum outfit into a clean white shirt and pair of dark trousers. She was wearing make-up and had tied her hair back neatly. She looked like a successful business woman. She had declined the opportunity to have a lawyer sit in with her. Her one phone call had been to her sister, to arrange childcare. She regarded Bridget defiantly across the table.

Bridget watched her for a while in silence, trying to decide how she felt about this woman. Now that she had changed clothes and applied make-up, she was even prettier than Bridget had first appreciated. Stunning, really. She might almost have been a model. The well-cut clothes showed off her slender waist, which had previously been disguised by the baggy mum-wear. It was as sharply defined as her high cheekbones. How had she managed to lose weight so quickly after pregnancy? Bridget was still trying desperately, fifteen years on.

Helen Claiborne was a consummate actor, that

was clear. And she had played Bridget for a fool, taking advantage of her sympathy for a poor, abandoned wife. It was almost as if the woman knew exactly how to manipulate her emotions for maximum effect. One thing was clear. Bridget couldn't believe a single word Helen had told her.

'Let's begin again, shall we? And this time you can tell me what really happened when you confronted Zara Hamilton on the evening of Thursday, 13th June.'

'I've already told you what happened.'

'Let's go back a little further in time, then, to that morning, when you sent this text message to Zara. She placed the printed message on the desk between them.

Stay away from my husband or else.

Helen didn't bother to look at the message. 'Seems fairly straightforward to me,' she said. 'Is it unclear to you in some way?'

'What did you mean by "or else?"'

'I left it ambiguous. Threats work better that way, I find. Why do you ask? Do you think that I planned to murder her?' She snorted with contemptuous laughter.

'What did you plan?' asked Bridget levelly.

Helen leaned forward on her elbows. 'I planned to warn that little slut to stay away from Anthony.'

'And if she wouldn't?'

Helen sat back. 'It wasn't Zara who was the real problem, of course. It was Anthony.

Anthony is always the problem.' She took a sip of water before continuing. 'He just can't help himself. A pretty little thing like Zara Hamilton bats her eyelids at him, and he loses all self-control. It's pitiful, really. I told you he's done this before, didn't I? I don't really know how many times. I've lost count. But this time it seemed to be more serious. I think he'd fallen head over heels for her. I told him, it stops now, and he agreed. But I know him too well. The thing you should understand about my husband, Inspector, is that he's a very weak man. He has little or no control over his impulses. He's quite childlike, I suppose. If someone offers him a bag of cookies, he just can't help himself. He takes one. I found it endearing at first. But this time he was too careless. Rumours started to spread. That's what made me so mad.'

'I see. You were not so much concerned about your marriage, but worried he might lose his job?'

She nodded. Her expression was still calm, but her eyes were hard and cold. 'If he was dismissed from his post he might never work in academia again. He was becoming too reckless. I wanted to teach him a lesson. That's why I threw him out of the house. I hoped that if he kept a low profile until the end of term, it would all blow over. But then...'

'Then Zara was murdered?'

'Exactly. Now everything's going to come out into the open. He's such a fool.'

327

'Tell me about what happened when you went to see your husband in college.'

Helen shrugged. 'It was just like I told you. I found him coming down the stairs from Zara's room.'

'At twenty past eight?'

'Yes. We argued. Then I went upstairs to see Zara. I knew that Anthony didn't have the strength to finish the affair himself. Zara had to end it. I intended to confront her and lay down my demands. Oh don't look at me like that, Inspector, I didn't plan to do anything terrible to her. But when I found her, she was dead. I didn't lie to you.'

'But you must have realised that your evidence would strongly implicate your husband in Zara's death. Was that your plan? To kill Zara Hamilton and then incriminate your husband as the murderer?'

'Kill her?' Helen scoffed. 'I absolutely bloody loathed that bitch and I'm not sorry she's dead – she got what she deserved, but I swear to God that I didn't do it.'

'The problem is I don't believe you.'

'That's your problem. You haven't a shred of evidence to pin this on me.' She stared at Bridget. 'Have you?'

Bridget lifted a page from her notes. 'There are discrepancies in your story. Last time I interviewed you, you insisted that you left the college at nine o'clock precisely. You were quite adamant about it.'

'Yes. The bell in the clock tower was chiming as I left.'

'And yet the CCTV at Tom Gate recorded you leaving at five past nine.'

For the first time Helen seemed to falter. 'No. No, that can't be right. I –'

'Five minutes would have been just enough time to kill Zara.'

'I didn't kill her!'

'And plenty of time for you to find her phone and take it with you.'

'Her phone? I didn't take her phone!'

'You took the murder weapon too,' continued Bridget relentlessly, 'but what you hadn't counted on was that another person was present in Zara's room. A witness to everything that happened there.'

That brought Helen up sharp. 'A witness? To the murder?' She trailed off, stumbling over her words. Then she seemed to become animated again. 'Then that witness must be the murderer!'

Bridget decided to press home her advantage. 'No. Now tell me again what you did with the murder weapon. If it's in your home we'll find it soon enough. We have a search team there now.'

Helen's voice turned icy. 'I told you. I didn't kill her. I don't know anything about the murder weapon, or her phone, or any witness. I think you just invented that to try and trick me.' She folded her arms across her chest, seeming to weigh her next words. 'The person you ought to be talking to is the dean. Why don't you ask him why he was entertaining the leader of the council and the planning officer on the night of the murder?'

Bridget was thrown by this sudden change in direction. 'Why should I talk to the dean?'

Helen seemed pleased by her reaction. 'You don't know so much, do you, Inspector? Have you heard about the new student accommodation the college is planning to build? Hamilton House? Funded by Sir Richard Hamilton?'

'Of course. How is that relevant?'

'Get your people to go through the college's financial transactions. I think you'll find that generous funds have been paid to certain individuals to get planning for the building approved by the council.'

'That's an extraordinary accusation,' said Bridget. 'And even if it were true, how does it relate to the murder of a student?'

'Because,' said Helen, 'the one person with the power to stop that building work going ahead was Zara Hamilton. If she had told her father her suspicions about what the dean was up to and threatened to publicly expose him, Sir Richard would have pulled the funding for the new accommodation in a heartbeat. The last thing he'd want is to become embroiled in a financial scandal.'

'You're accusing the dean of murder, in order to secure funding for a building project? I find that hard to believe.'

'Do you? Perhaps you don't know him very

well, then. He's utterly ruthless. The governing body only voted him into his post by a margin of one, and that was because of his promise to build new student accommodation. If the building plans don't proceed, the dean will be finished.'

★

Bridget emerged from the interview with Helen Claiborne feeling like she'd been the one being grilled. The interview had thrown up more questions than it had answered and Bridget felt as if she was walking on quicksand.

Why had Helen lied about the time she left Zara's room, and what had she been doing during the five minutes she couldn't account for? Had she simply climbed the stairs to Zara's room in a fury and battered the young woman to death? Then calmly left the college, taking the murder weapon and Zara's phone with her? And could she then have murdered Shannon and somehow planted Zara's phone in Adam's room? It seemed extraordinary, yet if anyone could do it, perhaps Helen Claiborne was the one. And what about her accusations about the dean?

She returned to her desk and put a call through to Kat at the homeless shelter. The woman sounded pleased to hear Bridget's voice. 'Any news about the murders?' she asked hopefully.

'We're making progress,' said Bridget. 'But I wanted to ask you about the future plans for the shelter.'

Kat's voice turned glum. 'Don't get me started on that. We're all just gutted about the whole thing. It's so unfair.'

'I understand that the council has given permission for the demolition of the shelter to go ahead?'

'Yeah, but the planning meeting was all a sham. Everyone knows that the city council are in the pocket of the college. The chief planning officer, Michael Protheroe's a crook. And the head of the council too. What's his name? George Romano.' She stopped. 'Well, at least that's what everyone thinks. Zara believed it too, and she knew that kind of stuff.'

'Do you know if she had any proof of money changing hands?'

'Dunno,' said Kat. 'If she did, she never showed it to me.'

Bridget thanked her for her time and hung up. It looked like there might be something in what Helen had said, but did it really relate to Zara's death? And what about Adam? How did he fit into the puzzle?

She left her desk and went to see what progress the rest of the team had made.

Ryan and Andy were back after interviewing the other rowers. They didn't look very upbeat.

'They all told us the same thing,' reported Ryan. 'Adam was at dinner with the rest of the rowing team at the time of Shannon's death. They ate together, then jogged down to the boathouse and went out on the river. He couldn't have killed her.'

'Are we sure this isn't just team solidarity?' asked Bridget.

'I checked with the kitchen staff,' said Andy. 'They confirmed that the whole team was eating that night. They get a special rowers' dinner once a week – steak to build their muscles, apparently. And they all remembered Adam being there. He's so tall, he kind of sticks out. It's a cast-iron alibi.'

If Adam hadn't killed Shannon then it was doubtful that he'd killed Zara. And he would have been stupid to keep Zara's phone in his room. So what was it doing there? Adam himself had offered no insight. He hadn't seemed surprised when she'd used it as evidence against him during their interview, but she got the impression he would hardly have raised an eyebrow if Blackbeard's treasure had turned up under his dirty laundry. Unless something else came up that implicated him, they'd have to let him go sooner or later.

She returned to her desk and flipped through the items in her in-tray, not really taking them in. Like before, the case was crumbling to dust in front of her. She leaned back in her chair and closed her eyes. All she really wanted was to put some headphones on and listen to something soothing. Some Debussy, perhaps, or Erik Satie. Instead her desk phone rang. It was the duty sergeant. 'I've got a Dr Claiborne with me, asking to speak to you.'

Bridget gritted her teeth. 'Tell him I'm on my way.'

She found a very agitated Dr Claiborne sitting in the reception area, sandwiched between a lanky young man and a hostile-looking older woman. She rescued him from there and took him into a private room.

'What's going on?' he asked. 'Why have you arrested my wife?'

She studied him closely before responding. The man was a wreck. His hair looked unwashed, his clothes crumpled. His fingernails had been bitten to the quick. The contrast with Helen Claiborne, at ease under Bridget's interrogation, her make-up flawless, could not have been more obvious.

'Do you think your wife is capable of murder, Dr Claiborne?'

He hesitated just a fraction too long before shaking his head. 'Helen's very... um, determined, but no, I can't believe that she would ever use violence to get what she wants.'

'Not even if she thought she was going to lose everything?'

He slumped his shoulders. 'You mean me, don't you?' He didn't wait for a response. 'I've been a useless husband to her, I know. But I do love her. And she knows that too.'

'She thinks you might lose your job because of your inappropriate relationship with Zara Hamilton.'

'Maybe. Perhaps she's right. I don't know

what will happen. You must think very poorly of me, Inspector.'

'Is there anything else you would like to tell me?' she asked.

'About what?'

'About anything.'

'No.'

'Then I suggest you go home to your children. Is your wife's sister looking after them at the moment?'

He nodded miserably.

'I'm sure they'd like to spend some time with their father.' She saw him out of the station and went back upstairs.

All she wanted was five minutes of quiet thinking time, but Grayson called her into his office as soon as she set foot in the CID suite.

He regarded her from across the sweeping expanse of his desk. 'I've just had Sir Richard on the phone demanding to know what's going on. He's threatening to make an official complaint about the investigation. He was expecting more progress by now and, quite frankly, so was I.'

Bridget nodded. 'I know how it looks, sir, but we've been busy tracking down various leads.' She stopped, unsure what to say to him. She'd hoped for a chance to think things through, but time had run out. She had little choice than to run with events. 'A new piece of information has come to light just this afternoon.'

'Explain.'

She laid out as succinctly as she could the hints

of corrupt dealings between the dean of Christ Church and the city council. Even as she spoke the words, she realised she was probably bringing her career crashing down in flames. Grayson stared at her as she detailed her suspicions. 'But I have no proof of anything,' she concluded lamely. 'We'd really need to bring in a financial specialist to look at the college accounts.'

Grayson regarded her thoughtfully. To her surprise, he seemed to be giving the idea some credence. 'George Romano, you say? And Michael Protheroe. Leave it with me overnight. I'll do some digging, see what I can uncover.'

'Thank you, sir,' said Bridget.

Before leaving the station she went to the cells and released Adam and Helen, then went home.

CHAPTER 31

When Chief Superintendent Grayson called Bridget into his office the following morning, she braced herself for a severe scolding, but he invited her to sit down in a manner that was almost conciliatory. He wasted no time in getting straight to the point.

'It seems you might be onto something. George Romano and Michael Protheroe. Leader of the city council and his chief planning officer. You're not the first person to mention those names to me. Romano's a shady character. He has fingers in far too many pies for my liking. And Protheroe's a creep. The two of them are quite unpleasant. But that doesn't make them criminals.'

'Sir?' It was too early in the morning for enigmas. She hadn't yet had her first cup of coffee.

'I was at a golf club dinner last night and happened to be sitting next to an old friend whose firm has contracts with the council. He's a big cheese in recycling and waste management.'

Ah, thought Bridget. When all else fails you can always rely on the old boy network.

'After a glass or two of wine,' continued Grayson, 'he told me something rather interesting.'

'And what was that, sir?'

'Apparently the leader of the council has had a recent windfall. He's just bought himself a rather nice villa in the south of France. I have the details here.'

He slid a copy of an estate agent's brochure across the table. The picture on the front featured a white Romanesque-style villa with a temptingly blue swimming pool, perched on a hillside overlooking the Mediterranean. The asking price for this little corner of paradise amongst the olive groves on the French Riviera had been one million Euros.

'I don't know what the salary of a council leader is these days, but I'm starting to wonder if I'm in the wrong job,' said Grayson. It was almost a joke and Bridget smiled. 'Do some digging. But keep it quiet. Don't even think about talking to the dean or anyone on the council without coming to me first. Understood?'

'Yes, sir,' said Bridget, jumping to her feet. She took the brochure with her.

As she left Grayson's office, Ffion entered the CID suite in her green motorcycle leathers. 'When you've changed,' said Bridget, 'I've got a little job for you.'

By mid-morning Ffion had dug out the required information. 'The villa is owned by a company,' she told Bridget. 'Ad Astra.'

'To the stars?' Bridget still remembered just enough Latin from her schooldays to translate the odd phrase. 'What do they do?'

'The company website says they run summer schools for students from disadvantaged backgrounds to help them get into Oxford, Cambridge and other Russell Group universities. Sounds almost like a charity, doesn't it? I phoned their contact number but just got a recorded message saying that all their places are currently booked.'

'Hmm,' said Bridget. 'Anything else?'

'Two of the company's directors are listed as Mrs Judith Romano and Mr Kevin Protheroe.'

'And are they by any chance related to George Romano and Michael Protheroe?'

Ffion flashed her a grin. 'How did you guess? Judith Romano is the wife of the council leader, and Kevin Protheroe is the father of the chief planning officer. Kevin Protheroe is aged 74 and lives in a care home. The company wasn't registered until six months ago. It hasn't run any of these so-called summer schools, and I can't find any actual details about them on the company's website. The whole operation is just a front.'

Bridget picked up the phone and dialled the Claibornes' number. She was pleased when Dr Claiborne himself answered. A baby was crying in the background.

'Dr Claiborne, it's DI Bridget Hart here from Thames Valley Police.'

'Yes?' He sounded wary, as well he might.

'Have you heard of a company called Ad Astra?'

'Yes,' said Claiborne, the relief audible in his voice. 'The college has been working with them as part of our outreach programme. You know, encouraging students from less privileged backgrounds, especially in the north of England, to apply to Oxford.'

'Working with them in what way?'

'I don't really know. I'm sure we gave them some money recently.'

'Are you aware of any work that the company has done in return?'

'Not as such. But I'm not really involved in that side of things.'

'I see,' said Bridget. 'Tell me about the proposed student accommodation block, Hamilton House.'

'Um, yes. The private rented sector in Oxford is so expensive, it puts a lot of people off, especially students from poorer backgrounds. The new building will enable us to offer accommodation to all students. But this building project is...' He hesitated, as if reluctant to go on.

'What about it?'

'Well, a lot of us think that it's more of a vanity project designed to bolster the dean's career.

The budget seems to be growing almost day by day. One hears things in the Senior Common Room, you know. I can't really say any more than that.'

'Thank you, Dr Claiborne,' said Bridget. 'You've been most helpful.' She put down the phone. If they could get a warrant to go through the college accounts, then they might be able to nail the dean and the council officials for bribery. But would that bring them any closer to catching the killer of Zara and Shannon?

★

There was always so much paperwork, or rather computer work, to do during an investigation. Sometimes Jake wasn't sure if he was a policeman or a data administrator. He sat at his screen, laboriously typing up his notes in the Holmes database. Opposite him sat Ryan, looking equally bored and fed up, banging clumsily at the keys of his computer with two fingers.

'Got any plans for the weekend?' asked Ryan.

'Not really,' said Jake. He supposed it would depend on the case whether he even had a weekend or not. His ex- had always complained that she could never rely on him being around at the weekends. Still, that was a pretty poor excuse for her to cheat on him. 'What about you?'

'That depends,' said Ryan cryptically, looking up.

'On what?' Jake followed Ryan's line of vision. Ffion was just entering the room carrying a mug with one of her herbal concoctions brewing. Her long legs crossed the floor quickly, hugged by skintight trousers. 'Good luck with that one,' muttered Jake under his breath.

Ffion sat down at her desk and began to type, her fingers flying over the keys. Jake stared at his screen but he'd lost his place and couldn't remember where he was. In front of him, Ryan hammered away noisily at his keyboard.

Ten minutes later Ffion rose from her chair, stretched her slender body like a cat, and strode from the room.

'Wish me luck,' said Ryan getting to his feet and following her out of the door.

Jake continued with his data entry, but it was difficult to focus. He pictured Ryan with Ffion in the corridor outside. What on earth was he saying to her? What was she saying in reply? He squinted at his notebook, but his handwriting was illegible. He really must try to write more neatly in future.

Five minutes later Ryan was back, his usual swagger notably absent. He sat down at his desk and resumed typing without a word.

'So how did it go?' asked Jake, trying to keep a straight face.

'Put it like this,' said Ryan grimly. 'I thought that fire-breathing Welsh dragons were just a myth. Turns out I was wrong.'

Jake laughed, and returned to his work with

renewed vigour.

CHAPTER 32

The parish church of St Mary the Virgin in Shipton-under-Wychwood was packed for the funeral of Zara Hamilton. Extravagant displays of white roses adorned the pillars and the altar, as if for a wedding. As Bridget entered the church, a dark-suited usher offered her an order of service embossed in gold leaf. She took it and slipped into a pew at the back from where she had a good view of most of the congregation.

Bridget had been just twenty-one at the time of her sister Abigail's funeral. It was the first funeral she'd ever attended, and she'd been bewildered and lost. Her parents had been distraught, leaning on her and Vanessa as if their whole world had collapsed. Bridget's world had collapsed too but there had been no one for her to lean on.

The students of Christ Church had turned out in force to say farewell to their friend. Many of the girls sat with their arms around one another, quietly sobbing. The boys sat mostly stony-faced, staring straight ahead. Bridget noticed Megan Jones in the company of a young man who was presumably her boyfriend, the one she'd been on her way to see when she encountered Zac hammering on Zara's door. Adam Brady sat at the end of a pew, leaning forward with his long forearms resting on his knees, head hanging down. Also sitting alone was Sophie Hinton, Zara's tutorial partner.

Bridget nodded and smiled to the head porter, Jim Turner and his wife Val, who were sitting on the opposite side of the aisle. Jim took his wife's hand in his and gave her a gentle pat as she dabbed her eyes with a cotton handkerchief.

Dr Claiborne and his wife Helen were a couple of rows in front of Bridget, sitting stiffly side by side but not touching or looking at each other. Bridget wondered whether they were managing to work through their marital problems. She hoped so, for the sake of the children.

Near the front of the church sat the dean and his wife, together with the college bursar and a few of the older tutors.

Could one of these people be Zara's killer?

The organist who up until then had been playing a selection of slow and mournful hymn tunes, paused then began to play the first notes of Nimrod from Elgar's Enigma Variations. It was the sign for the congregation to stand. It was a piece of music that never failed to bring a lump to Bridget's throat and a tear to her eye. As it grew from its simple beginning to something richer and more complex, Bridget mused that it was an appropriate choice. The death of Zara

Hamilton was certainly proving to be more of an enigma than she could have anticipated.

The music swelled and reverberated around the church as the funeral party made its slow and dignified way up the aisle. The oak coffin – carried by four pall bearers, one of whom was Zac – was adorned with huge white lilies that left a pungent, heady scent in their wake. Walking directly behind the coffin were Sir Richard and Lady Hamilton. Lady Hamilton's face was shrouded in a black lace veil reminiscent of Jackie Kennedy at the funeral of JFK. Zac's girlfriend, Verity, and Zara's younger sister, Zoe, brought up the rear.

The pall bearers laid the coffin on a bier in front of the chancel and the family took their place in the front pew just as the final chords of Nimrod died away. Timed to perfection.

The stage-managed service seemed somewhat at odds with the Zara Hamilton that Bridget had come to know. Zara had chosen a messy life for herself, dating an angry young man from a poor background, freely giving her time to help those less fortunate than herself, picking arguments with her brother and the college authorities, and becoming entangled with a married tutor. But didn't all of us lead messy lives? Bridget certainly had. Beneath the smoothest surface, there were always mistakes and failures brushed aside. No doubt Sir Richard and Lady Hamilton had no wish to be reminded of any of that today. They had already set about rewriting their daughter's life, ironing out the creases and the wrinkles, washing clean the stains.

The vicar welcomed the congregation, and the service proceeded with a selection of readings, hymns and music. An angelic-looking choirboy from the choristers at Christ Church filled the building with the sweet sound of Pie Jesu from Fauré's Requiem. Sophie stood and read Do not stand at my grave and weep with a quavering voice. In his eulogy the vicar spoke of the tragic loss to the family, of how beautiful and intelligent Zara had been, how kind and generous. No mention was made of her work with the homeless, as if to bring up such a subject would have been distasteful in this idyllic rural parish.

As the congregation sang the final hymn – The day thou gavest, Lord, has ended – the pall bearers lifted the coffin once more onto their shoulders and carried Zara from the church followed by the members of the family.

Bridget kept her distance as Zara was laid to rest in a quiet corner of the graveyard beside an ancient yew tree. She was here as an observer, not a mourner and had no wish to intrude on the family's private grief.

As the funeral party dispersed, she noticed a solitary figure remaining standing beside the old gnarled trunk of the yew. The girl looked so similar to Zara, it was unnerving to see her there, as if she were a ghost. It was Zoe, Zara's younger sister. Bridget went over to her and offered her hand. 'It's Zoe, isn't it?'

The girl nodded.

'I'm DI Bridget Hart.'

Zoe ran a finger through her fine golden hair. 'I know who you are. You're the inspector investigating Zara's murder. I saw you when you came to our house. Daddy was furious about that.' She spoke calmly and simply, without rancour.

'I'm sorry. I needed to speak to Zac.'

'Yes. He was mad too. They're both still mad at you.'

'I'm sorry,' said Bridget softly. 'I was just doing my best to find out who killed your sister. I still am.'

'I know.' A suggestion of a smile played across her sad features. 'There's no need to be sorry. Daddy's always mad at someone.' She started walking and Bridget went with her.

'This is a beautiful place to be buried, don't you think?' said Zoe as they walked. 'Zara loved this churchyard.'

'Yes,' agreed Bridget. It was a beautiful, peaceful place. It reminded her of the churchyard where her own sister was buried. 'Were you very close to her?' When she looked at Zoe, she couldn't help but think of Abigail. The age difference between the two sets of sisters was similar, but in Zoe's case it was her elder sister who had been killed.

'We were quite close,' said Zoe. 'But I could never hope to be as close as Zac was.'

'Twins,' mused Bridget. 'I can imagine.'

'Can you?' said Zoe. 'I doubt it.'

'Zara phoned you on the day she died, didn't she?' asked Bridget.

'Yes. She wanted to tell me that she'd finished with Adam. I think she felt bad about it really. Zara wasn't an unkind person.'

'When she phoned, did she tell you why she had split up with Adam?'

'She didn't need to. I knew that it would never last.'

'Oh?'

'There was only ever one person for Zara,' said Zoe.

She looked out across the graveyard and Bridget followed her gaze. Zac was standing alone beside some crumbling headstones looking utterly bereft. Zoe turned away and began to walk off. Gradually Bridget started to understand.

★

Bridget drove back to Kidlington with her mind racing. She needed to explain her theory to someone she could trust.

'Incest?' said Jake, frowning.

'Twincest,' corrected Ffion. The others stared at her. 'That's what sibling incest is called when it's between twins.'

'Like Jaime and Cersei in Game of Thrones,' suggested Jake, his eyes wide.

'There are other cultural and historical

references,' said Bridget, who had never seen Game of Thrones. 'Siegmund and Sieglinde in Wagner's The Valkyrie. Anne Boleyn and her brother, George. The Roman Emperor Caligula and, well, all of his sisters.'

'Yuck,' said Jake. 'Is this for real?'

'It's a documented medical phenomenon,' said Ffion. 'The correct term is GSA – Genetic Sexual Attraction. It's most common during teenage years when siblings are discovering their sexuality. Twins often bathe or sleep together, and are naturally curious about each other's bodies. There isn't always a clear boundary between intimacy and sex.'

'You seem to know a lot about it,' said Jake, frowning.

'I know a lot of stuff.'

'So how does this explain what happened?' asked Bridget. 'What if Zara dumped Adam not because of her affair with Claiborne, but because she had never really got over Zac? What if Zac was the mysterious other man?'

'So could Zac have murdered Zara to stop her talking?' asked Jake. 'He didn't leave the college until just before nine o'clock.'

'And Adam was definitely still in college at the time of the murder too.'

'What about Verity? What if she found out what had been happening between Zac and Zara?'

Bridget shook her head. 'No. The timings don't add up. Verity was chairing the ball committee meeting. She was seen on CCTV returning through Tom Gate at nine o'clock, and Helen Claiborne is adamant that she saw Zara lying dead at nine.'

While they were trying to puzzle it out, Bridget's phone rang. 'DI Bridget Hart, Thames Valley Police,' she answered.

'It's Jim Turner here ma'am, head porter at Christ Church. I thought I should let you know straight away. There's been a discovery.'

She listened carefully to his explanation. 'Thank you, Jim. I'll send someone over to pick it up straight away.' She hung up. 'Jake, you were in charge of the crime scene. Did you conduct a search of Tom Quad?'

'Of course, ma'am.' He frowned, looking worried.

'Didn't you think of dredging the fountain? The statue of Mercury in the middle of the quad?'

Jake's face paled. 'Oh no. What did I miss? Don't tell me.'

'Only the murder weapon. A purple glass paperweight. It was hidden under some water lilies. The groundsmen were cleaning the fountain ready for tomorrow night's ball when they found it.'

Jake looked devastated. 'Shit. Sorry, boss. I'll go and collect it right away.'

CHAPTER 33

There was no homemade shortbread on offer this time. Neither was Bridget invited into the dean's garden. Instead she was summoned to his study for a progress report on the murder inquiry.

It was tempting to refuse his request and remind him that she worked for Thames Valley Police, not Christ Church. However, it did give her the opportunity to speak to him without first having to ask for the Chief Superintendent's permission.

The dean seemed to have recovered his confidence after their previous tricky encounter. His sense of self-importance was if anything greater than usual. Perhaps he would reveal something useful if she allowed him to speak freely.

'I must say, I had expected that someone would have been charged with the murder by now,' he told her sternly, as if she'd failed to hand in an essay on time.

'Two murders,' Bridget reminded him.

'Yes,' he agreed, with obvious distaste.

'We're getting very close now.'

'Good. I hope so. As you'll have seen when you came into college, we're in the throes of getting ready for tonight's summer ball. The Christ Church ball is naturally one of the finest in Oxford.'

Bridget couldn't have failed to notice the preparations the dean was talking about. Tom Quad, normally so tranquil, was bustling with activity. A massive stage was being erected opposite the staircase to Zara's room, presumably for the live music acts which would perform that evening. The Tudor walls were being hung with miles of fairy lights, and Chinese lanterns suspended on metal cables were being strung across the quadrangle. No doubt Cardinal Wolsey was turning in his grave.

'Can you assure me that the crime scene will be completely cleared before the guests start arriving?' he asked.

Bridget had spoken briefly to the constable still on guard at the foot of the staircase leading to Zara's and Dr Claiborne's rooms. She had already asked him to clear away the taped-off area. 'No problem,' she told the dean.

'Good. Then I take it that your people won't need any further access to the college?'

'I can't make any promises. This enquiry is still ongoing.'

'Just as long as the ball proceeds without interruption and the college stays out of the headlines.' He pulled a gold pocket watch from his waistcoat and looked at it ostentatiously. 'Well, I shan't keep you any longer.'

'Actually, while I'm here,' said Bridget, 'there was another matter I wanted to talk to you about.'

'Oh?' said the dean, raising his eyebrows and giving her a supercilious stare.

'Yes,' said Bridget. 'It's about the plans to build new student accommodation.'

The dean frowned. 'What could that possibly have to do with the death of Zara Hamilton?'

'I don't know yet,' said Bridget. 'Possibly nothing. Or possibly everything. But it certainly has something to do with the large payments the college has been making to a company called Ad Astra.'

The dean seemed to shrink in size before Bridget's eyes. It was as though, like Alice, he'd fallen down a rabbit hole and drunk a magic potion. For once he had nothing to say.

'The relevant information has been passed over to the Serious Fraud Office. They'll be sending a team of forensic financial experts next week. Don't leave Oxford, will you?'

'Where do you think I might go?'

'I understand that George Romano owns a rather nice villa in France. Or rather, Ad Astra owns it.'

The dean blanched. And then, like the White Rabbit, he looked at his watch and said, 'I'm sorry, but I am going to be late for a meeting.'

★

Making her way out of the dean's lodgings, Bridget paused in Tom Quad. It was a perfect summer's day, the blue sky untouched by clouds, the bright sun already beginning to bake the yellow stone of the quadrangle. The college was closed to visitors today as it prepared for the ball. The quad bustled with activity as students gathered to watch the workmen busy with their final preparations. An air of celebration and excitement was coursing through the college. Term was over now, and tomorrow everyone would leave – some for the summer break, some for ever. Once they were gone the case would grow cold. People would forget what they had seen or heard. Zara herself would be forgotten. Time had almost run out.

In the middle of the quad stood the ornamental pond and fountain from where Zara's paperweight had been recovered. Forensics had confirmed this as the murder weapon, but it hadn't been possible to extract any fingerprints or DNA evidence from it. In the centre of the pond, the lead statue of Mercury looked towards Tom Tower. The statue's blind eyes had watched all the movements in Tom Quad on the night of the murder. He'd seen Zara and Shannon enter the college and climb the stairs to her room. He'd watched Helen Claiborne arrive, and then leave just as the bell, Great Tom, rang the hour. He'd watched the various comings and goings of Zac, Verity, Adam, Sophie and Megan, as well as the leader of the council and his chief planning officer as they went in and out of the college during the course of the evening. And he'd also witnessed the murderer flee Zara's room, pausing briefly to toss the glass paperweight into the pond before making their escape. Bridget had pieced together all of those same events. Now only the last piece of the puzzle eluded her.

Mercury was the messenger of the gods. If he could speak now, what message would he have for her?

She turned the facts over in her mind.

They were dealing with two separate murders but surely a single killer. Zara had returned to college at 8pm on Thursday evening, bringing Shannon Lewis with her. Apart from Shannon, Dr Claiborne was the last known person to have seen Zara alive, and had been seen coming down the stairs from her room at around 8:20, according to his wife. Helen Claiborne had supposedly found her dead at 9pm.

Shannon had been hiding in Zara's bedroom and must certainly have witnessed her murder. After trying to stop the bleeding with a towel, she had taken Zara's wallet and phone, dumped the bloody towel in the ground floor seminar room and run out of the college at 9:15. Shannon had most likely been murdered because she had witnessed the killing. She had probably brought about her own demise by trying to blackmail the murderer.

As for suspects, Zac had a clear motive to kill his sister. On the very morning of her death, in a text message exchange, Zara had threatened to make public a secret, quite probably their incestuous relationship. Zac had threatened to kill her if she did. And he had not left the college until just before 9pm.

Adam Brady had been dumped by Zara on the afternoon she was killed. He drank heavily in the college bar that evening, not leaving the college until five past ten. He'd then gone to the Oxford Union and had a fight with Zac. Adam was rowing with the crew who discovered Shannon's body next to the boat house, and Shannon had been killed with an oar. Zara's phone had been discovered in Adam's room, and the texts on her phone between her and Dr Claiborne provided a clear motive for Adam to have killed her – jealousy.

Dr Anthony Claiborne had slept with Zara on at least one occasion, and had been pursuing his student obsessively ever since. She had threatened to make a formal complaint about his behaviour, which would quite probably have led him to lose his academic post. He was the last person to see Zara alive when he went to see her in her room at 8pm.

Helen Claiborne also had a motive to kill Zara. By her own account, Claiborne was ready to abandon his wife and family for Zara. Helen had revealed herself to be ruthlessly single-minded and a consummate actor. She had admitted to being in Zara's room at 9pm, and no one could verify her claim that Zara was already dead at that time.

Last but not least, the dean of Christ Church, Dr Francis Reid, was implicated in bribery and financial misconduct in connection with the building of the new student accommodation, Hamilton House, at the site of the homeless shelter where Zara worked. Zara had actively opposed the construction, and had the power to stop the project by persuading her father to withdraw his donation. The dean had been hosting a drinks reception in his lodgings all of Thursday evening, and might easily have slipped out just long enough to kill Zara and then return unnoticed, throwing the murder weapon into the fountain on his way.

Bridget paced the quad restlessly.

On the other side of the quad beyond the statue the crime scene had been cleared, and so had the flowers and tributes that had been left for Zara. Her body had been buried. Yet still her murderer had not been found. Bridget's interview with the dean had yielded no new information. She needed a new lead, some clue that would enable her to obtain justice. She lingered in the sunshine, reluctant to return to Kidlington empty-handed.

Someone here knew the truth. Somewhere within these walls lay the answers Bridget needed.

Instead of leaving she decided to take a moment's respite from her busy schedule, and slipped inside the cathedral through its entrance next to the dean's lodgings.

★

Every Oxford college had its own chapel. Some of them, like Corpus Christi were small and intimate. Others, like New College, were built on a more impressive scale. But none of them compared in size or grandeur with Christ Church college chapel which doubled as the cathedral of the diocese of Oxford. The building dated back to the twelfth century, when it had functioned as the church for the former monastery of St Frideswide, patron saint of Oxford.

Empty of tourists, the cathedral was quiet today. Bridget turned left into the North Transept, pausing to look at the enormous stained glass window of the Archangel Michael slaying the devil in the form of a dragon. It was brutal and dramatic and did not offer the soul-soothing quality she was looking for. She continued on to the small Latin Chapel in the north east corner, with its finely carved shrine of St Frideswide. Sunlight filtered through the brightly coloured Burne-Jones window, casting colourful reflections onto the shrine and the surrounding stone floor.

There was one person in the Latin Chapel, and as Bridget approached she recognised Val

Turner, the wife of Jim Turner the head porter, who she had seen at the funeral. Val was sitting quietly, gazing at the shrine, her hands clasped in her lap. She turned at the sound of Bridget's footsteps and gave her a small smile of recognition.

'Mind if I join you?' asked Bridget.

'Please do,' said Val.

She slipped into the chair next to Val and for a moment they both contemplated the shrine in silence.

'I still think of her all the time,' said Val after a while.

Bridget didn't need to ask who she was talking about. 'I'm sure you do,' she said.

'I've known a lot of students over the years,' continued Val. 'Some of them have gone on to become famous. Politicians, actors, writers. I tell you, the stories I could have sold to the newspapers about the antics of some of those people!'

She cast a sideways glance at Bridget then, as if she might suspect her of selling the news of Zara's murder to the papers. 'But I never would,' she declared. 'I've lived my life according to one simple motto: treat people as you'd like them to treat you. On the whole they pay you back in kind.'

She lapsed into introspection, and Bridget was happy to sit in silence alongside her.

'This day has been looming over me for a long time,' said Val, after a minute. 'Today is my last day in college. It's my husband's last day too. I suppose it's time we finally put our feet up and relaxed a little. We've worked hard all our lives. Everyone says we've earned a long and happy retirement.'

She sounded utterly wretched at the prospect.

'I'm the college's longest serving scout, you know. I've been here for almost fifty years, and married to Jim for nigh on forty-five. Jim's already busy making plans for our retirement, but to be honest I can't summon up much enthusiasm. Sorry to sound maudlin, but it feels like the beginning of the end. I don't relish the thought of doing nothing except collecting my pension at the end of each month. I like to keep busy. What am I going to do with myself all day?'

'I'm sure you'll find something to fill your time,' said Bridget. 'You could start a new hobby. Get out and meet people.'

'Yes,' agreed Val. 'I'm sure you're right. It's the people I'll miss the most, you know, especially the students. Jim and I haven't been blessed with children of our own, so these young people have been my surrogate family. I've met all sorts, I can tell you, from all walks of life. But it doesn't matter to me where they come from. If they don't keep their rooms tidy, I give them a good talking to. I rarely need to tell them off more than once.' She gave a little laugh.

Val seemed to need no prompting to continue talking, and Bridget was happy to sit and listen.

'I always enjoy graduation day, helping the

students into their robes, seeing them go off into the world. But that's all coming to an end now. We'll get our golden handshake and we'll be off. I don't mind telling you, I'll miss this place more than I can say.'

Bridget patted her hand. 'I'm sure you'll find new things to do with your time. And you'll have lots of fond memories to look back on.'

Val sighed. 'At least I'll be able to do things at the right time from now on. It goes against my natural inclinations when everything starts five minutes late.'

'What do you mean?' asked Bridget, intrigued.

Val gave her a quizzical look. 'Everything at Christ Church happens five minutes late. Haven't you wondered why they serve dinner at six twenty and seven twenty, when quarter past the hour would be a more sensible time?'

'I hadn't really thought about it,' admitted Bridget. 'But do explain.'

'It's because Christ Church keeps to the old Oxford time which is five minutes behind Greenwich Mean Time. The bell in Tom Tower chimes at five past nine every night to call the students back to college before the curfew. Of course, they don't really have a curfew anymore. The students all have keys and can come and go as they please now, but Oxford likes to hang on to its traditions.'

Bridget stared at Val as the final piece of the puzzle slotted into place. She now knew who had killed Zara and Shannon, and why. She jumped to her feet. 'I'm sorry, it's been lovely talking to you, but I have to get back to the station. You've been most helpful.'

'Have I?' said Val, looking surprised.

'Absolutely. And if I don't see you again, all the best for your retirement.'

'God bless you, my dear.'

★

'So let me get this straight,' said Jake, a look of utter bewilderment on his face. 'You're saying that the bell in Tom Tower chimes at five past nine instead of on the hour?'

'Precisely,' said Bridget.

'I'd say that's more late than precise,' quipped Ryan.

Laughter rippled through the room. There was a palpable air of excitement, as if they knew they were closing in on their prey. The chance encounter with Val in the cathedral had cast a whole new light on matters.

What was it that the King of Hearts had said to Alice in Alice in Wonderland? 'Begin at the beginning, and go on till you come to the end: then stop.' Bridget and her team had done as the King advised, following the leads and the evidence, being led a merry dance. But now the end was very close, she was sure of it.

'We don't yet have enough evidence for a murder charge,' she told her team, 'but today is our last opportunity to talk to people before everyone leaves Oxford for the summer vacation. Our best chance to find our prime suspect will be at tonight's ball, but I don't want to go in all guns blazing. For one thing, we might frighten them away. Jake, you and Ffion can come with me. We'll take uniformed officers as backup, but let's try to blend in and keep this operation as low key as possible. I don't want any more trouble with the newspapers, or the college authorities. I definitely don't want to make an appearance on tonight's news.'

She glanced at her watch. The ball would be starting in a little over an hour. She didn't have long to get ready.

CHAPTER 34

Bridget parked behind the marked police car in Pembroke Square. From here she had a clear view of the guests lining up to enter Christ Church through Tom Gate. The young women, robed in lengths of sequined silk and pastel chiffon, looked like princesses out of a Disney movie. Some wore daringly low-cut gowns, some had extravagantly elegant hairstyles. Their dates for the evening mostly wore sedate black tie and dinner suits, although one or two of the more flamboyant men sported multi-coloured waistcoats and gaudy bow ties. Dr Roy Andrews, the pathologist, would have envied some of the fancier neck-wear.

Bridget had bought a gown for her own graduation ball but, due to Abigail's death, had never worn it. She still had it somewhere, in a box in the attic, but the memories it evoked were too painful. Besides, no amount of wishful thinking was going to make it still fit her. Instead she had changed into the strappy cocktail dress she'd worn to Jonathan's art gallery. Her high heels gave her a welcome extra couple of inches, but she didn't know how far she'd be able to walk in them. They were already pinching her toes. It wasn't exactly a suitable outfit for a ball, or an arrest, and she hoped she wouldn't have to do any running, but it was the best she'd been able to manage at short notice.

Beside her in the passenger seat Jake was looking surprisingly dashing in a black suit. He didn't own a dinner jacket, but Bridget had assured him that a black suit would do just fine. Superintendent Grayson had lent him a black bow tie that he kept in his office drawer 'just in case'. Behind them in the back seat, Ffion looked like a cat-walk model in something sleek and shimmering which she just happened to have in her wardrobe.

It was an obvious decision to bring Jake and Ffion. Their similar ages made them look like a couple. Bridget would have to go in alone. If this hadn't been a police operation, it would have been nice to invite Jonathan, but she could hardly take him with her to arrest a murder suspect. In any case she hadn't heard from him since she'd dashed from his exhibition to attend the murder scene at the river. He would probably prefer someone who didn't keep rushing off all the time.

'All ready?' she asked Jake and Ffion. 'Then let's go to the ball.'

With a nod at the two officers waiting in the police car, they crossed the road and moved to the front of the queue. A team of private contractors – burly men in black suits with close cropped hair and curly-wired ear pieces – were checking tickets and keeping the riff-raff out. They raised their eyebrows when presented with three warrant cards, but allowed Bridget and her team to pass without trouble.

Inside the college, the preparations that Bridget had seen earlier had now transformed Tom Quad into a wonderland of garlands, flowering trellises and twinkling lights. Stalls and kiosks ranged around the edges of the quad. In one corner a chamber orchestra was playing a selection of Strauss waltzes. A large stage was ready and waiting for the main entertainment that would begin after dinner. The college was already filling up with guests, and laughter and merriment echoed off the four walls of the quadrangle. It was still perfectly light on this midsummer's evening. Later, when darkness fell, the sky would light up again with fireworks. Bridget hoped that by then her work would be done and the murderer would be safely in custody.

She scanned the crowds strolling over the normally off-limits lawned areas, but could see no one she wanted to speak to. 'Let's split up,' she said to Jake and Ffion. 'Our suspect must be here somewhere. It's impossible for anyone to leave the college without being seen. Call me as soon as you have anything to report.'

Jake set off in the direction of the Meadow Building and Ffion headed towards the hall.

Ignoring the table filled with complimentary glasses of champagne, Bridget made her way along the edge of the quad.

★

Feeling ridiculous in his suit and bow tie, Jake stalked across the grass lawn, threading his way between the crowds. He didn't know what was worse, wearing a lounge suit to a black tie event, or having to come to such a posh ball in the first place. He tugged irritably at his bow tie, wishing he could pull the damn thing off. The plan was to remain low-key, but he felt sure that everyone was staring at him. No wonder. He had never felt so out of place.

He made his way through Tom Quad, past the Meadow Building and out onto the Broad Walk at the top of Christ Church Meadow. There, he stopped. He certainly hadn't expected this.

The meadow had been given over to entertainments for the ball. An ABBA tribute band was belting out the Swedish group's greatest hits, with students enthusiastically joining in at the tops of their voices. There was a carousel, a ferris wheel and, unbelievably, balloon rides promising stunning glimpses of Oxford's dreaming spires.

This ball was really quite something. He'd expected a rather stuffy affair, but he had to hand it to them. These students really knew how to party.

He mingled amongst the guests, politely disentangling himself from a group of female ABBA fans who wanted him to sing and dance with them. He scanned the faces on the carousel and waited for the ferris wheel to complete a full revolution. But there was still no sign of the person he was looking for.

He turned at the sound of raucous laughter. The men's rowing team was coming through the Meadow Gate, carrying their cox aloft like a mascot. Leading the way was Adam Brady. When Adam saw Jake, he detached himself from the group and came over.

Adam's previous hostility seemed to have all but vanished. It must have been the party atmosphere. 'Hey, mate,' he said, slapping Jake on the back. 'I didn't expect to see you here.'

'Me neither,' said Jake. 'How are things with you?'

A shadow fell across Adam's face briefly. 'I'm still coming to terms with what happened,' he admitted. 'I don't know if I'll ever get over Zara. I mean, there's never going to be anyone like her in my life again, is there?' He brightened. 'Still, time's a healer. And distance too. So I'm getting out of here, as far away as I can.'

'What do you mean?'

'I've had enough of all this.' He waved a dismissive hand at the college. 'After what happened to Zara, I don't want to stay here anymore. This place gets under your skin, it's too claustrophobic. I've been offered a sporting scholarship to Harvard and I'm going to take it.'

'Wow, good for you, mate,' said Jake.

'Hey, Adam, get a move on!' One of the other rowers was shouting at him to join them.

'Sorry, have to go. Got a balloon ride booked.'

'Have fun,' said Jake, as Adam ran off to join his teammates.

Jake scanned the faces on the meadow one more time, then made his way back into the college.

★

The seating plan was pinned to a board just outside the dining hall and Ffion stood to one side of the door as laughing, chattering students began to enter and look for their places. The hall was ready for a banquet fit for a monarch. Each place was laid with three sets of cutlery, glasses for white wine, red wine and port, a starched linen napkin in the shape of a bishop's mitre, and a name place in fancy cursive lettering. Decorative silver urns placed at intervals along the tables completed the sense of opulence.

Mr Shepherd & Woodward and the excitable girl with the long blonde hair were bustling up and down, ensuring that every last detail was perfect.

The hall was beginning to fill up in readiness for the banquet, but a quick inspection established that the person Ffion wanted was not there. 'Hey,' she said to Mr Shepherd &

Woodward as he scurried past, 'your bow tie is crooked.' She left him anxiously trying to straighten it in the reflection of one of the silver urns.

On her way out, she encountered Sophie Hinton on the grand staircase. The shy student was accompanied by a good-looking young man, presumably her boyfriend. The normally awkward girl seemed much more relaxed than usual. She smiled at Ffion as she approached.

'Enjoying yourselves?' asked Ffion.

'Yes,' said Sophie. 'I wasn't planning to come to the ball. Social scenes aren't really my thing. But then Tom' – she indicated the slim man in black tie – 'asked me to be his guest. So of course I said yes.'

'Good,' said Ffion, moving past.

Sophie stopped her with a hand on her arm. 'I hope I didn't confuse the investigation by telling you about Dr Claiborne. I only wanted you to find the murderer.'

'Don't worry. You did the right thing.'

Sophie seemed reluctant to let her go. 'Life will never be the same for me without Zara. I miss her so much. But what Zara taught me is that we have to find the goodness in our lives and then embrace it.' She gave Tom a squeeze.

'I understand. Now you two go and enjoy yourselves.'

★

371

Bridget was doing her best to blend in among the bright young things, a job she suspected she was doing rather badly. She stood by the wall at the corner of Tom Quad, scanning the faces of the guests, searching for one among many. It was such a large quadrangle, the biggest in Oxford, and there were so many hundreds of people moving about that it was an almost impossible task. But Zara's killer was here somewhere, she was certain of it.

There were fewer people in Peckwater Quad, since all of the attractions were elsewhere, but a small number seeking quiet had congregated there. She studied the groups and couples and at last she spotted the person she'd been hoping to find. Zac Hamilton.

He was descending into the quad from his own staircase, arm in arm with his guest. But the young woman at his side wasn't Verity. It was his younger sister, Zoe.

Bridget headed towards them, but Zac had already spotted her and was guiding Zoe over to her.

'Inspector Hart. I wasn't expecting to meet you here.'

The last time Bridget had seen Zac wearing black tie, he'd had blood on his shirt and a cut on his cheek. Now he was spruced up and immaculately dressed. But he'd changed in other ways too. He seemed to have lost that air of arrogance that had clung to him like a nasty smell.

Zoe was wearing a close-fitting gown that showed off her dainty figure. With her golden hair elegantly styled she looked older than her seventeen years, and more than ever like Zara.

'Verity isn't with you?' Bridget asked Zac.

He shook his head. 'I don't expect to see much of her tonight. She'll be too busy. As chair of the ball committee, tonight's her crowning glory and she won't let anything stand between her and perfection. Verity always aspires to be the best. And so I invited Zoe along. She deserves some cheering up. We all do.'

Zoe gave Bridget a wan smile.

'Do you know where Verity is now?' asked Bridget.

'No. But you might like to know that I spoke with my father and persuaded him to cancel his donation to the college. We agreed that it's what Zara would have wanted. The new building won't be going ahead now and the homeless shelter is safe. My family is making a donation to Shelter instead, in honour of Zara.'

'Good,' said Bridget. 'I'm pleased to hear it.' But she was already searching the faces of the now thinning crowd.

'And now, if you'll excuse us?'

Bridget hardly saw them go. Where was Verity? She had to find her.

CHAPTER 35

Jake had scoured every inch of Tom Quad, Peckwater Quad and even Blue Boar Quad, not to mention the meadow and its fairground rides. But there was still no sign of Verity. There was always the possibility that she'd done a runner, but somehow he didn't think she'd want to miss tonight for anything. In any case the uniformed officers stationed outside the college would arrest her if she tried to leave.

'Seen the boss anywhere?' asked Ffion, catching up with him by the Mercury fountain.

'No, I was hoping she'd be here in Tom Quad.'

'I'll give her a call.' Ffion opened her clutch bag to take out her phone.

Jake put a hand out to stop her. 'Wait. Look!'

'What is it?'

'Up there.'

He pointed in the direction of Tom Tower. The great tower rose high into the evening sky, standing head and shoulders above the adjoining buildings, the last rays of the sun just brushing its upper reaches. Above the gateway at its base and the huge arched window and clock face that stood over it, rose the octagonal belfry housing the bell of Great Tom. The belfry was crowned by a dome and spire, standing high over the quadrangle far below.

At the very top of the tower next to the dome, two figures had appeared. Young women, arm in arm. Verity and Zoe.

'Oh my God,' said Ffion.

Others had seen the girls too, and were staring up at the tower.

'We have to stop her!' said Jake. But Ffion was already moving. She darted across the quad, her high heels apparently no hindrance to how fast she could run. Jake followed, powering forwards, catching up rapidly with his long stride.

★

Bridget dashed up the stone staircase, cursing her tight dress, her lack of fitness, but most of all her heels. She kicked her shoes off and carried on up the spiral stairs, taking them as swiftly as she could in bare feet.

Verity's voice echoed down the stairwell from the rooftop. 'Look, Zoe. Didn't I tell you? The view's amazing from up here.'

'Stop!' gasped Bridget, her voice bouncing off the stone walls. But she knew that words alone wouldn't stop Verity. Panting breathlessly, she pushed on up, her soles slapping hard against the smooth stone steps. It was going to be a long way to the top.

By the time she arrived in the octagonal lantern which housed the bell, Great Tom, her heart was thumping wildly in her ribcage and her thighs were in agony. She paused for a second to catch her breath and to wipe sweat from her upper lip. She really must find time to exercise more often. She ought to have called for back-up as soon as she'd spotted Verity leading Zoe into the tower, but it was too late now. If she stopped to use her phone, she would be too late. She thought with longing of the uniformed officers parked in Pembroke Square, out of the sight of the drama unfolding within the tower. A wooden staircase in the corner of the bell tower continued upwards. Gritting her teeth she began to make the final ascent, doggedly putting one foot in front of the other.

She emerged onto the roof at the top of the tower, gasping for breath, and found herself on a precariously narrow walkway, high above the city. The setting sun shone in her eyes and she raised a hand to shield her view. Behind her, Sir Christopher Wren's dome was radiating the fierce heat of the day. In front of her, the parapet, not even waist high with its ornamental crenellations, overlooked the buses of St Aldate's in one direction and Tom Quad in the other, some hundred odd feet below.

Keeping her back to the dome, Bridget inched her way sideways around the tower until she caught sight of Verity and Zoe. They were on the Tom Quad side of the tower, peering over the edge of the parapet, far above the quadrangle. Verity was pointing out the sights of Oxford with her right hand. The dreaming spires were ranged before them – the tower of Merton College Chapel, the spire of St Mary's Church and the bell tower of Magdalen College beyond. At this height the famous spires seemed not to be dreaming, but had woken from their centuries-old slumber and were vividly alive, swimming in Bridget's vision. The ferris wheel spun slowly on the other side of Tom Quad, and a hot air balloon drifted across the darkening sky. Bridget clutched at the parapet with both hands and inched towards the girls.

But even as she moved, Verity reached out and seized Zoe by the shoulders.

★

Despite Ffion's head start, Jake caught up with her by the time she reached the wooden door that opened into the base of the tower.

'You go ahead,' she told him, stepping aside to let him pass.

'Okay.' He rushed headlong through the tower entrance and began to run up the twisting staircase, taking the steps two at a time. It was dim inside, but he charged upwards, heedless of danger. He'd messed up bigtime over that business with the murder weapon in the fountain, and he had a lot to prove. He passed through the chamber containing the huge cast

377

iron bell and belted up the final wooden staircase, emerging from the confines of the tower into bright daylight.

He grabbed at the stone parapet that edged the rooftop, his knuckles white. He was no more fond of heights than he was of corpses. The evening wind gusted at him up here, even though it had been perfectly still in the quadrangle below. Gingerly he peered over the edge and immediately wished he hadn't. Small figures like insects were gathered together by the roadside, their tiny arms pointing up at him. Model-scaled cars and buses glided up and down St Aldate's, carrying their pocket-sized passengers with them. On the other side of the road he saw two uniformed officers emerge from their toy police car and run towards the college. Help was coming, but for now he was alone.

He forced himself to look away from the precipitous drop and turn towards the rooftop walk. The circular path was narrow and precarious, slippery with rubble and the accumulated mess of nesting birds. The domed roof curved away to his right, the low parapet guarded the fall to his left, but seemed completely inadequate to prevent him from toppling over the edge. Its ancient yellow stone crumbled under his sweaty fingers and he jerked his hand away from it, afraid it would collapse under his weight. Overhead the blue sky stretched on to infinity.

A woman's voice called his attention back

towards the direction of Tom Quad, and he edged gingerly forward.

'Don't come any closer!' shouted Verity. 'I know you're there.'

He rounded the dome just in time to see Verity grab Zoe's arm and yank it sharply behind her back. The younger girl yelped in surprise and jerked forwards, almost losing her balance, her upper body leaning out over the low stone parapet, one foot leaving the safety of the walkway. Verity held her in place, half secure, half ready to topple. Jake came to an abrupt stop, but it wasn't him that Verity had seen. Her gaze was fixed on someone on the other side of the tower, hidden from Jake's view by the dome.

'I just want to talk to you.' It was Bridget's voice, perfectly calm, making it sound as if a rooftop conversation was an entirely normal event.

'Stay back!' screamed Verity.

Her attention was fixed on Bridget and on the struggling Zoe. She hadn't seen him. Jake dropped to all fours and began to crawl slowly around the edge of the rooftop.

★

Bridget could see nothing in Zoe's eyes but shock and terror. The girl was shaking like a leaf in Verity's fierce grip.

Bridget tried to breathe calmly and recall the training she'd received on dealing with hostage and crisis situations. But those role-playing exercises had all been carried out in comfortable conference rooms, not forty metres up in the air on a narrow walkway with a vertiginous drop to the ground. The people she'd practised with had been fellow officers, not a young woman who had already killed twice and perhaps felt she had nothing more to lose.

All sound dried up in her throat.

Verity turned her back to her and forced Zoe to lean further over the edge. The girl screamed. 'Stay still and shut up!' screeched Verity. 'You wouldn't be here now if you'd kept your mouth shut at the funeral instead of blabbing to the police.' She shoved Zoe again so that her entire upper body lurched over the edge of the parapet. Zoe screamed and fought back, but Verity had her pinned, her arm twisted behind her back.

'Verity, stop!' shouted Bridget, injecting as much command as she could summon into her voice. 'This has nothing to do with Zoe. Let her go.'

A cloud passed in front of the setting sun, and Verity laughed as the wind whipped at her dress and blew her long hair across her face. 'Let her go? This is my night of triumph. I intend to go out in style.'

'No,' said Bridget, easing forward. 'Talk to me instead.'

'What would you like to know?' sneered Verity. 'You must already know that I killed Zara.'

'Yes, I knew that. That's why I came here

tonight.'

'Then there's nothing more to discuss.' Verity pushed at Zoe again, trying to force her over the wall, but the girl struggled and clung on.

'It wasn't Zoe who gave you away,' said Bridget. 'It was Val Turner, the scout.'

Verity grew still, holding Zoe in place. 'What are you talking about? What could Val possibly have said to you?'

'She told me about Oxford time, and how Great Tom chimes at five past nine every night. It chimes one hundred and one times to signal the closing of the college gate. You returned to college at precisely nine pm, and the bell was still chiming when Helen Claiborne found Zara's body. I knew then that you'd had ample time to kill Zara.'

'Whatever.' Verity began again to push Zoe over the edge.

'Tell me why you killed her,' shouted Bridget.

The distraction seemed to work and Verity grew still again. 'Don't you already know?'

'I think so. But tell me yourself.'

'Okay.' Verity sounded happy to be given the opportunity to explain. 'Zara was a jealous bitch. Did you know that? Everyone said she was the golden girl, the perfect, selfless angel. She'd rather give her money to the poor than keep it for herself. But she was no angel. She had a dark secret. You know that now, of course. Zoe told you.' She pulled at Zoe's hair, making her cry out in pain. 'Zara and Zac were lovers. They thought

I didn't know, but of course I did. Zac couldn't keep a secret from me. But I didn't care. I would do anything for Zac. Lie for him, steal for him, kill for him.'

Bridget waited, motionless. She knew that if she broke the spell, Verity would stop talking and would try again to push Zoe over the edge. She listened patiently, every muscle in her body tensed for flight.

'Zara wanted Zac back. She was jealous of me. That relationship of theirs, it was horrible – disgusting and unnatural. It was over as far as he was concerned, but she couldn't let go. She thought that by telling me about her and Zac, I'd leave him. But nothing would ever make me leave Zac! I told her so. So then she threatened to tell everyone about what she and her brother had done. She used blackmail to try to get Zac to go back to her.'

Bridget recalled the texts between Zara and Zac on the day of her death.

You've got 24 hours and then I'll tell everyone
If you tell anyone about this, I'll kill you

'She was going to ruin everything. Zac and I, we had it all planned. He was going to go into politics, I was going to go into media. Together, we'd have been unstoppable. He could have been prime minister one day, but not if his sister's dirty secret had become public knowledge. Imagine what the press would make of that! There have been plenty of scandals in British politics, but nothing of that sort!'

'So you had it all planned. You left the ball committee meeting and went straight to Zara's room, intent on killing her.'

'She had to be stopped. She would have ruined his life and mine!'

'But you didn't realise that Shannon Lewis was in Zara's bedroom, and that she saw everything.'

'Shannon? Was that her name? Zara was always picking up bloody waifs and strays. She wasn't supposed to be there. I didn't know she was there until it was too late. The stupid cow tried to blackmail me. She wanted money to keep her mouth shut. I shut her mouth for her all right.'

'And you tried to frame Adam by placing Zara's mobile phone in his room.'

'Adam deserved it. Did he really think he was good enough to be dating Zac's sister? He was trash. He even left his door unlocked. How stupid is that?'

Out of the corner of Bridget's eye a dark figure had appeared, emerging from behind the curved dome of the rooftop, crawling low along the narrow walk. Jake. Verity had her back to him. If Bridget could keep her distracted…

'And yet you think that you were good enough to marry Zac?'

Verity's eyes narrowed. 'How dare you judge me!'

'Don't you think you've ruined Zac's life

yourself? Are you really the kind of girlfriend he wants? Does he know you killed his twin and that you're threatening to kill his other sister?'

'Shut up!' screamed Verity. 'You don't know what you're talking about!'

'What would he say to you if he was here now?' persisted Bridget. 'Release Zoe, Verity. Let her go. She's done nothing wrong.'

'No!'

In one swift movement, Jake was on his feet, closing the last few yards between him and Verity. He grabbed at her and she spun to face him, releasing her grip on Zoe.

Zoe screamed, tumbling forward over the parapet. She steadied herself at the last moment and pulled back away from the brink.

Bridget ran to her and took her by the hand. 'This way!' She hauled Zoe back to safety, away from Verity's reach.

Ffion had appeared at the top of the tower in her shimmering dress that seemed aglow in the evening light. Bridget handed the shocked girl over to her and turned back to see Jake struggling with Verity.

They were perched right at the very limit of the rooftop, jammed up against the edge of the parapet. Verity's scarlet gown billowed in the wind like a great sail. Jake grappled with her, but the fabric of the dress tore in his hands and she broke free. She darted out of his reach, then gathered her skirt and stepped up onto the parapet itself, hauling herself up by one of the fancy stone crenellations that jutted out every six feet.

An audible gasp could be heard from the quadrangle down below where most of the ball guests seemed to have gathered. They were clearly getting more for their money than they'd bargained for.

'Don't do anything stupid,' said Jake, inching his way towards her.

She balanced on the narrow stone span on heeled shoes, her arms stretched out against the deep blue of the sky. Her ruby lips wore a victory smile. 'Keep away from me. Don't come any closer.'

A voice from below roared out in anguish. 'Verity! No!' It was Zac. She turned to look down at him and opened her mouth to speak. But her words were drowned as suddenly, without warning, the bell began to chime. The tower reverberated as the great bell swung back and forth, striking the hour, and Verity reached out with her hand.

Whether she simply lost her balance or chose that moment to jump was not clear. Bridget saw the red dress as if in flight.

Jake lunged forwards and for one heart-stopping moment Bridget thought that her sergeant was going to fall. He leaned far out over the edge of the parapet, his upper body invisible, only his long legs still on the tower.

'I've got her,' he shouted. 'But I can't hold her much longer.'

Heedless of her tight dress and bare feet, Bridget rushed towards him and was joined by Ffion coming from the other direction. Both women leaned over the edge. Jake's hands were clasped around Verity's arms. Together they helped Jake haul Verity back onto the rooftop.

Down below in the quadrangle, the crowd burst into applause and cheers.

Bridget collapsed onto the walkway, her breath coming in great gulps, the relief in her arms palpable. As she lay on her back panting, she was only dimly aware of the welcome stomp of the boots of approaching police constables.

CHAPTER 36

Bridget woke to morning sunlight and the gentle song of blackbirds and starlings. She swung her short legs over the edge of her bed and drew back the curtains to let the daylight and the birdsong flood in. From her bedroom window she could see nothing but greenery – trees, shrubs and long grass – and the brightly coloured jewels of cornflower, cow parsley and field poppies. Late June in all its glory. Her garden was untamed and bursting with life, and one day soon she would try to cut back the honeysuckle and prune the rambling roses. But for now she was happy for them to run wild with abandon.

The rooftop ordeal was still fresh and vivid, but it was over and Zoe was safe. By the time the bell had stopped chiming, all but deafening them in the process, a team of uniformed officers had made it to the top of Tom Tower. They managed to handcuff Verity, who was by now putting up very little resistance, and take her away. Bridget had helped a shaken, but unhurt, Zoe back down the steps and watched her run sobbing into Zac's arms. Back at HQ, Grayson had praised Jake for his bravery and congratulated Bridget on the arrest.

The ball had come to an abrupt end. With its key organiser in the back of a patrol car, several of the guests in a state of shock, and police officers everywhere, the rest of the ball committee had been given no choice other than to bring the evening to an untimely close. All that time spent planning had gone to waste.

It had been late by the time Bridget had crawled into bed. She'd drifted into a light, dream-laden slumber in which young women falling from towers had featured prominently. Now that she was awake she had no desire to stay in bed. She could hear Chloe moving around in the kitchen downstairs.

Bridget went down to join her, and found her staring into the near-empty interior of the fridge. 'There's no food in, Mum. It's just as well we're going to Aunt Vanessa's for lunch.'

Bridget nodded. 'Let's head off early. I want to take you somewhere first.'

'Okay.'

She had never taken Chloe with her before, but now the time was right.

They headed north to Woodstock in the Mini, slowing as they approached the outskirts of the town. Blenheim Palace, birthplace of Winston Churchill and home of the Duke of Marlborough, was hosting a vintage car rally which had clearly attracted hundreds of antique car enthusiasts from miles around. They crawled towards the entrance to Blenheim at a top speed barely above that of the horses the vintage cars had once replaced. Once past, Bridget picked up speed again and soon they were in the heart of Woodstock, driving past houses of Cotswold stone, historic inns and antique shops.

Welcome to Middle England. Woodstock must have been the sort of place the former prime minister John Major had in mind when he dreamed of, 'long shadows on county grounds, warm beer, invincible green suburbs, dog lovers, and old maids bicycling to holy communion through the morning mist.' The old maids must surely have already passed into history by the time John Major quoted Orwell, but the green suburbs and dog lovers were still out in force.

Bridget parked the Mini outside the church of St Mary Magdalene.

'Is this it?' asked Chloe, peering at the tiny parish church with its square sandstone tower that had stood for a thousand years.

'Yes. This is where she is.'

They walked together to the churchyard at the rear, quiet and enclosed by trees and ancient stones. Only the sound of the songbirds broke the stillness. The grave nestled in the shade of a holly tree, dark with spiky, emerald leaves. Chloe read aloud from the headstone. 'Abigail Croft. Beloved daughter. Dearest sister. Rest in peace.'

Bridget knelt and removed the old flowers from the grave, replacing them with purple foxgloves she had picked from her garden that morning.

'You never talk about her,' said Chloe. 'Why is she buried here?'

'This was our church. My parents brought us here every Sunday.' The smells and sounds of the church had disturbed a trove of memories from Bridget's childhood and teenage years. Carols by candlelight in the freezing dead of winter. The annual celebrations of Easter and Harvest Festival. The solemnity of the Eucharist. Ancient words and rituals, once so familiar, now half-forgotten.

'You don't go to church anymore.'

'No. Not since Abigail's death.'

'And the police never caught the man who killed her?'

'No.'

Chloe closed her fingers around Bridget's. 'But you found Zara's murderer. And Shannon's. Just like you told me you would. You got justice for them.'

'Yes,' said Bridget, and a single tear ran down her face. 'Yes, I did.'

★

The front door flew open and Vanessa appeared from behind it like a jack in the box. She gripped Bridget tightly. 'I just heard what happened. It was on the BBC.' In Vanessa's opinion, the British Broadcasting Corporation was the highest form of truth. 'Tell me it wasn't you up on the tower.'

'It was me.'

'Oh my God. You could have died.' Vanessa wrapped both arms around her.

Rufus the dog bounded over, leaping up at Bridget and barking at the commotion.

'Down Rufus,' said Vanessa, still holding her tight.

'You're embarrassing me,' Bridget told her sister. 'And worse, you're embarrassing Chloe.' She gave her daughter a wink.

'I didn't even know if you would make it to lunch,' said Vanessa.

Her husband James appeared in the hallway. 'Well she's here now. And I think she deserves congratulations.' He leaned in to kiss Bridget on the cheek, and she gratefully took the opportunity to extract herself from Vanessa's hold.

'Yes, well, come inside,' said Vanessa. 'Lunch will be ready soon. And there's someone here who's really looking forward to seeing you.'

'Oh?' Bridget followed her into the sitting room.

Jonathan rose to his feet as she entered, and stood awkwardly by the armchair. 'Hi there.'

'Hi.' She realised suddenly that she hadn't called him or even sent a text since rushing off to attend the murder scene at the boathouse.

'Jonathan told me that you walked out of his exhibition,' scolded Vanessa. 'So of course I immediately invited him to lunch again.

Honestly, if it wasn't for me, you'd have no social life whatsoever.' She disappeared into the kitchen, leaving Bridget alone with Jonathan and Chloe.

'I'll go and find Florence and Toby,' said Chloe quickly, vanishing into the recesses of the huge house.

Jonathan kept a safe distance from her, standing self-consciously on the other side of the room. 'I didn't know if I should come to lunch today,' he began awkwardly, 'but Vanessa can be very insistent. After you left the exhibition I wasn't sure if you'd want to see me again.'

'I'm sorry. I've been rather busy.'

His warm eyes crinkled in a smile. 'I gathered that. I understand that congratulations are in order.'

'Thanks.' She felt like a tongue-tied teenager standing there. She groped for some words that would express her feelings, but all she could manage was, 'I'm glad you came.'

Jonathan's smile spread slowly across his face. It was contagious and soon she was smiling openly back at him. 'Good,' he said. 'I'm glad too. Perhaps we could try again? A concert, or a trip to the theatre, perhaps? Vanessa tells me that you're keen on opera. Puccini's La Bohème is showing at the New Theatre next Saturday. Would you like to come and see it with me?'

'Yes, I'd like that,' said Bridget. 'I'd like that very much.'

Killing by Numbers (Bridget Hart #2)

A work of art. A mysterious number. A secret worth killing for.

When reclusive artist, Gabriel Quinn, is gunned down outside a gallery on Oxford High Street, Detective Inspector Bridget Hart investigates the world of contemporary art, where paintings can change hands for millions in the auction room.

Bridget is convinced that the last words spoken by the artist – a mysterious code of 8 digits and a letter – are key to unravelling the mystery of his death.

But when her ex-husband, Ben, now a senior detective with the Metropolitan Police in London shows up with new information about the murdered man, Bridget's personal and professional lives are brought crashing together with dramatic consequences.

Set amongst the dreaming spires of Oxford University, the Bridget Hart series is perfect for fans of Elly Griffiths, JR Ellis, Faith Martin and classic British murder mysteries.

 Scan the QR code to see a list of retailers.

Bridget Hart series (large print ISBNs)
Aspire to Die (978-1-914537-01-1)
Killing by Numbers (978-1-914537-03-5)
Do No Evil (978-1-914537-05-9)
In Love and Murder (978-1-914537-07-3)
A Darkly Shining Star (978-1-914537-09-7)
Preface to Murder (978-1-914537-11-0)
Toll for the Dead (978-1914537134)

Bridget Hart® is a registered trademark of Landmark Internet Ltd.

About the author

M S Morris is the pseudonym for the writing partnership of Margarita and Steve Morris. Together they write the Bridget Hart series of crime novels set in Oxford. The couple are married and live in Oxfordshire. They have two sons.

Thank you for reading

We hope you enjoyed this book. If you did, then we would be very grateful if you would please take a moment to leave a review online. Thank you.

Find out more at **msmorrisbooks.com** where you can join our mailing list.